February 2018

Karma Blues

Ann Beltran

> Also by Ann Beltran
> *Nonprofit Girl*

This book is a work of fiction. References to real people, events, establishments, organizations, or locales are intended only to provide a sense of authenticity, and are used fictitiously. All other characters, and all incidents and dialogue, are drawn from the author's imagination and are not to be construed as real.

Karma Blues. Copyright © 2018 by Ann Beltran. All rights reserved. Printed in the United States of America. No part of this book may be used or reproduced in any manner whatsoever without written permission except in the case of brief quotations embodied in critical articles and reviews.

Cover illustration by Ying Liang. Aymi.ying@gmail.com ying.virb.com

ISBN 9781530334124

This book is dedicated to my ancestors

Acknowledgements

Many thanks to my readers who have generously given of their time to read entire drafts and provide feedback that I value. It's one thing to ask a friend to read a book, another to read a trilogy! You have all been so kind: Albie Beannacht, Martha Beltran Bermudez, Catherine Bradshaw, Dee Endelman, Ellie Holstein, Lisa Lungren, Elisa Ortiz, Cheryl Ryan, and Nicole Walter. Big hugs for staying the course with me.

A special thank you to my brother-in-law Patrick Beltran, author, editor, and publisher, for being a reliable, kind supporter in all my travails with the technology of self-publishing.

I'm happy to share in the story references to *The Four-Fold Way: Walking the Paths of the Warrior, Healer, Teacher, and Visionary*, by Angeles Arrien. For so many years, when I was a single mom, I would begin each season assessing the path I'd just walked, and anticipating the work to come. Her mantras became my mantras, encouraging and inspiring me to live fully.

I am in awe of the lost boys of Sudan. Having learned their story years ago while volunteering at the International Rescue Committee in Seattle, they still bring tears to my eyes when I read of their amazing accomplishments once resettled. If ever you doubt the resilience of the human spirit, or the ability of refugees to contribute to society, you need only search the internet for these heroes and read their stories.

And special thanks to the organizations and people who taught me the ways of nonprofits: Washington CASH in Seattle, and Leadership Institute, the Family Resource Center, and Hopelink in Redmond.

"Whatever action you performed in the past becomes your destiny now. Whatever action you perform now becomes your destiny in the future."
    Muktananda, "Resonate with Stillness," June 20

Sunday, April 1, 2007

Confronting yet another failed attempt to cast a male figure as her husband and her daughter's father, Liv was seriously considering whether they could just do without. *Aren't my family and friends enough?* She was tired of her recurring frustration of failing to secure in one person a husband whom she would care to be in bed with and stand to talk to, and a father who genuinely cared for her bi-racial, in-your-face, adorable child. After all they'd managed for six years. Family had protected and supported them. And Liv provided for most of their needs. Really, what was she looking for?

A firm knock at the door interrupted her meandering mind. Before Liv completely opened the door, Elyse was pushing it farther to grab Liv and do a twirl hug. "Hey girlfriend, I've got really big news – Cory proposed last night!"

Liv, still in her grey sweats, felt the mug in her hand tip and slop coffee on the carpet. Her contemplative eyelids of a moment ago popped fully open. "Oh my god! Oh my god, finally, I'm sooo happy!" She took Elyse's hand looking for a ring, and seeing none, raised her eyes.

"No, we're not doing an engagement ring – no blood diamonds for this couple. But I don't care. I'm just floored that after all this time – what has it been, three years? – all this time, with no particular occasion, he cuddles up and asks me while we're in bed. I'm still in shock!"

Friends since college, the twosome were approaching twenty-nine. Occasionally they still had a night out at a bar and whomever Liv didn't pull in with her Euro look – a northern coolness in sync with an increasingly pragmatic assessment of men, yet enlivened by a sunny smile that drew them in - Elyse did with her Hispanic attractions – warm, inviting eyes that signaled a good time to be had, while concealing an easily triggered sarcasm about ineffectual men. Both career savvy now, their interests covered urban Seattle life. Liv was deeper into the nonprofit sector. She'd left her job at the International Rescue Committee to work at a family multi-service center at the north end of Lake Union where she helped women improve their financial situation. Elyse was embedded in city hall moving from the neighborhood development program into serving as staff for a city council member. That neither had moved into an explicitly permanent relationship with a man suited their friendship. Although these last years, Elyse had come much closer.

"Here, sit down and share the shock. Do you want some coffee?"

"A little – I'm just so wired already."

Liv brought a cup out from her tiny kitchen alcove into the sunnier area of the apartment, located a floor down and a wing across from Elyse's apartment. The place had grown comfy and disheveled as IKEA furnishings became interspersed with second-hand treasures, and then layered with the scratches and stains of a child's activities, and not just any child, but as Elyse called Shakti, 'a wild child.' Meant mostly in fun, the assessment was initially based on the feral look the toddler embodied, tangled hair sans barrettes hanging over calculating eyes, dirt under her nails, and a premature willingness to let curiosity take her beyond her mother's comfort zone. Now, while the hair still needed taming, 'wildness' pointed more to a primordial uncompromising spirit, a challenging consortium of precocious and extroverted behaviors for a single mom. A child who thought she was always right.

"So, what moved him to propose? It seemed like you guys had a groove that wasn't going to change."

"Funny you should ask, because honestly that was my question too. When he whispered it in my ear, my first words were, 'you're kidding.'"

"And?"

"He was hurt a little and said, 'no, I'm not kidding. I think it's time.'"

"Time for what? Because of?"

"Here's the odd thing. I'd been thinking it was time too. Not that I said that to you, but I was. Maybe when he turned thirty and we had that party last August, the one you missed, I started wondering then, well, what now? Are we headed into something together? Will this just be status quo until my biological clock goes off? And then when his dad died this winter, it hit him hard. And I could tell he was having to change, be more attentive to his mom back East, asking me if we could go visit her, keeping up more with his older brother too. Family stuff."

"So that's what you think moved him to propose, but he didn't really say?"

"Not so far. But come on – I'm not going to interrogate him at one in the morning! I just said yes, a big yes, where I hopped out of bed and jumped around naked shouting, 'YES, YES!'"

Liv lowered her eyes and stared at her mug. "I didn't know you wanted it so badly." Each had always prided herself on having complete access to the other's feelings with rare notable exceptions. As well as Liv knew her friend, and kept up with her activities with Cory, she hadn't seen this one coming.

"Honestly, neither did I! Neither did I. But it was a huge rush when it sank in that he'd proposed, it just made me so fucking happy!"

Liv laughed and hoped she was concealing the negativity she sensed in her heart. Six years has passed since she'd ended a steady live-in relationship with her college boyfriend, Devin, the relationship she'd destroyed when she'd arrived home from Mumbai pregnant, carrying another man's child. Rama's. She'd chosen to have no further contact with him. Six years of totally immersing herself into motherhood, working to transform what had begun as a big mistake, at least to others. Years of a modest social life that were sporadically punctuated by sexual relations, varying in length and strength from exclamation points (one-nighters of passionate sex followed by little or no contact), to commas (ho hum repeaters who faded out), and worse, the three dot encounters (stretched over months with ups and downs that appeared to have some meaning but then fizzled out.) Indeed, it was just last night that a three-month sexual hiatus was almost broken when the nerdy Indian Microsoftie finally began some heavy petting aimed at getting her clothes off. History now. Just move on. That was an exit strategy she seemed to have perfected over time, first with Shakti's father Rama, then with Devin, and since then with others. Just end it when you know it won't work. Back to square one, although she hated that board game metaphor as though there were some 'right one' out there she needed to get to. More practically, she needed to remind her dad not to bother any more bringing computer geeks home.

Elyse sensed Liv was holding back. "Let me guess. I know you're happy for me, but it also makes you sad because there's no good man in your life right now?"

Liv nodded.

"What about Madhu?"

"Crashed and burned."

"That bad?"

"Unhuh. I will never fall into that trap again of thinking some computer nerd actually has lust in his veins, especially if he's from India and feeling guilty for having sex outside of marriage." Her gaze traveled to a stack of self-help books on her makeshift coffee table. Following last night's encounter, she'd searched for consolation, and seen the words 'a journey toward wholeness.' Yes, that was the crux of it, needing to learn to find completeness within herself. *The Four-Fold Way* was now on top of her stack, attracting her with its mantras for every season. Spring's was about healing: 'pay attention to what has heart and meaning.' *Last night certainly did not have heart and meaning.* Although considering how she'd derailed Madhu's awkward efforts to get her into bed, she found satisfaction in her ability to blend compassion and respect with honesty, realizing that the harder he tried to be macho the less attracted she was. She ejected him out of the bedroom, out of her apartment, and out of her life as gracefully as she could. In the past, she would have given it more of a try, but then had to deal with a deeper masculine wound at being rejected post intercourse. Better to do it up front.

"Well, we knew that wasn't going anywhere."

Liv snapped back. "But that's partly it – why do things have to go anywhere? Why are you so fucking happy that Cory proposed? Why does the be all and end all for us, for women, have to be getting married?" *Mad, yes I'm mad.* The attempts of well-intentioned others to set her up left her mad that someone, some societal culture producer/director, was demanding that she fill this role. And mad at herself for always falling into the trap. She made a vow as she bit with vigor into the stale doughnut and slurped her coffee with milk: *I'm good on my own. Make it work.* An inner mentor continued the advice: if someone comes along organically, naturally, well then great; if not, there will be other activities. *With whom? girlfriends?* Yes, just let yourself be, no more managing to gender structures. Be a great mom, a loving person to all. And create a life you love. *But I want a man in my life!* These were not new thoughts, but indeed a refrain that followed a melody that always ended on a low note. Yet, after another dismal evening, Liv felt more fiercely the need to break the shackles of others' expectations. And her own.

This inner dialogue had moved out loud so many times between Elyse and Liv before that it bore a label: 'feminist rants.' The rants were triggered as Liv would lament, "I need a father for Shakti," or Elyse would sense how her world had grown with her up-and-coming civil rights attorney boyfriend, Cory, and yet fear losing herself in his career, who she was and could be in her own right. Elyse would counsel Liv: look, you brought this magnificent child into the world on your own, and you don't have to sacrifice the rest of your life to some father-type who doesn't really cut it for you. You need to hold out for a relationship that rings your bells. Shakti's going to grow up fine with or without some guy trying to father her. Wait for the right person. And Liv would have back at Elyse: if anyone can hold her own in a marriage, it's you. And you don't have to get married, just enjoy the relationship. And even if you did have kids together, surely a civil rights attorney would appreciate the need to hold up his end of parenting, no?

Sometimes, their rants were about other women they saw capitulating, marrying down just to have a handy-man in the up-scale homes the women managers were buying, or a great looking stud at the parties they threw. They hated all versions of the Cinderella story. At the rant's foundation was the fundamental question whether a woman could and should be happy on her own regardless of the choices and happenings in her life, or whether women, well young women in particular, well Liv especially, needed to always be looking for that special something with a guy who would transform the repetitive travails of single momhood into some happy ending of couplehood.

They were both quiet. Elyse's bubble at the door had popped. "It's weird, I know, how I feel about the proposal. It just was such a release to hear it, like I'd been wondering if it would ever come, and suddenly it was there. Like I'd won some contest. I can relax into what I wanted all along, to have something together with him, to have a partner I can be me with. We can get on with real life, whatever that means." What Elyse was thinking that moment was living in a nice house, having a dog, and then having a baby. Stepping out of herself, she saw how attractive moving into a new life style, 'arriving' in a sense, was to her.

Liv moved, sat next to her and put down the mug. "You know I get that, I totally get that. And I am really, honestly, so happy for you. And I want that kind of relationship too. Today, this morning, not always but often on weekends, that's what I want too. And it just feels like it's never going to happen, that it's too complicated with Shakti, that guys I'm really attracted to don't want to become instant dads, and guys who might go for the whole package, the Liv and Shakti package, well, they're just too…"

"Boring, I know."

"Or judgmental. Or controlling. There's always some fatal flaw." They turned and hugged. "Elyse, please know I'm really happy for you. And if I don't get to be your bridesmaid and Shakti doesn't get to be your flower girl, I'll be crushed!"

Elyse laughed. "God, what kind of flower girl will she be! She'll doubtless steal the show. Where is she anyway?"

"She had a sleep-over at my brother's. She loves playing know-it-all older sister to little Jeff."

"How do Ryan and Mimi like their new place?"

"Oh, they're thrilled to be in a home of their own. The deal they got last year, almost no down payment and a low interest rate, they finally have what they wanted. They keep showing me the lower level they're fixing up to rent, and suggesting I move over there and be closer to work."

Elyse considered. Her concern turned to what would happen when she and Cory moved in to a place together between now and the wedding. That was all up in the air, but Elyse knew those discussions of a wedding date and a place to live would be coming up soon. She and Liv had lived here for five years as she raised her daughter while holding down a fulltime job. Elyse had been such a backstop, pinch hitting in all kinds of ways to help out with Shakti: babysitting, pick-ups and drop-offs at daycare, just being there to talk. Moving out would have a huge impact on their relationship, a particularly sobering consequence of beginning anew with Cory. Her mom liked to say as troubles had beset their immigrant family in Yakima, 'when one door closes, the Lord opens another.' But Elyse's happy event felt more like a door opening wide for her, and causing one to shut on Liv. "It's just occurring to me how me and Cory getting married, how it will affect us, like me not living here anymore."

Hearing that was like a full force six-foot wave knocking Liv flat. She sat back, dropping her head dramatically on the sofa. "Shit, you're right. Crap. What will I do without you? This is serious."

"I thought of it because of what you said about your brother wanting you to live there. Maybe you really should consider that. I mean, wherever Cory and I wind up living together – most definitely, still in the city – my habits will change and I can see where I might not be as available to you."

Liv brought her face close and used her sweetest voice. "Of course, you'll need to make dinner every night, and do his laundry."

Elyse punched her shoulder. "Just quit it. But seriously, there would be solid advantages if you lived in the same house as them. Think about it: Shakti and Jeff would have each other, lots of shared help with babysitting and meals. And you wouldn't have that nasty two bus commute anymore."

"True. I'm pretty sure there's a bus from Phinney Ridge that would go past where I work. Definitely a plus. And Ryan said he'd give me a good deal on the rent." Liv was already hosting an internal debate. "But what about my quote/unquote love life? Living downstairs from my brother? Shakti upstairs when I have a guy over and am engaged in indecent relations?"

"Well, you'd just have to date guys who have their own place, clean enough to spend time in. And you'd always have to drive over so you have a get-away car available." That reference sprang from the nights they'd picked each other up in rescue mode from a date gone wrong in some guy's pad, causing chortles over "the one who forgot to say he lived with his mother!" "That bastard with the SM set up!"

Liv moved to get another stale donut, offering half to Elyse. Together, they silently dunked. "Well, change is good I suppose. We couldn't have kept this routine up forever. Shakti enters first grade in the fall. The daily contact with Ryan, Mimi and Jeff would be great. I'd save time and hassle on my commute. Maybe I could finally get the grad school thing going. I can see a lot of it working out."

Elyse was shaking her head slightly in disbelief: "We're actually moving on. It makes me feel old."

"Me too."

"Maybe there'll be a single dad at Shakti's new school?"

Liv squished her face in disdain. "Right, I'll use one of those job descriptions we have at work, and post it on the school bulletin board: "Single mom seeking single dad."

"Just but don't leave out the requirements of sexy and good in bed!"

As Liv drove over to Ryan's about noon, she took a route past her workplace in Fremont and paused to study the bus sign. The 5 stops here. She'd check later to see where it stopped near Ryan's place.

Change. Maybe it's what needs to happen. Almost seven years had passed since she'd agonized over whether to abort her 'love child,' another Elyse moniker at the time, for Liv's lusty affair in India during her college internship there. Her decision to protect the life within then led inevitably to the next choice point as to whether to give the baby away. Liv journalled those following summer months, entries often generated by emotionally intense conversations with her family: her mom who as a teenager had given up Ryan only to reconnect with him when he was thirty; her aunt who had an abortion after being gang raped in college; and her half-brother who couldn't stomach someone giving up their own flesh and blood. And then there had been that time with Grandma that struck a deep chord about holding on to one's own thread of life in a world of adversity and trauma. Finally, Liv had started writing down conversations with her unborn child, which grew livelier once she learned that she carried a girl. As college ties were fading away, save for Elyse, Liv began succumbing to a deep relationship that was more meaningful to her than any other, except possibly that with her own mother Katherine.

Liv knew by the time she turned twenty-two that July, she was falling in love with the one who kicked her insides and made it increasingly difficult to sleep at night. She'd been so enthused and excited to meet the baby. When Shakti finally arrived that evening of November 14th, Liv, coached by Elyse, came face to face with the miracle of one becoming two. She'd been enthralled! To finally see the baby after looking at so many photos of fetus growth, to be able to touch the precious fingers and toes, to bury her nose in the baby's dark curls and smell the fresh life of her. The baby suckling at her breast was a stunning achievement for Liv: I made this baby. I'm able with my own body to keep this baby alive. While other mothers may have been experiencing a blue period, for Liv it was prolonged euphoria.

She'd welcomed the dependence that made her heart so expansive, so loving and giving. After regrets about how things ended with Devin, after rehashing her affair in India *ad nauseum*, her days became filled with thoughts and actions focused on another. Caregiving suited her, at least when it came to Shakti. And the delights! The pure joy of the little hands in hers, the snuggling and cuddling, the dressing and undressing, the playfulness, there was so much happiness in their togetherness. Her mom had said, "I would never have guessed you had it in you." Nor had Liv.

Of course, she had so much help with the baby, at home for over a year with her mom who cut her own work hours a bit. A family friend, Karuna, babysat too, as Liv re-introduced work into her life. Meanwhile, Elyse gave her psychological support in nearly daily phone calls. The move to an apartment in Elyse's building, Liv's parents covering the cost of daycare for several years, really it wasn't until after the first few years that Liv became pre-occupied with her single status. She wasn't dating as Elyse was, she didn't have a lot of friends her age. She dedicated all her energy to being a good mother, to vindicating herself in other's eyes, showing them that she could make good on her mistake – indeed, that it wasn't a mistake because what was not to love about Shakti and Liv together?

Fortunately, the crew at the International Rescue Committee and her refugee clients being re-settled in Tukwila fleshed out a lot of her days. She'd felt really at home there, operating out of the resettlement office, dealing daily with making life more understandable for her clients who were bewildered by technologies and systems Americans took for granted. Her favorites had been the 'lost boys of Sudan,' especially David and Jonathan. They'd taken turns doing part-time work for the IRC at different times, using their knowledge of the languages of Sudanese and Ethiopian people to help others out. At first, she'd felt motherly towards them, as though they were older brothers of Shakti. Later they became part of her social life with Elyse.

There came a point when, damn, she wanted to be with a guy who wasn't so much a brother to her, to have some fun, and not to have to explain Shakti to them. Her concern for the well-being of David became more than that along the way. But he had no time for girls, all work and study for him. And, in any event,

Elyse and she had made a pact not to flirt with David and Jonathan lest mixed messages only compound everything else they had suffered in their very long journey from being refugees on the run to being here in Seattle.

Instead, what began was the litany of set ups by her dad and mom. Gary and Katherine were both in hi-tech, he a consultant, she at Microsoft. The trickle of mostly young men her parents added to get-togethers in their home in Sammamish was now the stuff of family jokes: remember the guy – one of the first before Gary learned his lesson to mention in advance Liv was a single mom– the guy who went from draping his arm around Liv on the sofa, only to be out the door in a hot ten minutes after Shakti toddled in! By contrast, the forewarned older programmer came on super nice to Shakti, except she screamed and screamed until he left, convincing Liv that Shakti could see auras. Katherine kept eyeing young Indian men in her building until she learned from experience that a single mom with a half-Indian child actually didn't appeal much due to lack of purity. Even Ryan, Liv's brother, had tried a few fix-ups on the family boat, inviting Liv out *sans* child to meet some of his buddies from Fisherman's Terminal. One had fishy-smelling hands that were a turn-off; another couldn't stop talking to Ryan about boats and didn't even try to converse with Liv, as though she would be attracted to his technical know-how. Elyse had tried too. Cory had loads of attorney colleagues and while Elyse found many of them lacking in any real depth, occasionally one would stand out because of his interests in the world, or because he was Hispanic, or black, or Asian and offered that cross-cultural perspective that Liv craved. That one attorney from El Salvador had turned into a good relationship for Liv for the better part of a year. But he was too interested in the events and causes of Central America to stay for long in the Pacific Northwest, while Liv was not about to lose her support network at home or walk away from a good job. Losing Jose was big for Liv and it caused her to conclude that if a young man was intellectually and culturally attractive enough to her, he'd have more enticing things to do than settle down and be a father. That was certainly true of David who had his sights set on law school, and then returning to Sudan.

The cumulative effect of these experiences colluded with fresh challenges from Shakti's precociousness to bring Liv down. Not that she regretted her choices, not at all. But as her own mom had said to her seven years ago, whatever you decide, there are consequences. And the passage of time will confront you with them in ways you can't predict.

Now with change coming to her deepest friendship, with Elyse moving on to a home and husband of her own, Liv had to acknowledge the inevitability of it. And, how blue it made her feel. Life seemed like it was only going to get harder. Even if this move to Ryan and Mimi's place worked out and some aspects of life became easier, beneath the surface there were troubling concerns. Yes, great to share babysitting. But being part of her half-brother's family, living in his walk-in basement apartment, it didn't meet her need for self-fulfillment and independence. He would judge her, that was the fear. There would be clashes of parenting styles. She'd have trouble having a guy over for the night.

With a resigned spirit, she drove up to the hill-top house looking down to the locks below leading out to Shilshole Bay. It would be better than staying put and missing Elyse every day.

She parked and walked across the street toward her brother's home, assessing it and the neighborhood with a fresh eye. Plain beige house with some craftsman touches on the windows and doors. A real front porch. Pleasant. Sizeable trees. Some totally renovated homes down the street, others still on the funky side. Ryan and Mimi had been thrilled to find the place and take advantage of the market's easy loan conditions - a dream come true, especially for Mimi.

Together they'd made a lot of transitions over the past years: getting married, changing work and jobs, and then having a child two years ago. In their thirties now, Mimi, an untraceable adoptee from Vietnam, finally had her own blood relation and it was huge for her. Ryan, having reconnected with his birth mother, half-sister and grandparents going on ten years ago, didn't feel the birth of their child in quite the same way as Mimi did. But little Jeff arrived at the culmination of so many dreams that the milestone of his birth impacted him substantially too. He'd transitioned out of his dangerous but lucrative fishing work into a steady-enough marine repair business down at Fisherman's Terminal that paid a lot of their bills. Mimi left her work as an assistant producer at Paramount Theater downtown after securing her teaching credential. She loved her job as an ESL teacher and drama coach at a Beacon Hill school that touted enrollment from over thirty language groups. They were stable, financially and emotionally, when they brought little Jeffrey into the world.

His name solidified the family heritage that had broken when Ryan was given up at birth. He and Katherine, his birth mother, hadn't made much early progress in building more than a genealogically relevant relationship. Ultimately it was Grandpa Jeff of Scandinavian stock who really healed the family after the thirty-year disconnect begun at Ryan's birth. First, it was simply that Grandpa, a World War II Navy man, loved having a boat in the family. That was thanks to Gary, Katherine's husband, who made Ryan a partner in the boat. And when Grandpa shared his war stories at sea or the family's sailing trips, Ryan was an avid listener. In hearing his grandfather describe a near-death experience during the battle of Midway, Ryan's feelings surprised him, how happy his grandfather's survival made him. The grandson began claiming a heritage: they were people of the water. When Ryan lamented his financing problems in growing his marine repair business, the need to buy expensive boat lifts and lease space at the Terminal, Grandpa piped up and said he'd like to invest in the business.

This connection to his grandfather layered the veneer of legacy over Ryan's existing sense of responsibility to his family, and his own ambitions. A family business. Ryan would say he 'worked his ass off' to make it successful. While the dot.com bubble bursting diminished some of the luxury boat work, it had started coming back in the last two years. Coupled with his commercial fishing boat repair contacts, the business was doing well now. Well enough, that fulfilling Mimi's incessant desire to have a real home had come next. Life was good.

Liv noticed there was a walkway around to the yard in back. The house sat on the western slope of the street, two-storied from the front, but really three in the back with a daylight, walk-out doorway to the yard. The views were all out to the southwest which meant good sun on the days Seattle offered it. I'd have my own entry, was her first real affirmation of the space.

When Mimi opened the door, it was Shakti who threw herself at Liv. "Mommy, Mommy, finally you're here. I've got so much to tell you. Guess what I did to little Jeff, Mommy? I changed his diaper, poop and all!"

"That's great, honey," Liv affirmed with enthusiasm. She picked Shakti up for a hug and rolled her eyes at Mimi. "That must have been fun." Liv's sarcasm leaked through, causing a stare from Shakti, who not only knew when Liv was being phony, but also called her on it.

Mimi was laughing. "I'll describe it later – if you want to hear the details." She shook her head and mouthed the word, 'messy.' "Come in – are you hungry for some lunch?"

"Sure. All I've had is a stale donut and coffee. Oh, guess what, Elyse just got engaged."

"Really? To the attorney guy?"

"Yep. Cory. She is so, so happy, bouncing off the walls happy."

Mimi didn't want to spend much time on Elyse's good news, intuiting that at this fresh state, Liv might be feeling a little jealous, or even sad. "But what about you? How was the big date?"

Liv saw that Shakti's round eyes, sharing Liv's changeable sea colors, and popping out from a mass of dark brown curls, were totally attentive to what would come out of her mother's mouth next. Shakti was always on the alert for clues about what Liv called 'the daddy dilemma.'

Shakti was a quick learner and precocious in her behaviors, absorbing details of the adult world around her, eager to act just as the older girls did, especially her mommy. No sooner did Shakti graduate from going everywhere in strollers, then she began pushing her dollies, bunnies, and other stuffed animals around in her own mini-stroller while mimicking all her mother's actions. Just as Liv rarely left the house without her shoulder bag, backpack, and baby kit bag, Shakti accumulated her own assortment of purses and bags, flinging them over her bird-like shoulders with a sophistication that would make Elyse laugh out loud. In short, not much of what Liv said or did escaped her daughter's watchful intense eyes that caught all the details in high definition.

"Mommy, I made this for you!" Shakti eagerly held up a drawing, a primitive rendition of a little girl in bed next to a crib with a baby and then outside the house was a woman and man walking hand-in-hand. "See I showed you going on a date." The little girl was mostly a head of brown curls, just like the woman on the date had too.

"That's really good! Here's you and Jeff in the house and that's me outside, right?"

"Of course. See your hair."

"And who's that figure?"

"Oh Mommy, you know, that's the man from the date. Did you like him?"

This was always so hard for Liv. Early on she'd learned that for her own peace of mind, she needed to craft honest answers for her child. And for Shakti's sake, they had to be simple and not upsetting. Those first years after Shakti's birth had been easy, but then the questions had come. Liv and Elyse had a recurring discussion about how Liv should talk about Rama, Shakti's father in India. Elyse called it Liv's lusty affair, but for her it was more like destiny. Liv could never say she regretted what had happened. It was too real and meaningful, too much of a step out of a stale college relationship with Devin and into a world of defining choices and consequences, a world of being an adult. No, she wouldn't disown those choices. Especially not when the great feminine power of the universe, Shakti, was incarnated as her own child to love and care for. Given Liv's time in college longing to be more worldly and interesting, to not continue living the lifestyle of a white privileged girl, she and Elyse had long ago concluded that it was as though Shakti arose from Liv's own yearnings, a modern-day virgin birth of the thought becoming real. Except Liv was no virgin.

But how do you tell your inquisitive youngster at three years old about her missing daddy? Because of course, the questions started coming once Shakti was aware of daddies dropping off and picking up their kids at daycare. "Mommy, where's my daddy?"

That broke Liv's heart. That was the hard part of all this. Even before the question came, Liv ruled out claiming Rama was dead, unwilling to engrave that inscription on Shakti's life. She'd tested the divorce idea on Elyse, thinking that would be a common enough word among the children as Shakti grew up. But when Liv rehearsed the story, 'I met a man in India who's your father, but we're divorced now,' she didn't like the after-taste of that either. Elyse suggested that Liv could talk about it in a way that made Rama seem inaccessible to Shakti and avoid the questions about seeing him or him visiting Liv. In the end, it simply evolved as simple answers to questions Shakti posed.

Liv began a journal while pregnant and now in a second book she continued it, recording favorite moments, but also keeping track of what she said to Shakti about her father.

> Shakti: "Jason has a daddy. Do I have a daddy too?"
> Liv: "No, not right now." (Liv noted for history that Shakti was asking about a relationship in the moment, not whether she had a biological father.)
> Shakti, next day: "Why not?"
> Liv: "Because it just happens that way. Not all children have daddies all the time. Sometimes they have a daddy and then other times they don't. Right now, you don't have one. We have each other. And you have Grandma and Grandpa, and Uncle Ryan and Aunt Mimi, and Auntie Elyse. And we all love each other very much."

When Shakti was four, little Jeff was born. Then she began seeing her aunt and uncle and the baby together a lot. New questions arose.

> Shakti: "Little Jeff has Uncle Ryan for a daddy. Can I have a daddy too? Can Uncle Ryan be my daddy? When is it my turn to have a daddy?"
> Liv: "Well, your Uncle Ryan is sort of like a daddy to you. But really, for you to have a daddy, Mommy has to decide that she loves a man very much and wants that man to live with us."
> Shakti: "When will you do that, Mommy?"
> Liv: "I need to meet the person first and then go on dates with him and decide I like him."
> Shakti: "What's a date?"
> Liv: "A date, it's like time for just me and him to get to know each other. I might let you stay with Grandma or Elyse, while I go out and get to know someone."
> Shakti: "Do I get to meet a date too?"
> Liv: "If I think that's right for us."

With kindergarten, the questions got tougher. Some idiotic teacher, oblivious in Liv's opinion to current societal conditions, decided doing family trees was a great way to teach about familial relationships. By then, Shakti was savvy enough to absorb the idea of fatherhood, and that there must be someone out there already who was her father.

    Shakti: "Mommy, who is my father?"
    Liv: "Why are you asking?"
    Shakti: "Miss Martinez said everyone has a mother and a father. And when I told her I didn't have a daddy yet, that it wasn't my turn, she said, everyone has a father. So, who is my father?"

Liv had known this time would come, and again had rehearsed conversations with Elyse.

    Liv: "Yes, that's right, everyone has a mother and father. But sometimes mothers and fathers don't stay together. They're together for a while and then they separate. I separated from your father before you were born. So yes, you have a father."
    Shakti, next day: "Who is my father?"
    Liv: "Rama."
    Shakti: "Rama. Where does he live?"
    Liv: "In India."
    Shakti, a week later: "Mommy, where is India?"
    Liv: "Here, I'll show you on the globe. Here's where we are in Seattle. And all the way around the world, here's India."
    Shakti: "Is that far?"
    Liv: "Very far. Even by airplane."
    Shakti, a few days later: "Mommy, Marcella says that it's not possible for Rama to be in India because mothers and fathers have to be in the same place to make babies."
    Liv: "Marcella's right. Before you were born I went to India. And I met your father. And we came together and made you. And then I came home, and you were inside me. And then you were born."

Months passed. And then just last week, Liv recorded their most recent conversation.

    Shakti: "Can I go to India and meet my father?"
    Liv: "Someday, if you want to."
    Shakti: "Can we go now?"
    Liv: "No, the time is not right."
    Shakti: "Why not?

Liv: "Because...because I say so. Someday, when you're all grown up, then you can decide if you want to go."

Liv knew that the questions would keep coming and continued mental preparations to craft the shortest, simplest answers she could. At some point, she knew she would need to share the letter from Rama tucked in the journal pocket addressed *"To my child."* When she'd received the letter in response to hers informing Rama of his child's existence, she'd been tempted to open it. But it felt sacred. For Shakti alone, at the right time, eighteen Liv hoped, but the right time whenever that came. Someday, Shakti would comprehend the complete unvarnished truth and would make her own decision to read the letter.

In the meantime, Liv kept alive her correspondence with her friend, Arita, Rama's former co-worker still living in Mumbai. A couple of years ago, Liv learned from Arita that Rama married and had a job with the government working in agriculture. The news of his marriage pierced her heart and saddened her, surprising in its revelation of some latent hope or dream that was deeply buried.

Just a few months ago, Liv received an email from Arita about her latest feminist activist events, mentioning at the close the birth of a son to Rama. Shakti had a half-brother now! Liv immediately wanted to get on a plane and go meet this new relation. Of course, she couldn't. Wouldn't. She'd cried at the time, tears of both joy and sorrow.

"Mommy, earth to Mommy, did you like the date?"

"Oh, sorry, sweetie. I don't know where my mind went." Liv's eyes refocused on her daughter. "No Shakti, I really didn't like the man on the date." Shakti's drive to know if daddy material was in the making quickly transformed into sad eyes and a droopy mouth. She tore up the drawing. Liv looked at Mimi for help.

"Hey, where did Jeff go? I thought you were watching him?"

"Oh, he's downstairs with Uncle Ryan and that other man. They're working."

"Well let's all go and invite them to the excellent mac and cheese lunch you helped me make, okay?" With that, Mimi put her hand out to Shakti, who looked at her mother as though she'd flunked a test.

Liv knelt beside her. "I have to find a good one for us, darling. He has to be just right."

Shakti smiled and hugged Liv. "Okay, you'll try again, won't you?"

"For sure."

They all went downstairs to the basement space being remodeled into a mother-in-law unit. Mimi led to catch Shakti just in case she fell on the old wood of the steep basement stairs. They could hear the guys working, Ryan nailing up wallboard and his friend working on the sink's plumbing.

"Hey, you two, ready for some mac and cheese?" Mimi was excited to introduce Ryan's friend Eric to Liv. The first time Mimi met him down at the shop a few weeks ago – after recovering from how knock-out good-looking Eric was – she'd grilled Ryan with probing questions: is he married? Dating someone? A nice person? Do you think he and Liv would hit it off? Ryan teased Mimi, 'you mean I can't hire a new guy without him being Liv material?'

Eventually Mimi garnered enough information on Eric to think there was potential. Ryan described him as an old Bering Sea fishing buddy, 'a little wild' back then. But then Ryan put some context around that, pointing out that you had to be a little wild to go out on those boats up there. The younger crew usually wound up drinking too much when they had time off. Left unmentioned were flings with the native Indian girls since Ryan had done that himself each summer until he met Mimi. Nor did he try to convey his intuition about Eric, that he was more than wild. Ryan recalled one strip poker game where Eric mercilessly bullied the girl who didn't want to take off her bra. Of course, Eric had been drunk; it was all wild oats and guys grow out of that, as he had.

During the past winter, Eric turned up at the shop looking for work. Ryan hadn't seen him in over a year. Eric had heard Ryan's business was growing and made a pitch that he could use help he could trust. Ryan knew Eric was a highly reliable worker and knowledgeable about commercial fishing vessels, maybe not as fast with machinery as Ryan, but overall a good mechanic. They started going out for lunch once a week and that was when Ryan got a sense of Eric's current lifestyle. With some of his sizeable summer earnings, he'd picked up a fixer upper on lower Queen Anne with one of those low-down payment loans. As income permitted, Eric was renovating it and thought he might flip it and make a killing. After a beer or two, he'd sometimes lean closer to Ryan and share his latest male triumph: 'you should have seen this babe Saturday night! Really hot. Two dates and I had her in bed.' When Ryan suggested that some things never change, Eric dropped his braggadocio persona and opened up a little. "Yeah, it's fun, like the old times, but I'm looking at you, looking at where I am now not wanting to go to Alaska anymore, and I'm thinking, maybe it's time, time to settle down, have a boat of my own, and somebody I really care about."

After Mimi fastened on to Eric's potential and suggested introducing him to Liv, Ryan wasn't sure he thought Eric was right. But hell, that would be Liv's decision. Ryan didn't know though how to arrange a fix-up or deal with the existence of Shakti, so he continued to ignore Mimi's prodding. Then the house basement remodel presented a perfect opportunity to invite Eric over to make extra money, and wait for some natural meeting of the two, or three, to happen. With Shakti having a sleep-over last night, Mimi was on Ryan's case to get Eric over on Sunday so this 'natural' meeting could happen.

Eric turned his head from his crouch below the kitchen sink, little Jeff watching his every turn of the plumber's wrench, and yelled back over his shoulder. "Mac and cheese, yahoo! Got any dogs to go with it?"

"Yeah, I think we can fry up some puppies." Mimi and Shakti stepped off the stairs and she came running over to Jeff.

"Have you been a good boy? Are you bothering this man?" Shakti was the boss lady with her cousin, not for a second doubting she'd attained enough life knowledge to take control of him.

With her voice, strangely deep for a little girl, Eric pulled away from his last turn of the wrench to take her in. With the drama of the caterpillar in *Alice in Wonderland*, he said, "And *who* are you?" He took in her coloring and looked up to see Liv coming towards her. He noticed similarity in their hair and eye color, but as he checked Liv over very directly, as was his habit with women, making his back-of-the-napkin assessment the way some men penciled in key numbers of a deal, he didn't see much else in common between the two. Certainly not skin color. Nor the eye shape or nose. The woman was Irish looking, and had attractive reddish hair with some blond highlights, very fair skin. Striking, beautiful even. Unimpressive breasts but hips you would be able to grab on to. Looked good in tight jeans.

Mimi jumped in to make introductions. "This is Liv, Ryan's sister, and this little darling is Shakti…" Mimi paused, considering, and then took the plunge, "…Liv's daughter, Jeff's only cousin." Mimi scanned Eric's face to catch his first impression. She didn't see any change in affect, only his glances back and forth from one to the other.

Liv's focus coming down the stairs had been on the sliding glass doors to a yard - *wouldn't that be great* - when she turned her head and saw this Viking guy say something to Shakti. *God, he's good looking!* Even in his old wrinkled buttoned shirt, he could have been a model out of *Vanity Fair* ads. His blond hair rolled like waves back from a broad, high forehead that sat above piercing blue eyes. He was giving her the once-over now, looking her down and up, making her feel naked.

His wide smile at Shakti showed his well-cared-for white teeth. "No, Miss Shakti, Jeff has not been bothering me. My new apprentice is learning the trade."

"Apprentice? What does that mean?" Every Eric response brought forth another question. Liv, Mimi and now Ryan all watched in suspended animation, each processing Eric's encounter with Shakti. Ryan grew uncomfortable as a member of this assessment team and moved toward the stairs. "I'll wash up. Mimi, I'm starving, can you get lunch set up?"

"In a flash." Mimi paused considering the tableau. "Jeff, Shakti, want to come help me?"

Liv lowered her head, feeling uncomfortable. Then raising her eyes, with an "I'll help too" she met a steady gaze. She didn't know whether to say something more or invite him up, so she simply smiled lightly, turned, and went up to the kitchen. As she entered the workspace, Mimi was pulling out the frying pan. "How can I help?"

"You fry them up, okay?" As Mimi got the hot dogs out of the fridge and handed the package over to Liv, she sought to catch her eyes.

Liv feeling embarrassed looked up with a slight blush "I know. He's gorgeous."

"That he is for sure."

Liv wanted to ask if he was available, held off, but then whispered, "Does he know I'm not married?"

Mimi kept her voice low as she also kept an eye to Shakti getting Jeff into his high chair in the dining room. "No, neither of us talked about you to him." Now she tried to sound more removed from Liv's obvious interest in Eric, hoping to keep the lunch feeling low-key. "There's been no reason. I mean Eric works for Ryan at the business and the guys there, all they talk about is boats."

Ryan came out of the bathroom; Eric was upstairs now and took his turn. Liv did the final prep while Mimi got Shakti settled in at the table and working on her mac and cheese. Liv sat next to her. "What else did you do on your sleep-over?"

"We watched some Dora cartoons and then we ate chocolate cake. And I was really good and took a bath."

"You should have seen her face and hands with all the goopy frosting!" Mimi was laughing, keeping one eye towards the fry pan.

"Mommy, Jeff took a bath too. He has a penis." Ryan heard that too, and they all locked eyes and choked back outright guffaws.

"Well Shakti, actually I knew that. But let's talk about that another time, okay?"

"Okay, but I have questions, so don't forget."

"You know I won't."

Eric and Ryan were sitting down, and Mimi was planting the plate of hot dogs among the basket of rolls and condiments. "Help yourselves guys."

A contemporary photo of diversity in America emerged at the table, which despite its superficiality, Liv loved. Liv's craving for cultural differences was something she satisfied for the most part in her work. But here, in this moment tingly with possibility, using her awareness of Eric's perspective on them, she noticed their varied array of faces. Shakti looking Indian. Ryan, her half-brother, looking more Hispanic as his birth father had been. Despite freckles and a hint of red in his straight hair, his solid muscular body on the short side and rounded features led her at times to tease and call him Roberto. Mimi was Vietnamese, a pixie who five years younger than her husband could have passed for an adolescent - in a quick glimpse, almost a child. Jeff, unformed at this age, revealed no readily apparent racial heritage. A mix of Asian, Hispanic, Irish, and Scandinavian, it remained to be seen if any racial characteristics beyond a slightly sallow complexion would become dominant. For now, he was generically pleasant. Mimi said Jeff was what the twenty-first century person would look like.

    Ryan's priority was getting the near-to-complete remodel rented out. Oblivious at times as to what could be discussed around Shakti, he got right to the point. "What do you think, Sis? Do you want to move in downstairs?" He was ready to say more but Mimi touched his arm, moving her eyes to Shakti who looked up from her self-assigned task of supervising Jeff's lunch. Her eyes were big.

    At another time, Liv might have deflected the conversation, but with Elyse's news that morning, and considerations of the back yard and shared babysitting, she was ready to take the plunge. "Well, actually, I'm thinking it might be just right for us. What do you think, sweetie? Would you like to come and live downstairs?"

    Eric meanwhile was picking up on the absence of a wedding ring on Liv's hand, and no reference to discussing a move with a husband. This is getting more interesting was his thought, while an attraction to Liv was palpable. He started a mental list of follow-up questions on Liv for Ryan.

    "Really, you mean we'd leave the apartment and Tia Elyse and come here to live?"

    "Yes, that's what I'm asking. And I haven't had a moment to tell you but Tia is moving too."

    "Here with us?"

    "No, she's going to..." oh dear, Liv considered, I need to use the married word which only complicates the conversation with her. "She's going to move to a bigger place where we can still visit her, but it won't be in our building."

    "But we'll still see her?"

    "For sure, Shakti, Elyse will invite us over to her new place, and we could invite her here."

    Eric was wondering if Liv was lesbian or bisexual now.

"That would be okay then." Her little but quick mind was already calculating, "So we'd live here with Uncle Ryan and Aunt Mimi and Little Jeff?"

"Yep. That's right. We would live downstairs and they would live upstairs."

With that, Shakti slid off her chair and stood close to Liv. "Mommy, then I could be with them every day, and Uncle Ryan would be like a daddy, right?"

Oh dear. Liv regretted now not having squelched this conversation. The uncomfortable silence added another question to Eric's list: who was this little girl's father?

Mimi stared at Ryan, not wanting to come out with what might sound wrong to him.

Ryan subconsciously knew this was part of the deal, that in some way his presence in the house would help with Shakti. For him, it was part of the commitment he'd made to Liv when he'd so strongly encouraged her not to give the baby up for adoption. He looked at Shakti and his mind, focused on getting the rental solidified, melted into his heart. Shakti was looking from her mom to him and starting to look worried. "Come over here you ragamuffin."

Shakti moved to his side of the table. "What's a ragamuffin?"

Ryan swiveled in his chair and lifted her onto his knee. "A ragamuffin is a kid like you who always looks like she's never put a comb to her hair and dresses herself in funny clothes, like your mom's old t-shirt that's too big for you."

"Oh."

"I want you to know Miss Shakti that if you move downstairs, I'll see you every day and pick you up and hug you and then tickle you till you scream. And we'll get to do more things together because we'll all be so close. Does that sound good?"

A smile filled her face as her eyes lit up too. "But I'll tickle you first!" her tiny hands were now moving under his arms and chin.

He brought her close and then put her down. "Let's eat. My lunch is getting cold."

Liv relaxed. "I guess we have a deal then, Bro, unless you plan to charge me an arm and a leg for the place."

"What are you paying now?"

"A thousand a month."

"Honestly, if I rented it on the market, I'd look to make more..."

Mimi was pinching his arm hard now, determined not to let this opportunity slip away. "Remember we talked about how easy it would be to share babysitting, help each other with picking up items at the store, sharing meals sometime, how much fun the kids would have with each other...you can't put a price on all that...I just know I'd love it!"

Ryan broke out in a laugh. "I knew you were thinking all that, I was just playing with you." He faced Liv, "We'll be okay with the thousand, and you'll definitely get some upgrades, the yard, brand new appliances, a washer and dryer right in your place, even paint colors of your choice. It'll feel more like your own place."

Liv considered that washer/dryer remark, a possible overlap with her space. "So how would that laundry thing work, would it be where it is now under the stairs?"

Mimi intuited the issue for Liv's privacy. "We already figured that out in case we were renting to non-family. Some of that open space is going to get more chopped up so there's a tiny laundry room with access from the stairs, and there'll be a door to your place."

"Oh. Okay, maybe you can show me after lunch."

Eric knew now that Liv was a single mom, and no father was in the picture. He'd felt odd being there during this private conversation in his boss's family – and a tad ignored which hardly ever happened to him. To relieve his own tension, he interjected, "Ryan, I could help you with that. You know us boat guys know how to make things functional in small spaces."

That drew a chuckle from Ryan. "Always looking to get me to pay you for more things, you fox."

Following lunch, the ongoing sidebar was Shakti taking charge of Jeff to the point where Mimi wondered if this combo was such a great idea. Ryan, Eric, and Liv went back downstairs to discuss the design of the laundry room and consider the impact on the living area. Liv's mind moved quickly then to colors and how they'd be using the backyard. She'd get her mother involved in the décor and maybe, just maybe, it was time for a new sofa. She made a mental note to begin searching Craigslist for items. By the time she was ready to leave, her spirits were high. "I think it's time I gave poor Jeff a break from Miss Bossy. Thank you so much, Bro, I'm really excited about this now!"

"Yeah, it's a good next step, especially with Elyse moving out too. What's the deal there?"

"Her long-time boyfriend Cory proposed, so they'll be getting married sometime this year."

"Nice. Remind me what he does."

"He's a civil rights attorney. He does these big class action suits for women and minorities in the workplace."

"That can be tough until he gets paid. Is Elyse ready for that?"

"Oh, she's thrilled. He had a huge verdict last year, enough to give him a down payment on a nice house, and this year he's working on an even bigger case, involving women at Boeing I think.

So, she's not breaking off a lesbian relationship, was Eric's new factoid.

"Well, good. Elyse will keep working for their bread and butter money. Are they talking kids?"

"I imagine. We didn't get to that topic though."

Eric shifted. Ryan realized it was time to get back to work. "Okay, we need to keep making things happen here. See you soon. You can send Shakti down for a goodbye hug."

Liv brought herself close to Ryan. "You're the best. Thank you so much." She turned to Eric. "And nice meeting you and thanks for all the work you're doing to fix up MY PLACE." With that she grinned, and Eric saw that wide smile under equally wide vivacious eyes. *Gorgeous, this one could be fun.*

While Liv and Mimi dealt with packing up Shakti's sleep-over entourage, animals and dolls that accompanied her as though she'd conducted a royal visit, they shared ideas about what the move-in would mean.

Downstairs Eric settled in at the sink area again to test out his work. He knew the answers now to many of his questions, enough that he wouldn't risk showing interest in Liv at this point to his boss. As he continued working and got more into the specifics of the laundry room, he experienced a sense of comradery in doing this work. He liked these people. He liked working side-by-side with Ryan. An idea sparked: maybe I could even be a partner in the business. *Definitely something to consider. No need to rush with Liv. She's obviously open and fair game.* He knew that look she'd given him when she met him, that shock of attraction that was one he'd seen often, the feminine hunger for a man, a good time in the sack. *Careful! There's more at stake here now. Take it slow and easy. Plenty of time and opportunity.* He turned on the water at the sink yet again, double checking all the connections he'd made. A strong sense of satisfaction with his work welled up and surged into an expansive wave of his own potential.

    Once Liv was back in her apartment, and following a rather exhaustive conversation with Shakti about the move – yes, even those stuffed creatures who were currently not her favorites could tag along - Liv collapsed on the sofa, and called Elyse. With it going on four, ordinarily she and Cory would still be up to something before he returned to his own place on Capitol Hill to be positioned for his routine early Monday morning start. That often left weekend debrief time on Sunday evenings. "Hi, where are you?"

    "We're out at Shilshole, walking the beach. It's a beautiful day if you haven't noticed. You?"

    "Back home. Lots to share. I can't believe it's still the same day as this morning. Are you free tonight, or has the thought of wedded bliss so overcome Mr. Hot Shot Attorney that he's actually going to stay beyond dinner with you?"

    "Hardly, he's got some important motion in court tomorrow, so he'll probably drop me off early. I'll come by when I'm back, okay?"

    "Great, I can't wait to tell you about meeting the hands-down best-looking guy I've met in years."

    "Yeah, well, you know what I think about those types."

    "Anyway, see you about eight, after Shakti's had her bath?"

    "Sure."

Their debrief was packed with Liv's description of Ryan's apartment, interjected on a recurring basis with Shakti's own commentary. She was already projecting their new lives complete with Uncle Ryan tickling her every day and her ideas for a puppy or kitty in the yard. Only after tucking her away for the night, something Elyse and Liv enjoyed sharing Sundays, taking turns reading all the favorite stories, only after all the rituals did they return to the living room for their BFF shares that typically centered on men or work or what other women did.

"So, tell me about the gorgeous guy – how'd you meet someone today anyhow?"

"He works for Ryan at the boat repair, and he's helping out with the basement remodel. I came down the stairs to look at the space, and first noticed a body crouched by the sink. Then he turned, and honestly, oh my god Elyse, it was like seeing someone from a movie."

"Name?"

"Eric."

"Description with details?"

"Okay, so he's got this dark blond wavy hair, a really strong face with this perfect straight nose, and piercing light blue eyes, and..."

"Probably contacts."

"...and a really nice solid-looking body. And when he smiled at Shakti, it was like a toothpaste commercial."

"Sounds like Dudley Do-right from the Rocky and Bullwinkle show." While both too young to have seen it in the 60s, the reruns on YouTube had been popular in the dorm for a while.

Liv refused to let her enthusiasm lose out to sarcasm. "So, here's the thing, I mean he got the full dose of me and Shakti at once. And the way the conversation went about my moving there it was like all immediately apparent: me, single mom, Shakti."

"So?"

"So, if he calls or gets interested - which he might, maybe, I mean he looked at me like he enjoyed what he saw - well he knows what the situation is."

"We've had this talk before when we used to watch *Sex and the City*. If he's too good looking and looks at a woman in that kind of way, he's too good to be true. There's some huge flaw lurking, some gigantic ego or macho personality, and you'll be sorry to get involved with him."

Liv knew those conversations well. And yet - *who knows, everyone is different.* "I know. But look, it just lit me up a while, okay? Let's change the subject." Liv's body mirrored the shift as she rose to pour more wine. "Now that you're *engaged*..." Liv drew out the word and mocked looking at her birthstone ring as though it were a diamond, "... what did you do and talk about today?"

"You won't be surprised to hear that while I was trying to stay romantic a bit longer, dwelling on the warm, fuzzy stuff, remembering when we first met at a women's protest, Cory moved into his methodical prep mode as though a big trial was coming up, thinking about dates for the wedding, places, people...."

"That's not really you."

"No, it's not. I kept trying to stay with the spirit of the thing, like what would be fun, what would feel good that day: inside? outside? How big a party? Of course, there has to be music and dancing."

"Was he into that?"

"Sure. We visualized it all. But then he asked what these things cost. I don't know, but I recall people saying how expensive weddings have gotten. I said, well maybe it'll be several thousand dollars, like maybe $5,000 or more. That deflated him, as he wants to put most of his money into the house. He knows neither I, nor certainly not my mom, have much to kick in. Anyway, the mood down-shifted a little. We brainstormed places to cost out, like the Mountaineers Club or the Norwegian place in Ballard, maybe community centers? That's my job now."

"How many people are you talking about? You know a lot of people, and a party, to be the kind you like, like your friend Maria's wedding, you get into a hundred folks or more."

"We started guesstimating numbers. Both our families are relatively small, but we have friends from different settings, so it started adding up fast. Which I must tell you, Maid of Honor...."

"Or am I Matron?"

"Whatever you are, you need to know that Cory was talking about both law school buddies and climbing buddies, so I'm pretty sure Steve and Devin will wind up on the list."

"Shit." Seven years ago, Liv had left Devin standing staring at her at Seattle Center. She'd never written that follow-up letter to him that Elyse and Ryan thought she should, that even she herself thought she should. It just hadn't happened. As a result, her ex-live-in boyfriend, dating back to high school days, had never learned, as far as Liv knew, that she'd become pregnant on her internship to India and actually had a baby. All Devin knew was that Liv walked out of his life, having changed in vague ways he never understood.

"You never wrote that letter to him, did you?"

"No."

"Well, start prepping what you're going to say at my wedding when he figures out Shakti, the flower girl, is yours."

"Is he dating or married now?"

"Not sure, but when I saw him last at New Year's at a climbers' party, he seemed really happy with this girl named Eddi."

Liv went quiet. All she knew is she didn't want to attend Elyse's wedding without a date. Maybe, a really good-looking date? "Will you be inviting Ryan and Mimi?"

"Of course, and your folks. You'll have your support network there."

"Thanks. Selena? And what about David and Jonathan?"

"Definitely." Selena was a mutual friend of theirs. Elyse met her while working in her City of Seattle neighborhood services job, when Selena had just become a program manager at the Multi-Service Center of North Seattle, running the family assistance program there. It was Selena whom Elyse had sent Liv to, to see about getting a job after her four years at the International Rescue Committee. Liv had wound up with a job at the MSC working in the programs Selena managed, helping families with everything from welfare advocacy to financial literacy and employment opportunities. It was a natural next step after helping refugee families, and placed Liv in one of the largest social service agencies in King County. Once Selena moved over to the domestic abuse counseling area which also involved managing the temporary emergency shelters, Liv and she became fast friends. More recently, Liv was promoted to Selena's old job as program manager, and Selena became a deputy director managing even more programs including childcare. They were tight at work, both single moms for some time now with Selena separated from her husband. Regular girls' nights out including Elyse had solidified this feminist trio of women making their way doing good. "Is she dating anyone yet?"

"No, she's not sure she's ready."

"Sounds like she needs a push. Maybe time for another night out together and I can reel in someone for her, at least for a little frolic." 'Frolic and detour' was a term Elyse picked up from one of Cory's law books laying around, and she quickly adopted it to the dating scene of her friends. Elyse had a knack of turning their soirees into guy-baiting events if one of them was in need and looking for male companionship. On several occasions, she'd shown an uncanny ability to pick up vibes directed at her friends in bar settings. For a couple of years, she'd lowered the volume of her own emissions, not interested in giving Cory any reason to doubt her. But she could spy a guy interested in Selena or Liv and then with charm and finesse get the initial intros made. Not that many of these proceeded to a successful dating pattern, but it kept hope up and made them laugh a lot.

"Yeah, let's set something up. I'll see her midweek for lunch and hear the latest."

"When does she finish grad school?" Both Selena and Liv had reached that point in their nonprofit careers where another degree would help them move into better paying work. Elyse meanwhile was content with her own move from the city into politics and serving as staff for a City Council member. She saw her path as building on her city networks, solving problems that mattered to constituents, and eventually, maybe running for office herself.

"In December, if all goes as planned."

"You know, with this move to Ryan's you should think about grad school more seriously. I bet that Mimi would help you make it work, And you, with your parents, you know they'd help you pay for it. Or you could do student loans."

As Elyse spoke, Liv's internal calendar was agreeing: *maybe now is exactly the right time to focus some attention on myself.* "You could be right. Maybe that's an extra benefit to moving. I'll talk to Mimi about it. Although it's not like I know what I would study. In the past, well, you know, one time it was international relations, another time it was nonprofit management. Or should I break out of the nonprofit world and go into something else?"

"Right, like banking, or IT? Come on Liv, we know you're not going to like something that doesn't have a strong meaning you resonate with."

"What about human resource management? That's working with people."

"No, that's making people obey the rules. You'd hate it. Believe me. Those HR folks at the City are lovers of death: how many good ideas can we kill today? They're at their best when they're doing things so stupid they create laughs among the downtrodden – like the Performance Information System that was supposed to help us improve our evaluation process, except it met a sudden demise as soon as the nebbish who created it realized he was PISing on people. That was a good one. No, my dear, I don't recommend HR. Or anything financial for you."

"Well, what do you think makes sense for me?"

"I'm not sure either, but I'd say build on what you like about the jobs you've had, find a thread and follow it." Elyse tried to think but tiredness from her early exuberant rise was now catching up with her. "Time for bed." She always liked to end things on a laugh. "I know, what if you went into counseling, and ran men's study groups? It would be a really good way to meet guys!"

Liv in fact did laugh and enjoyed for a moment the vision of herself with a small notebook and pen seated in a circle of men asking them probing questions. "It would be a new angle on getting information for our never boring topic of gender relations." Lowering her voice, Liv continued, "And sir, what do you believe is the role of men in a society where women can do it all on their own? Do you see yourself as a protector? A provider? A sperm donor?"

Elyse's energy popped up with that. "Yes, I see the ball-breaking psychologist, Liv Anderson, conducting research and writing a ground-breaking book on post-modern gender construction."

"Me? A ball-breaker? Me, sweet Liv?"

Elyse hushed her and pointed to Shakti's bedroom. "Yes, you, my friend. You who cut off Devin at the knees. You who walked out on Rama in the truck. Bring this Eric guy on, and let's see what you do to him!"

"Enough. Out of here. Just out. Go sleep and let me sleep." With that they hugged, and Elyse left. Brushing her teeth that night, noticing in the mirror a new lightness in her demeanor, Liv assessed: what a difference a day makes. Last night, she'd been blue as one relationship melted and washed out of her life. Tonight, a new place to live, a handsome guy, possibly grad school. Life was looking better, way better.

Liv often read herself to sleep. Looking over her latest library and used book pile, Liv returned to *The Four-Fold Way*. What was that mantra from this morning? "Pay attention to what has heart and meaning." She loved that. The way of the healer.

The graphic for that chapter had a seasonal connection to spring. Checking the other ways, she saw that each was put in the context of a season and offered a special mantra. A bit of guidance for the year of change that was unfolding was heartening, as though some divine hand was holding hers while she migrated.

    Looking again at the opening page of the way of the healer, she wondered how this would apply to her life in this very moment. A black and white ink graphic depicted a native woman, balancing precariously in a very narrow opening between two cliffs, and reaching into the cliff's side to gather something. A poem by Antonio Machado accompanied it:

> *Last night, as I was sleeping,*
> *I dreamt – marvelous error! –*
> *that I had a beehive here inside my heart.*
> *And the golden bees*
> *were making white combs*
> *and sweet honey*
> *from my old failures.*

Bees inside her heart "making sweet honey from my old failures," evoked forgiveness, a pardon for Liv's past choices. Tears came to her eyes and then moistened her cheeks. *Yes, I haven't succeeded the way other women have, like Elyse has now, but that's behind me.* Optimism lit up her mind. No need to read more right now. The book slipped to the rug. Feeling very full, she slid between the covers, softly closed her eyes, and held the image of bees and sweet honey in her heart.

Wednesday, April 4

The beginnings of the Multi-Service Center's weeks were always hectic with new problems and clients who surfaced over the weekend. Which made Liv and Selena wait till Wednesdays for their weekly lunches. Tuesdays were staff check-in days to share issues and resources while they worked to stay on top of their short term and intermediate goals for MSC. For years now, they'd had an excellent Executive Director, Audrey Jiménez, who knew how to run a collaborative and focused work environment. Among staff, attitudes were positive and morale high. Liv knew she'd made the right move three years ago. She'd loved being at the Rescue Committee because it made her feel part of international work as she tended to re-settling refugees. But the relatively small office offered no opportunities for advancement. Her parents had strongly encouraged her to go to work for a larger organization with a career track and promotional opportunities, and better health benefits. And maybe a raise now and then.

After the dot-com bust in the early 2000s, her dad's IT consulting practice had suffered and caused her parents to look long and hard at their discretionary expenses, like Shakti's day care, like the boat. But as Liv knew, their abundant network rescued them in ways that simply weren't available to her refugees or now to her families in need. Grandpa and Ryan had both stepped up to share more boat expense and with Liv's own job change came a reduced rate for childcare. That combined with a small raise helped lift half the burden from her parents on that score. With Shakti being older, Liv had become more comfortable dragging her across the city in two buses at early morning hours. They were close if Shakti got sick. But it did make for a long and tiring day. With the move to Ryan's it was possible that Mimi on her way home from teaching would pick Shakti up, a special plus for them both. And one that might enable Liv's taking off to grad school one or two nights a week directly from work.

As Liv and her colleague walked to their favorite café on 45th street for their weekly lunch, Selena looked more like she was a feisty race horse, about to bare its teeth. Yet another domestic violence case had shown up Monday, and Selena was outraged: "The woman just got out of Harborview where they'd put her broken arm in a cast and treated her facial lacerations. It was bad, Liv, what her husband did to her. It made me sick inside. Her eye may never look the same again, plus there could be vision issues. So, first thing, we got all hands on deck to get her into an emergency shelter that night along with her two kids her mother had been watching. They're all so fucking scared. And meanwhile her job at the restaurant is in jeopardy. And the husband just lost his job, which is why he was drunk and became violent. The kids are only four and six. Imagine them watching that!"

"I don't know how you do it, helping people who are physically in such a bad way. I'm not sure I could."

"Of course, you could. It's just not what you're called to do." Although she knew that Liv was half-right and softer at the core. They'd had those conversations before, learning each other's backgrounds and comparing their choices. Selena had seen both sides of the world as she thought of it. There had been the good men in her mother's life and the not so good. And the evil one who fortunately her mother shed quickly. Selena had been born in Puerto Rico to a mixed African mom and mostly Hispanic dad. But he was a philanderer if there ever was one, and by two, Selena was taken by her college-educated mother to begin life anew in the States, first in Florida where relatives lived, and then to Seattle. Her mom had gotten into telecommunications and in the time of merger mania, she'd been able to land a promotion if they moved there. Their 'big adventure' was how mom marketed it to her. At thirty-five, her mom was ready for life someplace where more people got married, which she hoped was what a rainy Pacific Northwest offered, compared to Florida's Latin scene where relationships came and went too easily, at least for her. Despite a first rough winter of rain and dreariness, her mom did manage to find a good man she liked and married a white techie from Boeing. From sixteen on, Selena stepped into a different world, much more quiet and dreary, but one where nobody was getting beat up around them, where people didn't yell at each other in the streets, where she had her own room to study, and where she could go to school and feel like just one of the other bright kids with a big future. Boring but better.

Not that it kept her from making her own bad choices. The guys in high school who were more daring in their misdeeds reminded her of the Miami buzz, and they attracted her. The drugs, the petty thievery, the refusals to be bowed by school rules. She fought it though and made her way into college getting the grades that so pleased her parents. Believing that the army had reformed one of those high school boyfriends, Selena settled into a relationship that she thought gave her the best of both worlds. She stayed on track with her degree at UW, while Kyle was at army posts, training and improving himself. He persuaded her to marry after one tour of duty. By that time, right before 9/11, she had her first job after college at MSC. Her first promotion came, then another, and three years ago the baby arrived. Keelan. By then her husband was back from a second tour in Iraq and not the same guy, becoming violent with her and around their child. With her well-crafted sense of independence, she was not about to stay around and become a battered wife. Kyle had visitation rights and they were both in counseling. Selena hoped the worst was over. She just wanted to work hard, focus on Keelan as much as she could, and be really, really, careful about trusting a man again. Elyse's frolics and detours were fun in the bar, but she had no interest in seeing them through.

While Selena calmed down, Liv scoped out the café and latched on to one of the tables they preferred which provided more privacy. Liv had a lot to share about the weekend's thrust into new housing, and perfunctorily ordered her usual tuna sandwich, as she babbled on about the advantages. During the past few years, Liv had been a sympathetic listener to Selena's emotional and heart-breaking decisions. While Selena had enforced a "no whining" rule between them about the relentless slog of being a single mom, she nonetheless valued Liv's tenure in the tasks of juggling it all and her friendship in providing both advice and child care.

The punk-looking waitress with a streak of pink hair and triple earring posts brought their food, pausing an extra moment to look at Selena, as though she had a crush on her. Selena was hands down a knockout. She'd been created from a huge gene pool which gave her a warm inviting skin tone, and abundant, ever so slightly frizzed hair, both of which set off her dark eyes. Her lips were almost too big for her face, but no man ever saw that as a problem. And when summer came, and they finally shed their northwesters and cords for tank tops and shorts, Selena's lithe sexy figure took a ten to Liv's seven or eight.

"You have an admirer in case you haven't noticed."

Selena rolled her eyes. "I'm not going there. At least not yet. How about you? A different way to solve your problem?"

"No urges that way. Hey, guess who's getting married!"

"I know already, Elyse called me."

"What do you think? I mean, it's great, right?"

"It's always great when the proposal you want comes in. Then there's life ever after, happy and not so happy."

"Come on – you know Cory – really don't you think they'll make a great couple?"

"Actually, I do." Selena was smiling sincerely now. "I really do."

"Now we have to work on dates for the big event. I just met this great looking guy – but who knows – it's a long time till the wedding, likely September."

"You won't string along the Indian guy?"

"No way. That one's done. What about you?"

"No prospects really. I don't feel like dating. Keelan's a handful and I don't like bringing too many men into our lives."

Liv was quiet for a minute while she munched down some chips. "What if we did a group date kind of thing with David and Jonathan?"

"I think Jonathan's out of the picture."

"How so? I haven't spoken to either of them in way too long."

He calls occasionally, to check on me and Keelan. Last time, he said he's engaged - I'm sure he'll bring her."

"Well, we could share David!"

Selena screwed up her face.

"What?"

"Oh, he's so into law school. He's never available. I know."

"You do?" Liv's interest was piqued. She didn't know anything about David and Selena dating. A twinge in her heart belied her suppressed interest. He was supposed to be off limits to all of them.

"Yeah, there was this other wedding I needed to go to about four months ago, so I thought of him. I mean I think I'd had a yen for him going back even before Kyle and I separated. Not that I did anything about it. Not till this winter. I called him up and he was friendly enough and said sure, he'd go."

"And? That sounds like he was available?"

"Yeah, he did take me. And I was excited to be with him. But the message by the end of the evening when he brought me home was, 'I had a great time, but I really can't come in. I need to go home and study more.' And then when I pressed closer and looked up with pleading eyes, he just backed off and said, 'I really like you. But there's no place in my life right now for anything more.' And with that he was out of there."

"That sucks."

"Tell me about it."

Liv sat back. "He could still be a backup plan. He's bound to come with or without his own date. We can all hang together."

"I guess, but I'd prefer to have a real date, someone to cuddle up to after the party."

"Yeah, I know, I would too." They were quiet for a minute and then Liv remembered. "So back to the move, this is what I really wanted to talk to you about, the possibility that I could go to grad school in the evenings with Mimi's help."

"Fantastic!" Selena was a couple of quarters away from finishing her master's in social work at UW. "Have you figured out what program you to do? You weren't sure when we talked last year about it. Has the promotion and more staff responsibility clarified your thinking?"

"Actually, that's a good question, exactly how I need you to help me get clearer."

"Do you like supervising staff? Do you think you want to work your way up the admin ladder?" In part, this was what Selena herself was trying to do with her move a few years back out of supervising the family assistance work, the job where she'd hired Liv and which she now held. Selena wanted more hard-core case experience and pursued the master's in social work to have another credential and gain that 'in the trenches' perspective from working in basic services to the neediest. She knew she was tough: she could look life in the eye and not blink, however ugly and depressing the circumstances. But her long-term goal was to move through a wide swath of the agency's work and along the way learn enough to rise to an executive director position. Most likely in another large human services nonprofit. She knew she'd need years to hone her skill set in managing, not only a variety of casework and facilities, but also developing her leadership style with people. She was a big fan of Audrey and frequently noted her ways to Liv and others: look how she just got tough on that new person's absenteeism without being a bitch; look how she just ran that meeting and got us enthused about what we're doing – how did she do that? Both in the learning lab of work and through her grad work, Selena exuded confidence she would reach her goal.

With Liv, the career path would need to be different. First, at her core, Liv really wasn't someone you'd call tough. Yes, she'd made a hard choice in becoming a single mom at twenty-two, but fundamentally, she lacked determination. And the confidence that comes with achieving goals. For sure, she wasn't a natural leader. She'd have to learn her way into a skill set that would serve her in a real management position. She did that cocooning thing periodically, obviously not an extrovert like Elyse. Liv would go inside to think and give you an answer later rather than sooner. It made her look indecisive in meetings.

Which was exactly what Liv was doing now as she ate her brownie dessert deliberately: she was thinking about whether she liked supervising staff. "You know, I'm not sure I do. I mean I really like learning the program content and seeing what works and doesn't work for different clients. I like the challenges of learning the ins and outs of the federal and state safety net, and moving into advocacy for people in the system. That's been good. And I like the rewarding feeling of having helped. But I know I'd rather leave program logistics to others, have someone else handle the day-to-day setups for trainings in finding a job and finances. I'm glad to have others on my team who do that. But making things happen through others, managing them, isn't so much my thing."

"What's an example?"

"Take the new microcredit program Audrey might get us involved in. I love microcredit lending, the idea of it, what Muhammed Yunnus has set in motion around the world. And the idea that we might help participate in training women in getting into small businesses, I'm so excited about that."

"I am too, it'll be a great fit with the financial literacy trainings we do already and the employment assistance we support. But I bet it's that international connection that has you excited – am I right?"

Liv heard a thump inside as the arrow hit the target. Yes, she did love that aspect of it. Just as the Rescue Committee and refugees made her feel culturally connected to the rest of the world, the microcredit program would do the same. If she was ever going to get a chance to work globally, well anything that kept her mind and efforts in work of worldwide relevance excited her. Not that it seemed possible she'd ever leave Seattle, needing to raise Shakti and relying on her support network. "You know me too well. But when I think of doing grad work in international relations, somehow that just doesn't cut it. Like I could do it and what jobs would I be eligible for here in Seattle in two or three years?"

"Right. If you were living on the east coast, it would make more sense."

"That's just not in the picture though. What's working for me and Shakti is here, and that's my foreseeable future."

"Okay, so let's rule that out along with a management degree. But what about the certificate program at Seattle U in nonprofit leadership? You'd get to explore all the aspects of running a nonprofit, the financial side, HR, communications, marketing, and pick up some skill development, enough to help you manage programs and staff well, even if that's not your goal."

"Elyse has already turned the off button on HR. And financial? Really?"

"You know financial isn't just about accounting. I'm not talking that. But what do you think makes our programs run and pays our salaries?"

"Well, of course it's the grants and donations."

"Sure, and what are the jobs there? They're actually jobs a thinking type like you might enjoy, and which are highly transferable. Take grant-writing. That's a hugely important area to most nonprofits and certainly ours. Writing a good grant is not a piece of cake. It's tedious work in terms of compliance with long lists of deliverables the government or the corporation wants to see. But ultimately, and this is also true with the individual donors, it's about telling a compelling story about how the money will be used. Really compelling. It also spills over to the communications and marketing of the agency. Take a look at our publications and reports, the quarterly newsletter, the annual report, the special reports we do on topics. And now all the website stuff. Do you think you could be excited about the research and writing involved in grant work and publications?"

Liv was looking naively wide-eyed. "I never thought about it."

"Then I think you should. Go to lunch with Greta and look at some of her grant work. You'll need to work with her anyway to get the microcredit program off the ground. Review our publications and go meet Gabriella and Kaneesha. Basically, interview them and see what if anything excites you. Every nonprofit needs a writer who can excel at capturing their clients' stories and motivating the world to pay attention."

"To pay attention to what has heart and meaning."

Selena paused and put down the cup of coffee she'd just raised. "That's beautiful Liv. And something about that is very you."

Saturday, April 14

Ryan called to let Liv know that if she came over that morning she could choose the paint colors for her apartment. She sought her mom's advice, so mid-morning they both showed up at Ryan and Mimi's home.

Katherine was fifty-six and knew what was in store for her in the coming years, having scrutinized her older sister El's bloom-on-the-rose fade after fifty-five. Already Katherine covered her limbs with longer sleeves, wore fewer shorts, and over-applied body lotion to the alienating crepe-paper skin encircling arm creases and the elephantine folds at her knees. Depressing her far more seriously though today was her mother Colleen's lung cancer. A miserable way to go and the roughest part of it lay ahead these next months. Just thinking of her mom's passing would bring a tear, causing her make-up to burn fiercely in her eyes. Squeezing her eyes tightly this morning while driving at sixty on the freeways, she almost had an accident. She arrived at Ryan's grateful she made it without mishap but still slightly weepy.

Liv and Shakti were already there finishing breakfast. When Katherine entered the kitchen, Liv knew something was wrong. It wasn't like her mom not to have perfect makeup, and today she looked smudged and puffy-faced. "What's up Mom? Did something happen?"

Katherine didn't want to spoil Liv's decorating fun and focused her attention on her grandchildren to alter her mood. "Nothing's wrong that these two can't fix. How are you, Shakti? Come give Grandma one of your big hugs!"

Shakti came swiftly while Jeff clambered down from his chair, shouting, "Me too, me too."

Liv knew best to come back later to whatever distressed her mom. For now, until Mimi eventually herded the kids into an activity, they would dominate the scene with Grandma. Liv moved to clear up until Ryan interjected, "Come on, ladies, let's get moving. I've got a slew of sample paint colors downstairs and as soon as you figure it out, I can go buy it. We could even start today Liv, if you're up for it?"

"Sure, if Mom will help Mimi with the kids."

Katherine wasn't sure about that. "Let's just get on with choosing the colors." Liv went down the stairs to the apartment and noticed immediately how the stairwell with the washer and dryer and a little table were now all wall boarded off from the downstairs apartment. Her privacy buffer. Not bad, she thought.

Once through the laundry room door, she lit up. "Oh Ryan, this is really nice! There were new paned sliding glass patio doors to the backyard, ample space for a sofa and chairs, while farther back the small u-shaped kitchen area shielded by a half-wall created the standard space in front of it for a dining table. No carpet yet, but Liv couldn't help but feel a thrill about moving into all new space with nice black appliances and amber counter tops and what looked like wood cabinets, albeit only laminate. This was going to be a sweet place. The hallway to the left led to a bathroom and two bedrooms that occupied the space under Ryan's much larger living room and dining room. He'd configured it so each bedroom had windows out to the backyard. "I love it! It's wonderful, Bro!"

Katherine was immensely pleased too, content to have her children and grandchildren in one space looking out for each other. Ryan had taken his time to become enthused about them as family, but ever since what she and her husband Gary called 'the miracle of the sea,' referring to the shared boat, slowly they had all grown together. Just seeing this space made her heart full again, which started fresh tears.

"Mom, why the tears? I'm happy too, but what's up?"

Katherine looked at Ryan, trying to assess his patience. "I'll tell you after we pick the colors. That will perk me up."

Décor was territory that brought Katherine alive and her spirits rose discussing rug texture and color. Only to end in a dispiriting resolution: they finally settled on a semi-plush feel for the kids, and the shade of beige that is found in every new apartment complex. For the walls, Liv wanted something light with an accent wall for the kitchen and dining area. Amber worked well with the countertop color Liv had already chosen. For Liv's bedroom, she still had her green spread and linens from seven years ago. A light green paint that combined with the fresh white trim on all the windows and the view to the yard made her think of spring garden accents. New throw pillows would suffice for her.

With those choices made, Ryan sensed their potentially longer deliberations about Shakti's room provided the right space for him to go buy the paint. He was anxious to get this weekend-intensive remodel behind him, so he could be out on the boat. "Okay, I'm off while you two and Shakti figure out her room."

Liv turned to her mom. "Should I go get her now or do you want to talk first?"

Katherine considered. She did need to let Liv know about the changes coming. Once Shakti was there, that wouldn't work. The rooms felt so sterile. "Let's step outside and talk now."

Liv immediately became worried. Outside on the pavement deck were stacked green plastic chairs. Liv pulled down a couple, brushed them off and sat. From this level, you didn't see the canal locks below running between neighboring hills, or much of Shilshole Bay to the west. Nonetheless, with the house on a slope facing southwest, they could see across to the north side of Queen Anne hill. Mimi had already done some planting to conceal over time the eyesore chain link fence. The day was half-sunny and a touch of chill in the air made their REI fuzzy jackets feel just right.

Katherine settled herself. "So, here's the thing, sweetie. You know about Grandma's lung cancer."

Liv's usual image of her grandmother included her holding one of her ciggies. "Right." *Not that I've done much about it like going to see her,* came the familiar guilty mental refrain.

"It's getting worse now. And Aunt El to a great extent, and me not as much, we just can't handle all these visits to Bainbridge to see her. It's time consuming to get to the island. And then I feel bad leaving Grandpa alone with it all. So, El and I have decided that they need to come live with us for a while."

"In our house?"

"Yes. We would give Grandma your room, and Grandpa could take the other bed in the tiny room. It must be terrible for him at night trying to sleep. He looks so run down."

"When will this happen?"

"Soon. We're thinking next weekend."

"Wow. That is soon."

Katherine was pulling a Kleenex from her pocket. "The thing is… she's going to die." Her voice cracked, and her face twisted in pain. She began sobbing in a way Liv had never witnessed before.

Liv was close to her in an instant crouching by her chair. "Oh Mom." It was awkward trying to hold her. Liv pulled her chair closer and took her mother's hand.

"I just can't stand the thought of her going. And if you think I'm in bad shape, you should see your aunt. We just don't feel ready to let her go." Katherine dabbed away at her eyes as the Kleenex shredded. "Rationally, I know that we all go, but then it's someone you love, and it's just so hard. It feels like an axe lodged in my heart."

Liv was crying now too. She couldn't stand to see her mom like this. The minutes passed as Katherine worked her way through it, now wiping her eyes on her jacket sleeve. Liv didn't really know what it meant to her to have Grandma leave them forever. Her emotions were all interwoven with Katherine's condition. "Mom, I want to help you, how can I help you?"

Katherine tightened their clasped hands. "Be there for me. I need you. And I need Shakti. I need not to feel alone. And I'm sure Grandma and Grandpa need that too." She breathed in her sniffles.

"Of course, Mom, I'm with you a thousand percent. Whatever it takes."

"I've been thinking about it, honey. Your life is so busy with work and Shakti, and of course your dad and I always want you to have a social life. But this summer and maybe into the fall, it might be that sometimes I call. And you'll need to come. We don't know except in generalities how fast this will progress. But I doubt she'll make it to the holidays."

Liv was instantly and completely committed to doing what it would take. A fleeting thought about grad school came and went. Whatever it took, there was no way she would not be there for her mom. Katherine had been incredibly supportive during the early Shakti years. Liv's heart was clear and strong. "Mom, I'll be there. I promise. Once they move over, I'll come regularly on the weekends. And whenever you call, I'll come as soon as I can. Living here and having Mimi to back me up will really help."

Katherine inhaled deeply filling her body with fresh resolve. She stood. "I need a hug, a really big one."

Mimi happened to look down from kitchen window upstairs and see them clasped in each other's arms and rocking ever so slightly. She almost opened it to call out but decided against it, sensing something intense had transpired. Shakti came up behind her and looked too. "Let's go be with them, Auntie."

Mimi considered. By the time they got to them, a shot of Shakti might be just what they needed. And so it was. Their spirits rose and they all moved to Shakti's room to let her choose the paint color. As they arranged the paint chips in their hands and came to the pinks and purples that had dominated Liv's room growing up, she and her mom looked at each other. "Let's not." Liv stuck those colors in her pockets and let Shakti choose among the yellows and oranges. Shakti was decisive. "I want my room to be like walking inside the sun."

Saturday, April 28

Several more weekends passed with Ryan painting, moving on to carpet and tile laying last, and then the apartment was ready to occupy. No one anticipated the out-gassing problem of new carpet, which postponed the move until mid-May, with windows kept open when possible, and fans blowing to move the noxious air outside.

Liv was once again at her parents' home, as she'd been preceding weekends, ever since Grandma moved in. Katherine and El were exhausted physically by their full schedules, and emotionally by their grief. Ryan and Liv were having their own ups and downs between the positive changes coming with her move, yet at a time their family members were declining. For Ryan, he was especially concerned about Grandpa Jeff's state, and anxious to get him out on the boat. Anything to support him through this agonizing time of seeing his wife of over sixty years suffering and dying.

Liv's attention at work kept straying as she processed conversations with her mom and Grandma. Shakti was turning out to be the saving grace for her mom. Liv provided respite care for Katherine by simply sitting in the bedroom with Grandma resting, often sedated. Liv felt at peace being in her old bedroom. Her thoughts drifted over her own life, recalling times as a sheltered little girl being spoiled by her parents; making love in this very bed with Devin that last year in high school; lying here recalling what had occurred in India with Rama; living here again during her pregnancy and Shakti's first years. She emerged today from a reverie. *God, this room holds my whole life, and here Grandma is in my bed dying.* Colleen coughed as though wanting to be included in this conversation. Liv quickly rose to get her sitting upright in the bed. They all hated the incessant hacking coughing that sounded so painful for Grandma. Worse for her was the pain in her back and hips that made her so uncomfortable, and which told the tale of the cancer's metastasis to her bones. But Grandma was a fighter and she wasn't ready to go yet. She usually used her oxygen and made it to the table for meals. And they all still nursed the hope that chemo would work, both to diminish her pain and extend her life longer than the six to eight-month prognosis.

As Colleen coughed, and then moved and upset the breathing tube into her nose, Liv reached to adjust it. "This damn tube is what's doing me in." Grandma smiled at Liv with a bit of the devil in her. "Sit down, honey. But first, I need some water." When Liv returned with the glass, she sat on the bedside. Grandma reached for it to drink, and then, handing back the glass, laid her hand upon Liv's. "There's something that's been on my mind lately."

"Grandma, are you sure you want to talk, your voice is so hoarse?"

"I do need to talk about this, so voice be damned." Liv winced and moved closer thinking a whisper was less straining. The words and phrases came out in batches, as Colleen would pause to breathe. "I look at Shakti and I love her – you know that. And I see how your mom adores her... and how much fun she is for everyone...and then I see you, still alone, no husband... no one to be with you. And I worry about you.... It makes me wonder if I did the wrong thing... that day you were pregnant... I told you the story about Grandpa and me... and Eleanor... and not giving up the baby."

"Grandma, you shouldn't...

"Let me finish.... It's just on my mind that I planted this idea with you...that you'd have the baby... and some Prince Charming would come along and take care of you both... the way it happened for me.... And I feel bad about that... that I nudged you in the wrong direction.... You would be having so much more fun if you were still single... like your friend Elyse. It bothers me... I just wanted you to know that I'm sorry."

Liv was truly taken aback by this confession. At a loss for words, her mind buzzed between trying to recall what importance her Grandma's story might have had for her seven years ago - had it really tilted her toward keeping the baby? - and trying to find the right words to give immediate comfort regardless of any truth in what she said. Grandma was looking at her, and then dropped her eyes as if to say, so it's true.

Liv rallied, pressing her Grandma's hand tightly. "Look at me. Shakti is the love of my life. There is no place for regret. None. Please understand that. Really none. And relationships are so complicated anymore. I think it was simpler when you met Grandpa. Today, it's just really hard to figure out if marriage is such a great thing. Sure, it would be good for Shakti to have a wonderful father. But it's not like that breed is easy to find. And she's doing fine anyway. And even when I find a good guy, like Elyse has now, there are always going to be issues."

Grandma started coughing, the sharpness of it paining Liv's heart. "I know. I watch TV… and read books. But I still want it all for you and…" Grandma moved her hand away and folded it with her other, then brought them both up with energy. "…it's just that I feel guilty somehow."

Liv decided whatever the truth was at the time, she needed to redirect her grandmother's attention. "No, honestly, it wasn't your story that made me decide to keep Shakti, you have to understand that. I loved her from the very beginning when she was inside me. She is what caused me to want her, not anyone's story. I just loved her from the start. And I have never been able to regret creating her. And I certainly don't regret having her in my life. When it comes to men, I'm very, very choosy, I'm asking a lot. And I'm ready to hold out for it. Shakti fills my life and I'm really interested in still growing my career. I have a great family and friends."

Colleen seemed to be taking this in.

In her most firm voice, Liv demanded, "Don't ever feel bad for me! Don't think my life is not good just as it is. Honestly, Grandma, that really shortchanges me, and my life. You should be proud of me!"

Colleen's eyes became very open. She bit her lip as she sat quietly. "I hadn't thought about it like that."

Liv broke into an energizing smile. "I'm amazing and don't forget it." Seeing her grandmother perk up around the lips and eyes, Liv invited her to get up to join the others.

Later in the bathroom alone, Liv studied her face in the mirror. *I said the right things. She doesn't need to die carrying any guilt about me.* But Liv wondered, what was her state of mind when she was pregnant? As she dried her hands and looked at the book her mom kept near the toilet, it reminded her of the books she'd just packed for the move, including a journal of sorts. She resolved to pull it out that evening.

Returning to the apartment and getting Shakti to bed involved answering her newly recurrent line of questioning about dying prompted by Colleen's move into the Redmond house and her illness. Shakti was experiencing for the first time the grave illness of someone she loved. Due to their own apartment restrictions, she had never even had a pet that died, aside from her goldfish Gilley. Shakti's questions stressed Liv because they forced her to confront the absence of religion in their lives. While raised as a Catholic, Liv didn't practice. She hadn't been in a church in years, nor even had time to think about religion or spirituality. Given her commitment to honesty with Shakti, Liv came up short in response to the most innocently formed, yet probing questions about what death is, why people die, and where they go. She mostly put off her daughter tonight, pleading tiredness and promising to talk about it more another time. But Shakti would be relentless. Liv felt the need to think and write about what she believed and what seeds she wanted to plant in Shakti's mind.

Writing. I haven't done that in so long. She used to journal. Which reminded her, where is the journal from when she was pregnant? She went to the stacks of book boxes and started re-opening them, searching for what she knew was a small notebook with a deep blue cover. Finding it in the third box she opened, she sat on the sofa and paused at the title page lettered by her own hand: *"Conversations with an Unborn Child."*

She'd begun it on the day she visited her Grandma on Bainbridge Island, a visit when Liv was several months along. As she surveyed it, wishing she hadn't used the type of spiral notebook she always carried with her in college, but instead some beautifully covered bound journal, a wave of embarrassment washed over her. Embarrassment that she was going to open what now felt like someone else's journal. *Prying, I'm prying. I'm not that girl anymore. Immature, lacking confidence, uncertain in her decision to become a mother. I've changed so much.* That girl she was in college, she mostly liked her still. But she was afraid to turn the page and read what sounded naïve. Afraid, she'd judge her old self. Although how could she have been that clueless at twenty-one, having lived with her boyfriend Devin, and gotten pregnant in India by Rama?

She lingered, wondering: would reading her journal from what seemed a galaxy long ago, would discovering her past afresh, would she be reminded of truths then that perhaps were not her truths today? Would what seemed true then - the need to break with Devin or cut off contact with Rama - were those imperatives only how she saw things at the time? Today would she speak of her past choices differently, perhaps even with regret? Or would the passage of time have brought new perspectives that would instill meaning that wasn't there at the time? *Is what I think today more true?*

She turned first to the divider part way through the book that bulged out with the letters: a copy of her letter to Rama before Shakti was born, letting him know there would be a child of his in the world; and his letter back a month later. Both transferred through her friend in Mumbai, Arita. When Liv covered her letter to Rama with a note to Arita telling her of the pregnancy, she'd received an email right away. Arita expressed regrets as though somehow, she should have saved Liv from this fate. Foolish thought, as if the attraction she felt for Rama could have been short-circuited. What happened in the field was what wanted to happen. She pulled Rama's letter out from the pocket. His note to Liv surrounded a sealed envelope that was addressed "To my child."

> *"I too still feel the nights we spent together. I treasure them in a part of myself no one else knows. It amazes and pleases me that something has lived on from those moments. Whatever you decide, whether to keep the child or give her up for adoption, I have no say in that. It is your life choice. I will hold the child close in my thoughts. Here is my letter for the child.*
> *With affection and caring, Rama."*

She brushed her hand against her face to dry tears. *Someday, someday I don't know when, Shakti will open this letter. Will she wonder why I never tried to go back to India, to make it work with Rama? I was so sure at the time that route was fruitless, that Rama and me together was impossible. That I'd be rejected by his family and cause problems. I wasn't even sure I loved him. But should I have tried?* Her befuddled mind drifted, dismayed by revisiting the girl she was. Reading his note once again, she was struck by the lack of invitation into his life. *Maybe I was right.*

Moving to close and repack the journal, she recalled why she'd searched for it: did Grandma's story make her decide to keep Shakti? Liv turned the first few pages of the journal which quickly confirmed her premonition of the display of youth by the author.

> "It is the summer of 2000 and I am pregnant with you by a man I met in India. His name is Rama. I have no plans to ever see him again. (I will write more of that decision later, I'm just giving you context now for when you read this someday.)
>
> "I decided not to have an abortion because I couldn't bear the thought of squeezing life out of you. He, Rama, told me once of the preciousness of each seed (I had interned with his sustainable agriculture NGO) and I felt that way about you. You were – you are – too precious to me. It's been like that since I first learned I was pregnant and looked at drawings of fetuses. Sweet Pea, that's what I call you.
>
> "I'm starting this conversation with you now because I've decided to get an ultrasound and find out if you are a boy or a girl. And my family– Mom, Aunt El, and Grandma, and Ryan – have been talking to me and telling me stories. And I want you to know those stories.
>
> "And I have to decide whether to give you up to some nice family to raise or whether to keep you. It's hard for me to even write that – how does one 'give up' a baby? It's done a lot I know. But it makes a pain in my heart to write that."

Liv began turning pages to get a sense of the entries she'd made. There were ones recounting the stories: her mom giving up Ryan, her aunt's abortion, and Grandma's having kept baby Eleanor. Liv was searching for what she'd written about the latter to remind herself how important, or not, it had been to her.

> "I think Grandma told me this story to influence me to keep you implying that, 'you, Liv, wouldn't be here today if I hadn't kept the baby.' But Mom gave up Ryan and now he's part of the family, even though it took thirty years. But if she hadn't given him up, why Dad may never have married Mom and then I wouldn't be here either. So this test really doesn't help! While my existence is in the chain of consequences of their choices, Grandma and Mom made opposite choices. Not that their stories haven't impacted

> me, but not on the choice I should make. Their stories tell me that courage runs in the blood of the women of this family. They give me hope that somehow whatever I choose, it will be okay for me and for you, and that love is love. I could keep you and you could grow up to hate me for being a single mom or for marrying the wrong guy, and meanwhile you would have loved your adoptive parents. Really, it's totally unpredictable what my choice will lead to."

Truth there, thought Liv. So Grandma's story didn't sway me. Liv glanced at other entries, skimming and catching phrases: *"You're a girl! I couldn't be happier!"* Liv was reminded as she read that it was possible she would have made a different choice if it was a boy. But then:

> "Even if you had been a boy, I would have wanted to keep you as the seed Rama and I created during our love under the stars. I hold that time as having a divine quality that seems more important than some mundane calculations about my own life."

Really? Liv was caught off-guard being reminded that she had indeed felt that her time with Rama had a spiritual quality not to be denied. Nonetheless, she was taken aback by the writing. *Those were some long, lonely months that summer before Shakti arrived!* Liv was at her parents' home with only Elyse as her friend. These entries reminded her how introspective she'd been waiting for the baby to come. And spiritually minded. That was why she'd given the name Shakti to her child. Everything was coming back to her, a pre-occupation with the spiritual then, dormant now. She found the entry on Shakti's name.

> "Perhaps there is a force greater than any one of us in our situation, a force I ignore at my peril. I've come to believe now, a few weeks remaining until your birth, that I should not diminish what felt real with your father, that something meaningful happened those nights, and that it was you. There is no choice really. There is only keeping you that is real, that seems both divinely inspired and

> *compassionately human. I must affirm the life within me. You are my precious holy spirit.*
>
> *"Now I want to find a name for you that will always remind me of these thoughts. An Indian name to suit your heritage."*

Liv's head was shaking, and her mouth dropped open, surprised at how dramatic her thoughts had been. Yet still – she believed what she'd written, despite embarrassment at her sincerity. She considered the context again, being home, cut off from college friends and the baby's father. Her inner life got a little...well... weird.

A later entry, three days before Shakti's birth in November:

> *"My search for names of Indian goddesses gave me so many ideas, Devi, Kali, Lakshmi – I liked them all. I looked in an Indian bookstore and searched through volumes by gurus, making notes on the goddesses. It consumed me last week. Now I have the right one. Arita wrote me of the women's movement she volunteers with, "Stree Shakti – The Parallel Force." Here is what I learned about Shakti: the divine creative force of the universe, the mother of the universe both feminine and masculine, the source, the power of becoming – this is called Shakti. In some books, it's more explicitly the feminine principle of energy which moves the masculine principle of consciousness into action. I'm satisfied that Shakti should be your name and that it will call forth from you great feminine power.*
>
> *"When I told Mom that I would be calling you Shakti, her face pinched up – I think she'd been hoping for Deborah or Natalie – but then she checked herself and said, 'That's a strange name. Does it have a meaning? Why did you choose it?' It was hard to get it out at first for fear of being laughed at or criticized. But if I'm going to give it to you, surely I need to be strong in my communication of it. I said, 'It's the Indian name for the feminine creative power of the universe.' Mom was concerned that I would be drawing attention to what I had done in India and I surprised myself with my own sense of righteousness: 'I'm not running from or hiding my actions. I created a child in*

> *India and that's part of who I am, and Shakti is a divine creation.' Mom stared at me.*

Liv guessed she would have stared too.

> *"I hope you like your name!*
> *"This will be my last entry. I imagine someday I will give this to you. Soon we will have real conversations. I wonder what you'll be like, what you'll say. I'm eager to meet you!"*

Tears were forming in the wells of her eyes. But then Liv laughed out loud. *My god, I was a piece of work then.* She thought about Shakti lying asleep in the next room and her heart spread wide open like a diorama to display all the ways she loved her daughter, the one who posed questions of life and death to her now. *Even if I was woo-woo then, I didn't make a wrong decision.* She marveled at that impassioned girl she'd been, so compelled by the divine force. *Maybe that's where I should look for answers to Shakti's questions.* Once they settled in their new place, Liv vowed to go back to the East West Bookshop and see what she could find that was helpful. It was time to get spirituality back into the family.

Sunday, May 6

The last Sunday before Liv moved out, Elyse returned for their shared ritual of putting Shakti to bed, reading stories to her, and then having their own girlfriend check-in. They'd already missed a few Sunday nights together since Elyse moved into an apartment with Cory. They'd wanted to buy a place, but it was too much, too soon, so they settled on a new Denny Regrade apartment that kept their commutes easy.

"You have to come see it, Liv. It's cute, but tiny - staying near to work meant more than having an extra bedroom for now." Cory's law office was only a long walk down to Pioneer Square while Elyse was hopping a bus to city hall where the staff of city council had offices.

"You are certainly the urban couple now. Living the dream!" Liv meant it, raising her arms in a joyous pirouette. And then she noticed the doubtful expression on Elyse's face.

"The dream? I don't know. It's good. It's different." She looked at Liv almost as though she wasn't sure to trust her with more.

"Elyse, what are you holding back? What is it?"

The tea kettle sounded off, and Elyse moved among the boxes to pour their tea. She hesitated to speak of her deepest fear. *Am I making a mistake?* She'd always been the knowing, mature friend to Liv. Revealing her own doubts made Elyse ill at ease, despite an overpowering urge to talk about her situation. When she settled, she chose the table and Liv joined her there. "You're the only one I can say these things to, and as always this is just between us, right?"

"Right. Like it's always been."

"Okay, so ever since we moved in together, it's like, no it's not like, the truth is I feel uncomfortable."

"In what way?"

"In the relationship actually."

Liv was surprised, and yet not really. She knew her friend well enough to know that after being an independent woman, partnering in marriage, even with someone you really, really loved, that would not be easy for her. "What's going on for you? Give me an example of what's uncomfortable for you?"

"Well, take this weekend. Cory has a big week ahead starting with depositions in the race discrimination case against Seattle City Light. He's up against some big guns. Thorough preparation is what it's all about."

"But you've had weekends like that before where he's not very available because of work."

"Yes. But we're finalizing a lot of wedding plans right now. There are things that need to get done, a place confirmed – NOW – and he's too busy for it and ..."

"But you're used to making plans about things."

"It's not the doing of things, it's his attitude. It just seems different now, like of course ELYSE can do it, because I'm busy with more important things."

"Are you sure it's his attitude and not your feeling defensive or overly protective of your boundaries? I mean, maybe it's you seeing you need to change some in this relationship? That's to be expected, no? When you get married, roles can get redefined?"

"That's what I've thought sometimes too, that it's more about me than him changing. Listen to this: I had this dream a few nights ago. It was out in some place like a ranch in Idaho or Montana. And there's this horse in a corral outside a barn. Really gorgeous horse, but wild. I can still see the crazed eyes, the fear of being held captive. And then someone is trying to tame the horse, you know, get a saddle on him and ride him. And the horse is bucking and not wanting anything or anyone to touch him. Then it was as though I was the person trying to tame him, looking out at him. But then it wasn't me, it was Cory. I woke up then, but later the same night I went into the dream again - maybe more consciously - and I'm the horse, and I'm thinking it's Cory taming me, and then I see from the horse's eyes and it's me I'm looking at."

"Wow, that's an easy one."

"I know."

"The whole thing of getting married is feeling like you're having to be tamed and made to comply."

"Exactly. And the thing is, I love that horse the way he is. I don't want to be some compliant woman bullied by marriage, taking on all the marital to do's while my husband becomes a workaholic and leaves it all to me."

"But that's part of the attraction, no? I mean there's the basic attraction that brought you together, but there's always been this admiration component you have for the work he does. Remember, we joked about you two becoming a Seattle power couple, big-time civil rights attorney and you a city council member." Liv paused, considering how she could best support her friend: is marriage to Cory the right thing for her and should I help her accept the changes? Or do I encourage her to rethink it? What choice is right for her?

"You're right. If I'm going to marry someone, I do want to be with a man I really respect for the work he does in the world. And Cory is the real thing. But if my handling the wedding virtually alone is any indicator, I'll be handling a lot of other things for us, like raising kids, and watching my career stay on hold."

Liv wasn't sure what to say to that. No doubt that child-raising consumed your life. "Are you sure you'll have kids?"

Elyse scrunched up her face. "Of course we'll have kids. I want them, he wants them."

Interesting, Liv thought, for all Elyse's time with Shakti, I don't think I've ever heard her say she wants kids. "Really? You really want to have children?"

At that Elyse laughed. "Sister, do you really think I've spent all this time with Shakti to do you a favor? Haven't you noticed how much fun I have with her?"

"Yeah, of course. I just didn't realize you wanted one of your own." Liv was gaining her sense of what to do for her friend. "If you want kids, if you want to respect the work of the man you love, then you're going to have to tame yourself Elyse. You're going to have to give on a lot of small stuff to achieve what you want. You're going to have to accept the role of making things happen, of not being a workaholic yourself, and of creating space for balance in your life. And it may slow down, it most likely will slow down, your own goal of being a player in city politics." Elyse looked attentive, so Liv continued. "There's no point in your complaining about your loss of control or added responsibilities that are a time-suck. It just goes with the territory you want to head into. You need to accept the bridle and the bit, and the saddle, and someone riding you. Assuming that you both want to make the same journey - which I believe is so."

Elyse slumped in the chair, her hands around the tea cup on the table. "You're right. I know you're right. It's just hard for now."

With a pointed gaze Liv leaned in across the table. "As Selena would say, 'no whining, my friend.'"

Elyse sat quietly. A smile reluctantly arrived. "It feels like our table has turned, Liv – remember when I used to tell you what to do?"

Liv smiled back at the truth of it. She was the one who had to experience the humbling consequences of her choices, to see her plans, albeit vague ones, for a professional future evaporate when she chose to become a single mom. She'd had to change her focus to the short-term needs of the moment, while envying Elyse's ability to move with intention into an exciting future. And Liv knew that while her advice just now was sound, there was also a dollop of *schadenfreude* in knowing that her best friend would now have to face some of the mundane trials that Liv experienced, of sublimating one's ego, of bridling one's desires to a life that constrained you.

Elyse was ready to change the subject. "So, give me news. What's going on with the move, with school plans?" Her eyes had some sparkle now. "Give me a chance to tell you what to do."

"Well, the move happens next Saturday. Finally. There will probably still be noticeable off-gassing from the carpet, but with summer and windows open, I don't think there will be irreparable effects on Shakti's brain."

"Whatever happened, or didn't, with that friend of Ryan's, the good-looking guy?"

"Nothing. I thought he might call. But who knows, he may be over sometimes, and we'll have another chance to talk."

"And grad school plans?"

"I'm not sure what to do. I wanted to start in the fall, and I should have applied already. But with Grandma's move to Redmond, and Mom needing me, I'm just not sure this is the right time to go for it. I'm trying to get more experience at work, writing things up, the new microcredit training program. The grant writer is happy for me to help and then there's solicitations to donors and articles for the newsletter and website. I like telling the story of it all, more than I like the logistics of getting everything lined up. So, I don't know, maybe I'll just wait and apply the following year. There's a marketing and communications master's program at UW, or maybe I'll go back to Seattle U for their certificate in nonprofit leadership. I'm not sure."

"I just don't think you should keep putting more schooling off, especially now with the built-in help of Mimi."

"I know. But I need to be there for Mom and Grandma. That's what's most important to me."

Elyse stared at her. *We really have gone our separate ways. She's so about relationships, and being there for people, and I want to make my mark on the world.*

"I know what you're thinking. I'm never going to amount to much and I'll be stuck in the middle of some nonprofit the rest of my life." Liv felt her fur rise. "We're just different. It's not about rising to some position or place for me. I just want to be true to myself, to what and whom I value and care about."

Elyse rose and came next to Liv bending down to hug her. "I know that about you. I admire that. The world needs us both."

"Thanks for saying that."

Liv moved to make their second cup and decided to shift the conversation back to the wedding. She wanted to re-enthuse Elyse about the plans. "So where are you going to have the wedding? Who's marrying you?"

"Not sure. One option is one of Cory's best friends from law school who has a license to marry people from the Universal Church. And if we do early September, maybe we could pull off a short ceremony outdoors. But I'm also checking into churches too, trying to find a liberal pastor. And then if I get the paperwork in tomorrow, we'll lock down the Mountaineers' Club for the party."

"I assume it's going to be a dancing party?"

"Of course!"

"How many people?"

"A hundred and twenty or so." Elyse paused. Time for Liv to face up. "Devin and Steve will definitely be invited since they've been climbing buds of Cory's since law school. Have you started thinking of what you're going to say to Devin?"

"How about nothing? Just intentional casual avoidance."

"I'd give that low probability of working out. You'd better have a Plan B."

"A nod of acknowledgment? Look, he's going to have a date. I'll do my damndest to have a date. There won't be any need for conversation."

Elyse thought Liv was in denial. But at least the seed was planted. "I just don't want the wedding party to be difficult for you or unpleasant for anyone."

"Naturally. I agree. I'll give it more thought."

"You know who else confirmed they're coming?" Liv's eyes perked up with interest. "David and Jonathan!"

"Great! It's been at least a year since I've seen them. I've already talked to Selena about our default plan for a group date. Hey, we'll have to start practicing our old moves from when we used to all go dancing together. We were pretty good, mixing up some of the African stuff with all our other moves. Remember how much fun that was, teaching those guys butt bumps and dirty dancing!"

"Some of their stuff was pretty wild too." Elyse's eyes went to some distant past that energized her. "Remember this one!" And up she jumped and started a wide-legged foot stomp that blended weirdly with a salsa shimmy that sent her breasts wriggling. "Those guys were naturals."

Liv joined her in some hip gyrations but nixed putting on music. "Definitely I need practice – but not now or we'll wake up Shakti. So, did you talk to both of them?"

"Yeah. David and I talked more. He's finishing law school now and Cory said he'd talk to him about his plans." Elyse grimaced. "David actually wants to go back as a staff person at one of the refugee camps. He's getting more active too in the Sudanese People's Liberation group in this area."

"That sounds dangerous, like he could go over there and wind up in the middle of a civil war in South Sudan."

"I didn't get into it with him. You should call him. But he's not leaving – if at all – until the end of the year. So you'll see him at the wedding if not sooner."

"I need to pay more attention to what's going on there now – and to him." Liv paused. It was just so hard to squeeze out time for old friends, but she resolved to invite him to dinner once she got settled in at Ryan's place. "Anyone else to surprise me with?"

"No, the rest will either be very familiar, like Selena and others we've done things with, or total unknowns." Elyse paused. "My advice though - definitely have a date."

"Because of the Devin thing?"

"Yep. You need to feel at your best that day with nothing bringing you down. Because I'm sure he'll bring his girlfriend and Steve will bring his, and they'll all look like they're at the top of their game. And I don't want my best friend moping, okay?"

"Okay, I've got my party orders."

"And don't forget to call David. He'd like to hear from you."

"Really, he said that?"

Elyse's head was turned away at that moment, but she slowly brought it around and stared sideways at Liv. "Just don't go there. He's never been available, and nothing is going to change."

After Elyse left, Liv felt exhausted. As she readied herself for bed, she was closing up boxes too, thinking about what clothes to leave out for this week and which to drive over to the new place in mid-week trips. Her mind returned to Elyse's admonishment about David. She was right of course.

Ever since he and Jonathan had resettled in Seattle in 2001, David had always been focused on school. He was one of the 'lost boys of Sudan,' although when he and Jonathan arrived, they were older war orphans from the Sudanese genocides, hardly boys anymore. David was twelve when his village was destroyed by the Janjaweed tribesmen and government helicopters. He'd joined so many others, many children, in the incredibly long trek across the desert, from one refugee camp to another, with many losing their lives to crocodiles, starvation, and disease. Those who made it to the U.S. and other locations were real survivors.

Liv had gotten to know David better once he came to work part-time at the Rescue Committee, while he gained his high school equivalency diploma and then began college. She found him so easy to talk to. He had this amazing spirit. After a while, she and Elyse started having them over for Sunday dinners and going to each other's' parties. She loved hearing about Sudanese culture, and learning the political scene there. His whole experience of being among a nomadic herding tribe for the first years of his life, then being in life threatening and miserable conditions for another six or so, and then having to rapidly come into modern culture as they relocated to the States – the whole thing blew her mind then, and still did. These guys were remarkably adaptable, especially David. To Liv, he was one of the finest human beings to walk the planet.

When he first arrived and was studying for the GED, she knew that he had some Ethiopian girlfriends. Nothing major though. And Selena, Elyse, and she swore an oath not to flirt with any of the lost boys or send them mixed messages. The women held a special charge to teach the guys the ways of American life, while always being kind and concerned for their welfare. Over time, Liv went from 'I feel protective,' to 'I admire him,' to 'I wonder what it would be like to be held by him.' As he grew and changed and racked up his degree and went to law school, she was in awe. But, then each one of them became focused on important life choices and spent less time together. Once David entered law school, they didn't see much of him at all. The guy was totally focused on returning to Africa to right wrongs.

Lying in bed, thinking about David, Liv really wanted to see him, to get her own fix on where he was. It was time to get together.

Saturday, May 12

When Liv opened the door for Ryan at nine, she was surprised to see Eric's face behind her brother's shoulder. "Hi Bro! Hi Eric."

"I brought help along for the heavy stuff. Eric and I can manage the furniture better than you and me."

"I was a little concerned about that. Thanks for being willing to help us out, Eric."

"No problem." Eric had in fact been waiting on the moving date as his next opportunity to show up in a low-key way. He'd offered to help Ryan weeks ago, but then nothing happened until two days ago when Ryan brought it up. Eric wasn't sure he recalled very well what Liv looked like, but he knew he'd made up his mind to check things out with her more after they'd first met. The girl he was dating now, Kirsten, she was fun, but young and too much into playing games. He was old enough to appreciate direct, honest communications. As he entered Liv's apartment and turned to take in the size and volume of the stuff to be moved, he took her in also. She bent over to give the little girl directions on staying out of the way. *Not bad at all, actually beautiful.* Turning her face upward to him, the width of her smile felt like it jumped off her face to embrace him, disconcerting him and causing him to turn to Ryan. "Hey, we start with the bed first right, mattress against the back wall of the truck?"

Ryan had borrowed a modest sized truck from a buddy. "Yeah, that's right." He turned to his sister. "I don't see as many boxes and loose items as I expected."

"You haven't noticed then the trips I made almost every evening to your place bringing whatever fit in the car. A lot of Shakti's stuff is moved already. We're pretty much down to big or heavy." With that she looked at Eric, and again was aware that he was outrageously handsome. She'd forgotten. "I'm so glad you're helping!"

They got on with it quickly and it didn't take much more than an hour to get the bed, sofa, chair, some tables, bookshelves and the book boxes loaded. "Man, you've got a lot of books I'd say." Eric wasn't one to read much besides magazines.

"That I do. And I hate to let go of them."

Liv was already cleaning the apartment, trying to direct Shakti either out of the way or towards wiping off marks on her walls. Not that it helped. But the lesson was good. "Boy, Mommy, these marker lines don't want to come off."

"Really? Well, you should think twice then about what you want to put on the walls in your new sunshine room."

Shakti appeared to process that idea. "They'd have to be the right colors."

So much for teachable moments thought Liv. She followed the guys in the truck, ferrying her own carful of smaller awkward items like lamps, and then the last of the clothes from the closet laid out on a sheet in the back. The plan was for Mimi to come back with her and help finish cleaning while Shakti and Little Jeff watched the guys re-assemble things. Of course, Liv needed to give the critical directions on where things would go.

Once in the new apartment, she laid out where the larger heavier furniture would go. Eric was following her through the rooms and complimenting her on the paint colors. "I really like the kitchen area, very functional. And the dining area jumps out nicely with that accent color." He looked at her, taking in the flushed excitement in her face about having a new place. He increasingly liked what he saw. "Maybe you could give me some advice on paint colors for my place?"

"Where is your place?"

"I bought a home across the ship canal on lower Queen Anne a few years back. You could see it from here if it weren't under the cover of trees."

"Queen Anne? That's pretty special."

"Yeah, well, the house was run down. A total fixer-upper. And I've put a lot of work into it and still there's a lot more to do." He liked the way she looked at him wide-open and honest. "So, if you want to do me a favor in return, you could come over on a Saturday morning and be my color advisor."

Liv smiled. "That would be fun. Sure, I'd love to."

Ryan interjected, "Come on, Eric, we got some heavy lifting to do."

Liv turned to find Shakti who was in the middle of her new room twirling in circles. "Come on, sweetie, let's find Mimi."

Saturday, May 26

Two weeks later Liv drove over to Eric's. His follow up call topped off an upbeat time. She'd made herself put in two school applications, just to see if she could get admitted, plus she'd unpacked and arranged her new flat. The sofa looked awful - that would be her next major purchase. Now she was holding the thought, tentatively, that she might have a knock-out date for Elyse's wedding.

Eric provided detailed instructions on getting to his place taking the back entry on to the hill from Highway 99 and making some quick turns to find his tucked away, shadowed home. Pulling up, she saw why he'd been able to afford otherwise prime realty. A steep incline led up to the garage, and the cottage-like home was dwarfed by a ring of gigantic trees looming over it. She imagined one toppling over during a fierce storm. The house itself looked dumpy from the outside: flaking decades-old paint, sorely in need of scraping, replacement of some boards, and several layers of new paint. Despite all the disadvantages, its craftsman cottage design offered latent charm.

Eric knew from experience that girls were suckers for his home renovation projects. Get them in the door and their little decorator genes would fire up, thinking how fun it would be to play house with this handsome muscular dude who rode a motorcycle and sailed boats. In short, he knew the house was bait. The only downside was that when a romance cooled, and he was no longer interested, they knew where he lived. He'd had one, no two, of his exes show up at inopportune moments. But he couldn't resist reeling them in with the house. Like flying fish jumping into a boat.

Liv climbed the stairs to the porch noticing three planks already replaced. Unsure of herself, she took a deep breath before knocking.

When Eric opened the door, his light blue eyes were very alive to her. He quickly took in what she was wearing and how her hair tied back showed off the soft curves of her face. She didn't spend much on clothes for herself, when she could be spending or saving for Shakti: blue jeans, t-shirt, and jacket, were her uniform on the weekends. "Hey, you're on time! Good thing I got up early myself. Come on in and I'll show you the place, from attic to basement - if you're up for it."

Liv's smile came from a complex state of excitement and uncertainty. "Whatever you want ideas on."

"How about some coffee first?" He was striding through the living room, then a dining room, and into the kitchen. She saw a hallway and bathroom off to the right of the dining room, where the bedrooms likely were.

The first rooms were dull and rundown, not much having been done to them. A new navy leather sofa stood out, but the seriously gross carpet compromised the entire appearance of the rooms. She was taken aback as she stepped into the kitchen. You wouldn't have known it was the same house. Bright with new big windows, all the appliances were new, as well as the fawn large-tiled floor, and handsome oak cabinets. The walls were bright white, except for one that the appliances backed into which gleamed in high gloss, a rich azure blue. A great complement to the golden tones of the cabinets and countertops. A small table and chairs by the window overlooked the overgrown backyard. "Wow."

"You like it?"

"Oh yeah. It's so different from the rest of the house."

"Little by little, I'm making a dent. Hey, sit down and I'll get that coffee for you. I tell you it's been slow-going with this remodeling. When I first moved in a few years ago, I had to spend my time and money on boring but important stuff, a new furnace and insulation, patching holes in the roof, and making sure the stairs were safe. Oh, and plumbing that worked. But last year I finally got to have some fun with the kitchen. It's really cheered the place up."

"For sure. How much of the work did you do yourself?"

"Well, ripping out the old is kind of fun and not that hard. And plumbing and electrical is easy enough for me. But I let the professionals install the cabinets and counter tops – there's not a level floor surface in this place." Placing her coffee down, he pushed the sugar and milk toward her, and then sat himself.

"Those big trees all around look a little scary."

"Tell me about it. This last winter I thought for sure one would come crashing in. Do you know how expensive it is to have trees cut down though? It's on my list for this year. If business keeps going well at Ryan's, I should be able to swing it come fall."

Liv felt comforted by his work in this home, sensing that Eric must be a solid guy to own the house and be moving ahead with such discipline on all these improvements. He wasn't just a pretty face.

Eric could see the wheels moving in Liv's brain as she continued to look around, comment on details of the kitchen, and generally recognize that he was a guy of substance. It worked every time. Bring them here in the morning, and they want to come back at night.

"I'd say your taste is pretty good, I mean the kitchen came out great. I doubt you need any advice from me." Liv suddenly wondered if a hot lady had been here a year ago helping him pick out colors. Discomfort began to creep in.

"Actually, I had several friends come by and give me ideas. I like that, getting input from different people." Beth was really the one who'd chosen the color. But she was history now.

"Do you have your own ideas, sort of an overall vision of how you want your home to be, like a statement it makes about you?"

"You sound like an interior decorator for sure! But it's smart, what you're asking about. I saw some new condos going up along 99 and stopped in, and I realized that they were way too clean and sparse for me, with no molding, and everything sharp angles. And they had all this metallic and glass furniture in them. That's definitely not me. I like the clean lines and functionality of a beautiful sail boat, but I still want my home to feel cozy when I walk in on a rainy miserable Seattle day. And I love the colors of the sea, all the blues and greens." He was noticing that her eyes were leaning more green than blue with the sun on her face. He liked that. She seemed familiar.

Liv was watching his lips as he spoke, becoming mesmerized by his voice, as it tuned her in to another dimension of him that was strong, and suggested a deep inner space.

"Come on, let me show you around. I have some ideas about what to do next, and I'd like to hear yours." As he took her out to the backyard, she assessed it as potentially cute. Even if a couple of big pines came down, it would still be sheltered and offer privacy. Needed a deck though. Walking back through all the rooms of the house, she heard every one of them crying out for a fresh coat of paint. And the floors! Each ached for either new carpeting or a chance to show hard wood. The bathroom demanded a total make-over. A room in the basement adjoining the garage was ghastly, but tidy in the tool area. Liv didn't say much as the house silently messaged her, while Eric spoke aloud of the fixes he had in mind.

He was enjoying watching her eyes observe and take things in before she started throwing out her own ideas. "So, that's the place. What do you think? What room should I tackle next?"

Back upstairs now, she was noticing tidy stacks of magazines in the corners. The beat-up coffee table showed recent interest in a boat magazine and one on motorcycles too. She'd noticed the total absence of books in the house, except for some 'how to' paperbacks down in the tool area. *At least he reads something.* "Well, this is just a gut reaction, but I think getting the rest of this open area fixed up would be next, at least for me. So that when friends come over it would be pleasant for socializing."

Eric almost said, not the bedroom? But he caught himself. Usually the girls who came complained about his depressing bedroom, and that he needed to get his mattress off the floor and make it more fun. Put in a flat screen TV, have end tables to put things on. And they weren't fond of the bathroom either. "Not the bathroom?"

Liv considered. "That would get one of the most expensive other rooms done, but if you're going to be spending money on removing those killer trees, maybe cheap paint in these rooms is a good indoor project. By the way, are there hardwood floors underneath this carpeting?"

"Yeah, I think so. But I haven't really checked it out. Why? What are you thinking?"

"You can talk to Ryan about it, but I recall them looking at house that needed work like yours and they pulled up a corner of the carpet. They could see that the floors were probably good enough, but they'd have to get them fixed up and stained. Mimi just didn't want that extra move-in work, not after they saw the place they're in, where all that work was done already."

"Yeah, but staining two sizeable rooms, that's expensive too."

"I imagine so. But you know you could pull out the carpet - it's really disgusting, must be decades old. Then do the walls. That way the floor color and wall colors would be a better match. Then come back in another year and actually do the staining."

"That makes sense. Hey, let's see what they look like." With that, Eric went to a corner of the dining room unencumbered with any furniture and tried to pull the carpet up. "There's a reason I haven't tried this before," he said laughing. "Let me get the right tool." Liv was having fun with the spontaneity of this. When he returned and pulled the quarter round molding up with a crowbar, and then pulled up the nailed down carpet and pad a foot or so, he saw some nice-looking white oak floor boards. "Bingo!" He smiled up at Liv. To her surprise, he kept going and began pulling off whole strips of molding from the area and more carpeting, until he had revealed several square feet of floor.

    Liv was totally engrossed watching him move through the task so quickly and efficiently, anxious she'd triggered a big mistake and huge stains would appear. "Oh my god, it's really nice!"

    Eric sat back on his haunches and laughed. "To think I've had this under my feet for years now, and I didn't pull this stuff up. I feel stupid. You know, I'm going to get a friend over today or tomorrow and just get this vile stuff up and out." He stood up and surveyed the flooring and looked right into her eyes. "Thank you so much! Now I owe you lunch. Want to head over to the diner at the hilltop and let me treat you?"

    Liv was slightly amazed at how well this had gone. "Sure. Maybe. I should check with Mimi about when she needs me back. She's watching Shakti and I'm already concerned I'm abusing my new housemate." In a minute, she had Mimi on her cell. "How's it going? Good. They do play nicely together as long as he likes being controlled by her. Say, Eric wants to thank me with a quick lunch now. You'd love the discovery we made about his floors, nice looking oak floors under some foul carpeting. Would you mind if I didn't get back till say two? Thanks so much."

    Mimi had been on pins and needles about the non-date and was thrilled it had led to lunch.

    Meanwhile, Eric was using every moment to have at it. "Here we go, you take that end." And with that, they both pulled the carpet much further back to reveal more hardwood. "Man, it's in really good shape – what luck!" He was genuinely excited and went for his cell. "Pete, how soon can you get your ass over here? I'm pulling up carpet. It won't take more than two hours or so. Great! See you at four." He smiled this huge grin at Liv, while he moved toward her, and touched her elbow. "Come on, I need to feed us." When they came down the stairs, he paused. "I don't suppose I could get you on my motorcycle?" He looked at the sky. "It's a beautiful day and the diner's not far." He noticed her hesitation. "I'll take side streets and go slow." He saw from her reluctance she wasn't the cycle type. But he also knew that getting her behind him, holding his waist, and leaning into him, was his next best move. He watched her think about it, avoiding his eyes.

 Liv had never been on a motorcycle, well, once in India on a motor bike. And she hadn't liked it. *I'll probably get hurt. I can't do that to Shakti.* "Sorry, I don't think so. Honestly, I'm afraid."

 "Sure you don't want to try? I'll go slowly like I said."

 The shifting of her head revealed an internal debate. "No, I don't think so. How about if I drive to the place and meet you there?"

 "Ok, if that's what works for you." He gave her directions and then also said he'd go first and she could follow and see what a safe driver he was. He opened the sagging door of his garage, and there it was, a big black cycle, shiny as could be. She noticed the generous passenger seat behind his and watched him reach for one of two helmets on a shelf. *Who's he been riding with recently?* He put on a light weight leather jacket, then walked the bike out, swung a leg over, buckled up his helmet and revved the motor engine. "Are you really, really sure you don't want to try?"

 Liv felt dull. Boring. Ashamed. She walked to the garage shelf, got the helmet and put it on, and climbed behind him, as though she'd done it a hundred times.

 Eric laughed out loud, gunned the motor a little, told her over his shoulders to hold on to him, and off he slowly went. He stopped soon to give more pointers, like leaning into the turns with him.

 They arrived at the diner in ten minutes. Liv pulled off her helmet. *God, that was fun!* The pure thrill of doing something new and different pushed aside her maternal guilt and reminded her there were people in the world having a lot more fun than she was. As he removed his helmet and looked at her to gauge the effect, he saw a head of wild curls that had come free from their band and encircled a face that beamed a wild-eyed smile. "I think that was a success!"

"I can't deny it. It was a blast!"

The popular diner was crowded. Once seated, the waiter recited specials for the day, checking Liv out with some interest. She saw the guy give a thumbs up to Eric, alerting her that this was not the first time Eric brought a woman along with him. She wasn't bothered that he had a constant string of girlfriends in his life. But she'd never competed for a guy, and she wasn't about to start now. *Watch yourself.* She cautioned herself to keep this on a 'he's your brother's co-worker and kind of a fun guy' basis. Just thinking that brought her up short: the last thing she wanted was to have her brother and Eric trading stories about her.

As they waited for her omelet and his burger to arrive, he volunteered how he'd gotten into motorcycles up in Alaska. She noticed how easy it was for him to talk about himself and make easy conversation. "I just love that feeling of the wind in my face. I know it comes from so much time out on the water with my dad, here in Seattle, and then fishing in Alaska. The motorcycle is the closest I can come to that on land. It's just visceral, a whole-body experience. For me, that's beyond fun – it's being a hundred percent alive." As Eric spoke, he watched Liv listening and not interrupting: what was she thinking now? Those sea-colored eyes of hers, they hid a lot just the way the ocean did. "Hey, I'm talking too much. So, what do you do for fun?"

"Fun?" Liv hated this question, a frequent one with new dates. She always wanted to say, I don't do fun. She couldn't recall ever even thinking, except with Shakti, let's go have some fun. Fun was a shallow word. She'd simply respond she liked being with other people, with her family and friends. That began to capture what was genuine for her: she thought about whom she wanted to be with, and then what happened was interesting, or happy, or sad – or sure, fun. She hesitated to say that Shakti was fun most of the time as that was scary to guys, interjecting her maternal status as though inviting them to join her in a familial way. Really, there wasn't a good answer to give to Eric's question.

Eric sensed her struggling. "Okay, let me rephrase that: what do you like to do besides reading books, because I know you like to do that a lot since I carried a ton of them around the other weekend. Do you like watching videos? Being on Ryan's boat?" It was dawning on him that she probably didn't have a lot of free time being a mom. He wanted to avoid that territory though but then touched on it: "Playing with your kid? She looked like a lot of fun to me."

Liv smiled. "Sorry, I went spacey. It's a bad habit of mine. Sure, I like all those things. And spending time with friends. I just don't have much free time. Though being at Ryan's may free me up a little more." Should she go on? Why not, no reason to not be herself with him. She clearly wasn't his type, so maybe they could be sort of friends. And he'd oblige her by being her date at Elyse's wedding. She leaned in a bit, "What I'm really focused on right now is trying to get another degree, so I can get a better job."

"What kind of degree? What's your job anyway?"

Liv's description of working in a nonprofit trying to help other people filled the rest of the meal. Eric knew little of her kind of work, so it was all news to him. He thought only government workers helped the down and out.

"Right now, I coordinate..." she hesitated to claim 'manage,' "...some needs assessment for clients, help them decide on training classes, either ones we do, or others do. Basically, help them with their next steps towards financial stability once their housing and child care problems are solved."

"So, these 'clients' you call them, do they pay for this?"

"No, that's the point. We get funding so those without money can still find a way out of their situation through skills enhancement." By now, Liv knew what she was dealing with in Eric: basic lack of understanding about the role of nonprofits as a safety net, and in some cases, a launching pad.

Eric leaned forward a little. "Isn't that like a hand-out then, freebies for people who haven't pulled their..." he paused while he quickly did a word search to substitute for 'shit,' "...their act together?" He knew he might be baiting her a bit. But in his experience, you were responsible for yourself, for your own shit and getting it together. And his ideas of her clients were blacks and Hispanics on welfare. He and his dad had it rough when Eric was growing up. When his mom died of breast cancer when he was ten, his dad eked out an existence often working two jobs and not coming home till late. Neither of them really knew how to cook. Eric had to grow up fast, make do without the niceties. Eventually, he just ran with the other white guys in Ballard, took a lot of odd jobs, learned a good work ethic, and cooked up canned food concoctions. Proud of himself that he graduated from high school – 'I did it for Mom' – he took to working on the water and running with a different group of white guys. He really hadn't much to do with people of any color, except for an occasional native Indian American or Asian guy. He'd been surprised one day to overhear Ryan speaking in Spanish to a worker and realized that his boss was part Mexican. His dad had disliked the Mexicans, and bad-mouthed them, but not as much as he hated blacks. Why? Eric couldn't have told you because he just accepted it along with all the other things his dad said. There were a lot of people living off other people's taxes, and they were mostly a different skin color. That's what Eric knew.

It was a bit of a shock to realize he was out with a girl who dealt with those people. And she had – he knew you didn't say half-breed anymore like Dad did – a mixed race kid. *God, Dad would not like this girl, that was for sure.*

Liv was simmering, starting to boil. *Hold on, hold on.* Take a breath, she coached herself. She'd met people like Eric, not a lot, but a few other guys she dated, who didn't appreciate the lives of other people, and how if you don't have many assets, whether dollar-based or family, neighborhood or societally based, you just get stuck in systems you have no choice about and no control over. She was learning - both Elyse and her mom coached her - that you need to meet people where they are, given their own experiences and background, and bring them along. Not erupt, or call them some name like stupid, or racist. A quick chat was happening in her head, while her emotions were complicated by the desire to have this guy as a date at the wedding. Eric looked quizzical, she was taking so long to answer. Finally, after deliberately slow chewing, "We..." come on, she told herself, own it, claim your voice as Elyse always told her, "...I see it more as a hand up. People get stuck, and when you hear their actual stories, it's through no or little fault of their own. Take this one woman..." she chose not to say 'Hispanic' "... I met her yesterday. She was the child of migrant farm workers on the east side of the mountains, got a barely adequate education, got raped by a guy..." she chose not to say 'white guy' "...and is now a single mom with a three-year-old. She's about to finish her GED and you know what she wants? She wants to be a nurse. And that's going to take more schooling, and she's trying to figure out how to make it work. She needs affordable housing, of which there is almost none, good daycare, a full-time job with benefits better than what she has at

Wendy's, so she and her little girl can get healthcare, and God knows how, but time to study for school."

"Okay, so what does a hand up look like?"

"For starters, we'll see if she qualifies for some subsidized housing, and then if there's some skills training which on top of the GED would get her a better job."

"I suppose you give her food stamps too? My dad used to always rant and rail against people on food stamps."

"Her child qualifies for food stamps, and also some healthcare. Depending on her income she may qualify for food stamps too."

"I'm surprised she didn't just get an abortion and solve some of the problem at the front end." Eric saw Liv's features scrunch together in major disapproval, if not horror. He needed to quickly regain ground. "I meant if it was okay with her religion. But probably she's Catholic, no, so abortion wouldn't have been a choice?"

Liv looked down at her plate, took a deep breath, and repeated something her mom had told her: they just don't know, they just don't know.

"Hey, I'm sorry if I offended you. I didn't mean to." Boy, he thought, this one's touchy.

Liv looked up. There was a lot she wanted to spew back in his face. Like in case you didn't notice, I too chose not to have an abortion. But she knew his view in some ways was no different than Elyse's which had been to counsel Liv to make the hard choice to abort, and then move on with your life. "It's okay." She didn't know what else to say right now. It wasn't okay, but this wasn't the time or place to deal with it.

"You sure?"

Her thin smile said, 'of course I don't mean it.' "Let's just move on."

By the end of the meal and her trip to the bathroom, Liv was once again struck by how most people don't spend any time thinking about what it takes to help the poor and vulnerable. Always a rude awakening. And it wasn't just Eric who thought her work was odd, or even wrong because the needy are takers. The 'American myth of the individual' is what she called it, that somehow with no help from anyone or any systems, people were self-made. At least as far as she could tell, Eric just wasn't well informed or thoughtful. Lacking information. Trying to assume responsibility for the tense conversation, she second guessed herself: maybe I should have told him about the microcredit program I'm helping to set up? He might appreciate that, seeing he volunteered how he'd like to have his own boat repair business, and how some business training would help him to get going. By the time Liv took her place again on the motorcycle, she concluded that she'd have to figure out better ways to come at him with the stories. So he could learn.

Eric meanwhile remained foggy about this whole nonprofit thing. He was used to girls talking about their bosses in large companies like banks or the phone company, or to girls who were waitresses or barmaids and wanted to have fun. Or girls who were teachers. He'd dated a grade school teacher once. Or there was that trainer girl from the gym, they'd been good for a while. But he really didn't know what to make of Liv. He got that, as a single mom she'd need to make more money, and that education can help with that. But she was different, just a strange girl. But not really a girl anymore, with the responsibilities she had. Interesting is what she was. And now that he'd been seated close and across from a feisty version of her, he imagined she'd be fun in bed.

When they parted company at his driveway, his enthusiasm for pulling up the carpet returned. "When I've got it done, I'll have all of you over for pizza, so you can see the results."

"I'd like that. We could get out the blue and green paint chips then and plan a painting party." Liv paused. "That would be fun!"

Their parting left them both wondering what sort of relationship they might have just begun. Liv surprised herself later that day recounting to Mimi how much fun she'd had, at least for a while. And Eric pled that he was physically tired that evening over dinner at Kirsten's place when she noticed how quiet he was. His excuse was sore muscles from all that carpet pulling. But he also was recalling vividly a different face that was beginning to captivate him.

Thursday, June 14

Several weekends passed before Eric got around to putting down fresh quarter round to edge his golden floors. Returning home each day, he felt immensely satisfied with the clean, honest feel of the wood. Resting with a beer in hand, he was reminded of the impetus for this effort, and debated whether to follow through on a pizza party for Liv and family. He usually didn't have people over except for girls, so the idea of Ryan and Mimi coming over too, and bringing the kids pleased him, making him feel more adult, a single guy having friends over. And it supported his under-the-radar but persistent present goal of joining Ryan's business in a more substantial way.

And, what the heck, he could give the Liv thing another go. He knew he'd roiled her, but hanging out with family and pizza and beer on a Friday night might repair the damage. Not that he was so into her. But when he'd pushed his credenza around to get the carpeting up, it made him focus on those wedding photos of his mom and dad, especially that close-up of his mom. That's it, he'd thought, Liv's attraction. Damn, if some combination of her fine features and sparkle didn't connect with vague memories of his mom. When he'd picked up that sepia-toned portrait to look at it more carefully, his heart stopped for a moment. That strong wave from his adolescence arrived, the one when he'd wish he still had a mom to give him a hug, make cookies for him, and come to his games. *Maybe Liv had shown up for a reason?* Not that he was a woo-woo kind of guy, not at all, but he was not immune to the hint of romance in the serendipity of all this. *Did Mom send her my way?* Goofy idea he knew. He'd never say it to anyone. But enough of a nudge to give him a reason to try again with Liv. If we just don't talk about her work, we should be okay. He considered how to make the invitation, through Ryan? Directly with Liv?

He settled on a heads up to Ryan the next day, and then that evening called Liv. "Hey, it's Eric."

Liv was taken aback when she glanced at her cell and saw it was him. She was dead tired and just gotten Shakti asleep. After three weeks, she'd given up on ever hearing from him. She'd blown it with her talk of work, or so her logical brain calculated;

but her heart affirmed her speaking her truth, or at least not speaking in a way that ignored her truth.

She eased down into the plush comfort of her new dark green sofa. "Hi, how are you? How did those floors come out?"

"That's why I'm calling. I promised you a pizza party for your great advice. Could you and Ryan and Mimi come over next Friday?"

"Oh, thanks. I know I'm free, but I'll have to check with them. You know though if we all come, we'll need to bring the kids."

"No problem. They like pizza too, right?"

"Of course, absolutely."

"Okay, so see if it works for this coming Friday. I'm anxious to get on with painting the walls now. I picked up some paint chips today for your designer eyes to choose from."

That sounded nice. Personal. "Great. Let me run up and check. Call you back in a few." Liv flew up the stairs and found Mimi relaxing at the table. "You'll never guess who just called!"

Mimi already knew as Ryan was under strict orders to relay all Eric's remarks about women, dating, and Liv to Mimi. "I'm guessing Eric."

"What do you know that I don't?"

"Only that he mentioned to Ryan today that he wanted to have us all over to check out his new floors. I assumed that would include you."

"So tomorrow works?"

"Definitely, I'm really excited about it." To say that Mimi had discovered the strength of her matchmaking urge was an understatement. She'd been on top of the Eric/Liv thing as though she was a mother eagle with two beautiful eggs in her nest. She'd been after Ryan to uncover Eric's past, his dating preferences, and his opinions, before she put any of her plans in action. She had to be certain he was right for Liv. Especially after the Saturday non-date at the diner talk that Liv confided in her, Mimi was concerned that Liv would require any serious candidate to hold her same view of the world. Mimi knew too many couples, Democrats paired with Republicans, Asians with Latinos like her and Ryan, to know that you needed to not let too many ideas and opinions get in the way of basic attraction, compatibility on how to spend time, and ability to enjoy life together. The great unknown for her at this point was how Eric would relate to

Shakti. If Eric hadn't sprung with the pizza party, Mimi had been ready to plan a boat outing together.

Mimi need not have worried on that score as Eric had plenty of the kid in himself. Whatever his views about society and race, he didn't apply them to kids, until they got older and became a problem in one way or another. Kids were just kids. Fun. Silly. He liked to tease them. Indeed, that next night, Eric distinguished himself with his ability to get down to their level, play with them in his yard, watch their eyes grow big as he explained the motorcycle, and drive Liv crazy with requests from Shakti to get on it for a ride down the driveway. "You've unleashed a monster," she laughed into Eric's eyes.

"You've got to plant the seed for fun early," he shot back.

Then there was the dancing. He'd found some old cassettes of music they'd all grown up with in the 80s and 90s. His disco interpretation of John Travolta had them howling. He got Ryan going with some salsa. Liv, knowing she needed to be on top of her game for the wedding, and feeling relaxed by her second beer, tried out her sexiest salsa moves – thanks to Elyse who had taught her well freshman year in the dorm. Mimi was pleased with the fun element Eric brought, pleased that Liv was loosening up, and especially pleased that Eric had not only engaged with the kids but was a hit, particularly with Jeff.

As the salsa music continued, and her body replayed the old moves, Liv's desire rose. Good thing everyone's here she thought, or I'd start making stupid choices. Whatever was ahead for her and Eric, it had to last till the wedding in September. She felt the need to hold back and play this out slowly.

After they all left, Eric opened another beer and laid down on the sofa. Victorious, that was his sense. Not only had he thrown a great little party and had his boss over to have a good time, but he also knew he'd totally endeared himself to Mimi. And saving the best for last, he felt over the hump with Liv. *She wants me, I can feel it.* There had been that look she'd shot him as she shimmied her shoulders and shook her breasts. *What there was of them. The hips were good though.*

Friday, June 29

Eric let a week pass without calling. He was seeing Kirsten as usual Saturday night, but her calls during the week were starting to annoy him. He didn't like her to call during the work day, but she had, wanting to see if they could plan this outing with her friends for Sunday to Mt. Rainer. Next thing she'd have his entire weekends tied up. Other girls had done that to him, where before he knew it, they were taking over his life. That usually led to a scene where he'd just break it off. He was of a mind to try something different this go around, see if he could control his time and juggle dates with Liv into the dynamic with Kirsten.

Come Friday after work, he judged the timing was casual enough to call Liv and ask her over to help him make the final paint choice, which they'd totally forgotten about at the pizza party. He'd bought three small sample colors since then and painted stripes on the wall. "Hi. Hey, I know this is late. But I've got some actual paint stripes on the dining room wall and I'm wondering if you could hop over to help me make a final decision. I want to start painting this weekend."

"Oh gee, I wish I could. But I'm on duty with the kids tonight while Ryan and Mimi have a night out at a play she wanted to see."

"You guys trade off like that?"

"Yeah, a lot. And if I'm not careful it gets too one-sided my way." She hesitated to suggest dropping by tomorrow as she was heading over to Redmond after breakfast.

"How about tomorrow morning first thing?" It wasn't really the context he wanted though: Friday night created lingering space. Saturday morning space was busier.

"Hmm, I need to take off to my folks first thing. I promised my mom I'd give her plenty of time for everything she wants to get done." Liv considered. That sounded lame. Maybe she could just fill Eric in on the family situation. "Really, I'd love to help, but this weekend..." she debated whether to say 'actually weekends this whole summer', and paused. "This weekend and quite a few over the next months are going to be..." *don't say filled up* "...well, they're going to be full at times due to my grandma's health. She and Grandpa are living with my parents now. She has lung cancer and not that long to live."

"Oh, that's a bummer."

"It is. It's hard on everyone, because we're a tight family, and we're all sad to see her suffering. We're trying to perk her up as much as we can. My mom has cut back on work hours, my aunt too. And I'm going tomorrow to give them a break and bring Shakti who always cheers people up."

"So how long do you stay when you go?"

She wanted to convey flexibility although she'd told her mom she'd come every Saturday morning and stay through Sunday dinner if she wanted. When she'd committed to it, it felt big to her. Like she was doing something meaningful to be there for those who had been there for her during the pregnancy and after Shakti was born. In reality, the last two weekends had been relaxing and almost fun with family members passing through the house at different times. And Grandma would only last so long. Then there'd be this big hole in their lives, and Mom and Aunt El would be sad. Grandpa of course too. Better to focus on making the most of family this summer and not put much energy into dating, had been Liv's thinking - other than trying to make the Eric thing work for Elyse's wedding in September.

Meanwhile, her mom was consoling her that in the fall, when Shakti left her daycare kindergarten and started first grade at public school, Liv would be meeting a whole new set of parents and surely there would be divorced fathers among them. Or so Katherine comforted herself, despite her misplaced attempts all these years trying to get Liv married off, as though the average young man would want both Liv and instant fatherhood. But now, Katherine reassured herself: Liv will be entering a new community of parents with kids, a whole public elementary school full of them providing statistical certainty that there would be single dads seeking new mothers for their children.

With Eric seemingly wanting to continue contact with her, Liv opened to the possibility that life was presenting a different option. "Oh, how long I stay will vary from week to week. I just need to make sure Mom gets the break she needs. Sometimes it all gets too much for her. She and Dad will start going out on the boat more. But again, it's just about letting them know when I'm busy."

Eric was thinking that he wouldn't mind at all if Liv was non-demanding of his time. He could keep seeing Kirsten which had its pluses, an enthusiastic babe in the sack, always parading around in her new bras and thongs. And then he could see how he felt about Liv over time. "Sounds like this weekend won't work then."

"Not really. But hey, tell me what your reactions are to the colors you put on the wall."

"Okay." Eric walked over to his dining room wall and turned the overhead light on. "I really like the dark blue, but I'm concerned it's just going to be too dark in here, particularly if I use the same color in the living room. It's like a lighter shade of my navy sofa so maybe that's not good either."

"I'm guessing you're right. What about a light blue option?"

"Yeah, I put one up. But it's sort of nothing. I guess the room would seem more airy. But it doesn't excite me."

Liv was recalling the gold of the floors, the deep azure blue in the kitchen and the old brown dining table and chairs. "Any other samples you put up?"

"There's a blue green shade, although that might turn out overall to be too dark too." He considered. "It's close to the color of your eyes, only darker."

That released a small thrill. "You know, you could put on the primer coat in both rooms, which is a pretty strong white, and then see if you like the way that lightens up the rooms. And then try the samples again or some new ones. Doing the primer would take a chunk of the weekend."

"That's true. Not a bad idea." He heard the kids in the background shrieking. "What's up over there? Is Shakti annihilating poor Jeff?"

Liv laughed. "No, they're just doing their favorite thing these days which is hide-and-seek."

Eric was enjoying the ease of being on the phone with her. Her voice was on the deeper side, with a lilt in it suggesting she sang alto, and could reach up to higher notes. His mind was racing: where can I take this conversation now? He'd been puzzling that week over the kid – or rather over Liv in her early twenties getting pregnant by some Indian guy. Approaching Ryan casually about it just hadn't worked, with no openings at work to bring up his sister. Which all things considered for now was likely best. His mind turned to Shakti – maybe that's the way to learn more. "Has she said anything more about the motorcycle?"

"Oh yeah. She even drew one this week, colored it red and all. You've definitely planted a bad seed in a fertile mind."

"Shakti. I've been meaning to ask you – what kind of name is that?"

That question immediately shifted her external focus on the kids to the background and lit up the internal FAQ section of her brain. Here we go. *Make sure the answers come out right.* Her answers to 'frequently asked questions' regarding status as a single mom and Shakti's existence had been carefully crafted over time as each new dating experience taught her how not to answer, and where not to go. Elyse had helped, vetting possible responses. Liv's initial desire to gloss over and hide things, engaged in a long dialogue with her emerging feminist desire to claim her voice. Appropriately of course, while not delivering too much information. Yet to be true to herself, have no shame, and stand for what she loved.

Eric noticed the pause. "Was that a bad question to ask?"

"Oh no, I was just making sure I knew where the kids had gone and that the door to downstairs was locked. Jeff's at that age where he could really take a bad fall on those basement stairs. No, people often ask me about her name. It's an Indian Sanskrit name that refers to the divine energy in the world." She'd learned not to call it feminine energy, at least for the first answer. She'd also learned to stop with that and see where people, especially guys, wanted to go with that.

"Hum." Eric wasn't sure where to go now. He really didn't want to start singing Shakti's praises, as despite his superficial ability to interact with kids at their level, it wasn't like he was really into kids. They were okay in small bites, but he certainly didn't want Liv getting off on how much he liked her kid. But he didn't want to change his tack yet towards getting more background info on her. She obviously didn't mind hanging out on the phone with him. He felt kind of sorry for her constrained life, trapped by child and family. She seemed to want to spend time with him. She looked so happy when they danced. In for a penny, in for a pound. "So, her dad is Indian? I mean I've just been wondering what the situation is with you and Shakti. Is her dad around?" Eric was thinking of all the Indians he saw around Seattle, hi-tech types he figured.

Fair enough, thought Liv. If we do have a few real dates, he might as well know. She focused on what he asked and didn't plunge into her whole story. "Yes, her dad is Indian, and no, he's not around." Then she decided to volunteer more. "He lives in India." Now she was curious if he'd go further down the road with this.

That got Eric wondering how Liv had ever connected with him. He decided to stay the course a tad longer and tighten his tack. "Is that temporary? I mean, look, I'm just wondering if her dad is any help to you. No one ever mentions him, and it seems like you're pretty much on your own, like a divorced single mom."

Liv wondered how truthful to be. This is the hard part, right, that I'm not divorced, indeed never been married. "No, her dad and I long ago went our separate ways. He's not in the picture. I'm your basic single mom."

"That must be rough at times."

"Yes, sometimes it is. But I have all this family that helps take care of us in different ways. That's why I have to be there for Mom and Grandma now." She relaxed, having brought them back to safe territory.

"That's nice. I don't have much family or involvement with them. My mom died when I was young from breast cancer, and my older brother and dad brought me up - sort of. But I don't see much now of either of them. My brother's off in the war in Iraq. And Dad, well he's gotten pretty sour on life and not fun to be around. I guess a real family is nice."

"Especially with the way Ryan and Mimi are so much a part of the family now." *Whoops, I slipped!* Eric likely didn't know about Ryan having been given up for adoption. Big boo-boo.

"I don't understand."

Shit, how do I keep this short and simple? Damn, why did I let down my guard? She figured that talk of his own family had opened her up. She really didn't want to get into her mom having an unwanted pregnancy and giving Ryan up. Not now anyway. She took a deep breath, and intentionally pitched her voice to sound nonchalant. "Oh, it's a long story. We can talk about it some other time."

Eric got the message. Enough. Get off the phone. "Sure, well, let me know if your weekends ever open up."

"Since Mimi and I trade Friday nights, I'm most likely free next Friday and could come by then and look at those paint colors. Unless it will be already painted?"

"Let's see how far I get. Why don't we check in next Friday?"

"Sounds good."

"Okay, later."

"Bye."

Interesting, thought Eric, Ryan and the family weren't always together. He wondered what that was about, maybe Ryan was a son from a prior marriage. So then maybe he was raised by his dad, away from Katherine for a long time? That was probably it. His mind turned back to Liv: okay, six or seven years ago she got involved with an Indian guy – I wonder what they're like in bed? Was he a really dark one? What's a young girl doing hooking up with this dark dude from India? What did that say about her? Kind of intriguing. Eric had done some of that himself with those Alaskan Native American girls. But that was different.

It was dawning on Eric that, beneath Liv's restrained personality, there might be something more sensual. At one and the same time, her breaking boundaries appealed to him and slightly repulsed him. An internal voice was clear: no way do I want to be playing dad to a colored kid! He imagined the scene with his dad: if I took up with Liv, he'd probably stop speaking to me. Eric, while imbibing his dad's racist views, at least had learned to temper them by trying to be open to people different than him. Like in Alaska. He'd gotten that it was a rough life for that girl he'd hooked up with his last summer there. She had something going for her. Actually, he liked her. And he'd enjoyed the difference of her darker breasts and shiny body. But to blend races in a long-term relationship? Not for him. Nor taking on mixed kids. The light bulb went on: if there's no dad in the picture, then Ms. Liv is looking for one. *It ain't me, babe!*

Sunday, July 1

As Liv drove through the usual traffic mess on Mercer that Sunday evening on her way to Elyse's place in the Denny Regrade neighborhood, she considered a quick call to Eric. After all, he was just up and over Queen Anne hill to her right. Maybe it would work for her to just stop by now at five. When Elyse had called to say she needed to talk and have a Shakti fix, Liv could tell that her mom was genuinely okay with her taking off early from Redmond. Katherine felt bad enough tying up one of Liv's weekend nights, let alone asking her to stay through Sunday night dinner.

Liv was content with how the weekend had gone. She'd freed up her mom and dad, enabling them to dine out last night and have time to themselves, as well as go shopping today. At first during her weekend stays, Liv made awkward attempts to fill the time for Grandma and Grandpa. But mundane activities of life were really the best formula: keep Grandma on her routine, up and out of bed and in the family room; and, let the combination of TV, meal prep, and arts and crafts for Shakti make the long time less heavy. Grandma had her comfort demands, trips to the bathroom with her oxygen on – or off – as she willed it. "Get that damn thing out of my nose, and just let me alone." Then there were naps for her and Grandpa and time for Liv to go online. Really, it wasn't so challenging to be a caregiver. Yet. The chemo had started this week, and her mom talked of cumulative effects that could increase Grandma's fatigue.

Colleen's lung cancer at Stage 4 meant metastasis of the cancer to other parts of her body. While the bone pain was bad, they all especially feared it spreading to the brain. Katherine watched her mother like a hawk, ready to detect alterations of activities based on tumors growing other places. Was she slurring her words? Getting confused? Having vision issues? Katherine's anxieties would feed into Colleen's so that by the time Liv showed up on Saturdays before lunch, the air was thick with tension. When Liv arrived, her mom would fill her in on what she'd been noticing during the week: Grandma getting weaker in some ways, needing her oxygen more, being unsteady on her feet. Grandpa meanwhile was feeling cooped up here in Redmond, missing his walks outside their condo in Eagle harbor and chatting with neighbors there. While the view of Lake Sammamish was lovely, there just wasn't much to watch. He was depressed about Colleen's condition and frustrated with his own inability to make it better. Gary discovered that including Jeff in meal preparations was a good diversion, as well as a foundation for life as a widower.

Fortunately, Shakti was mostly oblivious to it all. Her natural childish ways often lit up the day. Drawings she did of the household revealed fresh exaggerated perspectives from the vision of a Lilliputian; the stories she concocted about her stuffed animals and dolls revealed her own sense of being royalty; and the cartoons she watched generated adult conversations about the pros and cons of Donald Duck's fierce anger compared with Dora cartoons and more politically correct characters.

For her own contribution, what Liv sensed she added to the mix, at least at times, was that she was the adult in the room. Which of course on the surface was obviously untrue and hubris on Liv's part, and she knew it. But from her perspective, the others were all just so emotional at times. She'd arrive and find her mom either sad and teary, or ready to pound the wall. Her dad would be hiding out in his office, exhausted after a week of hearing Katherine's concerns, laments, and complaints about her parents. And her grandparents were locked in this cycle of depression and anxiety for each other, embarrassment over their needs, and frustrations about not living on their own. What Liv brought to the household situation was a certain emotional detachment. Not that she didn't love them, especially her mom. Quite the contrary. Liv brought a steady love, a compassionate love born of her encounters with the refugees and her current vulnerable clients. She felt for them but not in a way that disturbed her own spirit. Some might call it compartmentalization. Or say she was not being *sympatica*. But the most astute would have seen the foundation being constructed of the detachment advocated by Indian sages: steady in the sense of the passage of time, that all things come and go, and that focusing on the moment and being present was the desired state. She'd just begun reading *The Power of Now* by Eckhart Tolle and was affirming its message in her own life.

At her best, which of course was not all the time, in fact perhaps only a few moments here and there, nonetheless, at her best, she was a calm, deliberate and equanimous voice on the weekends, managing the household as she saw her work colleagues managing the after-school day care. The people around her needed down-time, naps, snacks, and activities to pleasantly stimulate them. And if interpersonal relations got stressed, well then, time-outs. She was struck by how well that worked for Shakti – oh, time for a distraction! And how well that worked for the others in the house.

    She was pleased this Sunday when before she left, her dad whispered in her ear, "Thank you so much. Your help makes such a difference for us all." Yes, the thing with Grandpa needing his own TV had been a coup. They had an old box TV in the garage and really the only thing between Grandpa's getting to watch 'his shows' was finding some room in the house for this ugly old appliance. His bed was in Dad's office. Meanwhile the prim and proper living room was never used. Getting her mom to agree to have an old TV set on one of her fancy glass tables and moving things around was a bigger negotiation than Liv anticipated. But victory was hers! She succeeded in bending the silly rigor Katherine enforced about the living room being just so, and started it on its way to being an alternate area for hanging out with Grandpa and his TV. The TV of World War II movies, and the History Channel, which rescued him from Grandma's tireless game shows, soap operas, Oprah, and chic flics. "Hallelujah!" was what he said. And Gary was appreciative of a place to sit away from Grandma and his wife's Sunday sniping about who was right about how to make a good tuna fish salad, or whether Grandma needed to get back on her oxygen. Liv with her functional approach to using their space had created some positive new outlets for the stress and knew her dad meant it when he'd whispered his thanks in her ear.

    Of course, that had to be balanced against the sharp tone she'd taken with Grandma last night. By the end of the day, and the usual weekend battle with Shakti to maintain her schedule of being in bed at eight, it hadn't helped a bit when her grandmother piped up in in front of them both: "Oh, can't she stay up with me on a Saturday night?" Liv's direct, "NO, she can't" had not gone down well. Something to work on, she considered, acknowledging to herself that her preferences were no different than her mom's in not wanting the perfection of her living room disturbed by the men, leaving icy drinks to form circles on end tables, Grandpa leaving behind his plastic toothpicks for his teeth, Dad leaving the newspapers in a mess. It was loss of control for both of them. With that realization, Liv reflected, God what a loss of control Grandma's going through. We like our lives arranged just so, and the little deaths of an image of a perfect room, or a child kept on a beneficial schedule, only prepare us for the big one.

And it wasn't going to get any better between now and the end of the year. Liv was already being nagged by imagining the fall months, when Grandma would be much worse. Did it make any sense for Liv to enter grad school then? The weekend demands on her time from her classes would be enormous. Maybe this just isn't the right year for grad school. *When I know I'm doing the right thing by my family, why should I screw that up by loading on school work?* She knew Elyse would be upset with her for putting it off yet again. But thinking of her book on the power of now, she saw 'the now' lay clearly in focusing on family. Grad school could wait.

As Liv reached the bottom of Queen Anne hill with Elyse's to the left and Eric's up the hill on the right, she pulled into a no-parking spot to call Eric. He was only a mile or so away and Liv could offer to check those paint colors.

"Are we here, Mama?" Shakti looked up from the Walkman game she'd been playing, another one of Gary's techie kids' gifts.

"Almost, I just want to call Eric and see if we should drop in. He lives close to here."

Liv pulled up Eric's last call to her on her cell and decided it was time to enter him as a full-fledged contact. "Hi, it's Liv. I left my parents early and I'm on my way to visit my best friend Elyse who lives in the Regrade. Did you want me to swing by and check out colors?" Liv heard rhythmic music in the background and a woman's voice saying, who's that.

"Oh." Pause. "Well, actually I have a friend over myself, so now's not a good time. But hey, putting up the primer was a good idea to see how much light I want to keep in these rooms. I'm liking the brightness."

Liv felt a shade embarrassed and diminished. But she wasn't really surprised about a girl being there. "Okay. Talk to you another time then. Bye."

"Sure. Bye." Eric didn't want to say anything too revealing in front of Kirsten.

"Mama, are we not going to see the motorcycle?"

"No, honey. Eric's busy. Let's find a closer parking spot to Elyse's." While Liv had been to her place several times since she moved over here in the spring, the frequency was diminishing. Their Sunday night ritual was no longer a ritual, but a valued exception to new habits of living now that Cory and Elyse were co-habitating. It depended on whether and how late Cory was working that day. They'd chosen a new apartment building to live in for their first year together. Not to Liv's taste, but pleasant enough with tall glass and bright colors in the lobby. They were up on the sixth floor. Shakti always insisted on pressing all the code numbers to let them in and then the elevator buttons.

Elyse came to the door quickly, and swinging it wide, bent down right away to pick up Shakti. "Hey, look at you! Are you ready to tell Tia Elyse about all the trouble you got into today?"

"Auntie, you know I'm no trouble. They all love me."

"Now Miss Shakti, you know you can be both lovable and trouble at the same time."

"Honestly, she's right, there weren't any problems this weekend. In fact, Shakti is always showing me the way to help take care of the grown-ups." Liv was meanwhile gazing around the living space noticing new items, and how pleasant everything looked. "You really have made this attractive! I like how you arranged the den with the bookcases and computer table."

"We've had disagreements due to not liking some of each other's things, but we're not too invested in stuff, either one of us, so no big deal. I just hate all his climbing gear spilling out of this closet, and he thinks I have way too many shoes. Anyway, come sit down and I'll get dinner." Elyse had plenty she needed to share with Liv but that could wait while she got their chicken enchiladas dished out along with some beans and rice. There were chips and guac too which Shakti loved and a cheese quesadilla for her.

Liv was struck by how much she'd been missing these Sunday nights together. "Hmm – your special enchiladas, I can't wait!"

"Talk to me while I do this. You want a beer too?"

"Sure."

"Do you want to hear the family stuff or..." Liv paused for effect, "...or the Eric stuff?"

"Eric?" Elyse turned her head from the oven. "Eric. Why do I know that name?"

"Because it's been a while, like maybe three weeks or more since I mentioned him. He's the motorcycle guy with the house on Queen Anne. Works with Ryan."

"Oh, yeah yeah yeah. I remember. So?"

"So, he called."

"You have a date?"

"No, no date. But I'm thinking there's something there, maybe. Sort of. He's got a girlfriend, at least I'm almost sure about that. But, at the same time he seems interested in getting to know me. We talked on the phone Friday."

Elyse interrupted. "He just called to talk?"

"No, he wanted me to come over and use my 'designer' eyes to help him out."

Elyse's own eyes opened taller at that and a smile spread across her face. "That's a decent, non-generic compliment."

"He wants me to check out paint colors for his walls. Remember, I gave him the idea about pulling up the carpeting, and then we had a pizza party over there."

"Check out my paint colors, honey," Elyse said in a deep masculine voice. "Sort of like come up and see my etchings some time."

"Maybe. I mean it seemed like that, like if I came by on a Friday night, maybe we'd hang out a bit."

"Anything else to give hope about his being interested?"

"You'll be proud of me. He got into the frequently asked questions thing and I got all my answers right: direct, clear, and focused with no extra information given away."

"Bravo! Interesting that he was wanting to understand your status."

"Yep. It's clear to him there's no..." with that Liv lowered her voice so Shakti wouldn't hear, "...no father in the picture."

"You think that will scare him off, that it's too much to get involved with you?"

"I don't know. Of course, the other thing that might also hold him back is me being his boss's sister."

"True. Very true, now that I think about it."

"Anyway, I'm just hoping we slowly get to know each other and that it will be easy for me to ask him to the big wedding. Which by the way, remind me of the date."

"It's the weekend after Labor Day, September 8th. Only about two months away – I can't believe it." By now they were seated and eating. Elyse didn't want to ignore Shakti, so she got into what kind of dress Shakti wanted to wear as her flower girl.

Shakti had taken it all literally and been noticing flower names in a book at school. "I'm not sure if I want to be dressed like a petunia or a marigold. I like them both."

Elyse about blew out the food in her mouth laughing. "You think the flower girl actually dresses like a flower?"

"Sure. How else?"

"You have a point there. But sometimes the flower girls are called that because they carry a basket of flowers and maybe even drop a few petals as they walk up the aisle in front of the bride."

"But what do I get to wear then?"

"I thought we'd pick a dress out together. Usually a flower girl wears something special, a little fancy. Won't that be fun?"

Shakti was having trouble letting go of the petunia look in her mind. "I guess."

"It'll be fun. In fact, we're all going out together soon to look at dresses."

Liv looked across the table at Elyse. "We are?"

"Yes. You have to make time to go with me."

"And when exactly would that be?"

"When we decide. Come on, you two, get with the program. I need a bride's dress, Shakti needs a dress, and so do you Liv, as my something of honor."

"You know, I just spaced on the whole dress thing. I guess somehow I thought you'd just buy something and put us in it!"

Elyse angled her head with a look that said you must be crazy.

"Sure, sure I get it now. Of course, I buy my dress and Shakti's. What look have you got in mind for your own dress?" Liv associated Hispanic weddings with these big, fancy dresses, silky, lots of lace, and beads.

"Simple, really simple."

"Simple sexy?" Liv was thinking strapless, showing bulging breasts, and inviting your husband to rip the gown from you and make love in the car, but she dared not tease like that when Shakti was around, so she gave Elyse the look instead: you know the ones we laughed about at others' weddings.

"Well, maybe strapless, not sure yet. I don't want my mom to have a fit over my dress."

"There's also simple, like the Grecian goddess flowy kind of thing, chiffon floating around with maybe beaded edging, maybe an empire waist?"

Elyse's eyes drifted as she imagined. "Yes. Maybe. Look, I've got some magazines over there I'm going through with tons of dress photos. But what kind of bridesmaid dress do you want?"

"Me? Mostly I think they're kind of dorky. I do like the simply flowy look..." which looks like a sexy nightgown was the unspoken thought. "How about we choose ours – alone – and then we can find something for Shakti."

"Okay, what about next Friday night?"

"Not sure. That might be a good time to advance things with Eric. Look, why don't you settle first on a couple you like and then I'll come with you for the final selection?"

"Maybe." Elyse rose to serve seconds. "How you doing, Shakti? Need anything else?"

"I wish my mom would say what she's thinking. She's always asking me to tell her what I'm thinking. But she just makes all these funny eyes at you and she doesn't say what she's thinking. It's not fair."

Liv sat back grinning, turning her hands upward in the air. "I guess you nailed me!"

"What were you thinking about the dresses?"

Liv didn't want to get into all the variations in sexiness with her six-year-old, so she went and got the magazines to distract her daughter. Flipping the pages, she said, "Look, there's so many kinds of wedding dresses. Why don't you look through these, and then pick out your favorites?"

Shakti liked that idea and took the magazine over to the big chair. Elyse was smiling at her. "There's so many beautiful ones, you find three you like."

"Okay, Auntie."

Elyse poured more beer and served up another half enchilada for each of them. "I have some other wedding news to share with you. We did get the Mountaineers Club, so that worked out. They have a caterer's list they suggested, and I'm talking to a couple of them."

"Great. Now who all is standing up for the wedding? Is it just me and Cory's brother?"

"No, we both felt we should include family on my side too and we thought about my sister-in-law, you know Tessa in Yakima. That made Cory think over his friends to get a second guy." Elyse paused, considering how to break the next news. "One thing I love about Cory is he actually thinks a wedding is a community event, that we're inviting our family and friends to support us in our marriage."

"Nice."

"I believe that too. Especially since neither of us is big on god, it feels right to have a sense of ritual and purpose to what we're doing."

"And so..."

"So, he couldn't make up his mind between choosing his law partner, Mickey - or one of his climbing buds." Elyse watched Liv tense up. "Don't worry, not Devin. Cory really doesn't know him that well, he's just always been Steve's friend who comes along sometimes. But Steve has been Cory's good buddy all through law school. They've done a hundred climbs together..."

"So, Steve is going to be one of the groom's men?"

"Exactly. Does that freak you out?"

Liv considered. She wouldn't be paired with him but with Kelby, Cory's brother and the best man. "Is there going to be a rehearsal dinner kind-of-thing?"

"Probably. I mean we haven't even talked about that yet."

"No, it doesn't freak me out." She looked over at Shakti and then whispered across the table, "If there is a dinner, then he'd get the word about Shakti first, so by the wedding next day, Devin would already know and not be freaked out. I mean it might actually help in some way? What do you think?"

Elyse agreed in a soft voice back. "You're right, that could give Devin foreknowledge, and he wouldn't be so shocked at the wedding." Picking up the volume, she added that Cory then decided he really wanted his law partner and Steve, so she was now having to come up with a third bridesmaid. "I haven't been at city hall long enough to have really close friends there, and I was thinking about asking Selena."

"I think she'd love it! And what about the ring-bearer? Who's going to do that?"

"Neither of our families have boys quite old enough yet, although Shakti could probably keep a young ring-bearer in line. Couldn't you, Shakti?" Elyse called over towards where she was sitting with her face in the magazine.

"It's so confusing, Auntie. I like all the dresses. But especially I like the big veils. Will you have a big long veil?"

"Maybe."

"I would love that. Can I have a veil too?"

Elyse looked at Liv who saw the need to nip this in the bud. "No, honey, the veil is only for the bride."

"Did you have a big long veil, Mommy?"

Keep it simple. "No, I didn't honey."

"Why not?"

"Because I didn't want one." Liv turned back to Elyse to change the subject. "Are you doing a …" she paused to give full emphasis to the word, "…a real honeymoon?"

"Let's say we're taking a trip which I'm working on right now."

"Where to?"

"Hawaii, but I don't know which islands we'll go to. "

"Wow, that's special. I've always wanted to go there again. I barely remember anything from when my parents took me as a kid."

"September should be nice, not too hot."

"How long, a week?"

Elyse rose and collected their plates to put in the sink. She knew she wasn't supposed to whine, but if she couldn't whine to Liv, then whom could she complain to? "I want to do nine to ten days, so we can do some island hopping. And Cory's wanting to cut it back."

"How come?"

"The climbing crew, Steve, all of them he goes with, they're talking about climbing Denali, Mt. McKinley, in Alaska, in the spring."

"But that's a while away."

"But Cory says there'll be lots of practice climbs in the coming months, some climbing even before spring to toughen up. Basically, he's counting days and watching his time, so he has enough space in his work schedule to do all this climbing."

"Yeah, but you only get married once – hopefully."

Elyse was pleased with the support. "Exactly, so I'm annoyed about the focus on the climbing thing during the year we're going to be looking to buy a house and settling in together. It seems like such a bachelor thing to me. Is that wrong to think?"

Liv was quiet. She didn't want to feed into conflict between Cory and Elyse, although she appreciated her friend's point of view. Elyse was doing all the wedding planning, so Cory could work more. Couldn't he compromise either his work time or climbing passion? Didn't he know you need to give up things along the way, that in choosing love, it meant you can't hold on to everything else you like? Liv knew this territory well and judged him as somewhat immature to not see his commitment to Elyse as changing his life. "Did this just develop, or have you been talking about it for a while?"

Where to start, thought Elyse. She'd been holding back from Liv a host of frustrations about Cory's attitude toward getting married. Elyse wanting him to compromise on things, usually involving his precious time, and Cory trying to have it all, at least in her opinion. Let Elyse find the apartment, let Elyse arrange the wedding, let Elyse plan the honeymoon. She was sure she knew what was coming in the future: let Elyse take care of the kids on Saturday while I work or climb, let Elyse manage the home economy. He already had her paying the joint bills. She knew full well by now what this marriage was going to be like, like having an extra part-time job at first, and then when the first bambino came along, if she was going to continue working, then she'd have two full-time jobs. The proverbial handwriting on the wall was in her face. Every give and take between them was building her case, as though she were the lawyer in the family marshaling evidence. "Liv, there's been a lot that tells me very clearly that the work in this marriage is going to be very one-sided; and yet I can't bring myself to seriously raise a question about going forward."

"That's easy. I'll do it for you." Liv spoke softly knowing that at any moment they could be getting a Shakti interruption. "Are you sure you want to get married?"

Elyse looked over at Shakti. "Let's find a time to talk, some night maybe on the phone?"

"Sure, just make it after 8:30."

"I'll let you know what nights Cory is working late."

As though it were a cue for stage entry, the door opened bringing in one hunk of a mountain man. He dropped his backpack, called out for Elyse, and came towards the kitchen. "Hey, Liv, you're here too, nice to see you. Is the little demon with you?"

A frowning face looked up from the chair. "I'm not a demon."

Cory sniffed the air. "Any of those great enchiladas left for me? I've been to the peak of the Brothers, I'm ravenous."

"Of course, yours are in the oven." Elyse came to him and hugged him home.

Liv held back to take them in as a couple. Of course, Elyse would marry him. Something about his climbing clothes, how the washed out green turtle neck met his strong jaw and contrasted with his dirty, longish, slightly curly hair, how the old brown cords made his body seem more robust than his suits did. Plus, the light in his hazel eyes, the ruddy color in his face. He created a field of nature around him that contrasted favorably with what seemed an apartment too contained and sterile for living as a true human being, as a man of nature and of the mountains. Of course, Elyse wanted him. Under that grubby baseball cap was a brain smart enough to tackle big corporations and win for the little guy. He'd always exuded a magnetism that made Liv want to see him at work in a court room. No wonder he could win big verdicts. In a flash, she took it all in and knew that Elyse had found her match in Cory, and that she would bend more than he would. But wouldn't it be worth it to have such a partner in life? Yes, of course, Elyse should marry Cory. My job, Liv affirmed internally, is to help her think about how not to overly compromise those parts of herself that matter most in the coming months and years. Let her vent – a little. But re-direct her back to what she acknowledges she really wants. She's creative. She'll find ways to make it work.

Liv slowly rose and gave Cory a perfunctory hug. God, he stunk. "You need a bath!"

"How right you are! Shower first, or grub?" Was his question to Elyse.

"Come on and sit down and eat. I'm more used to your climbing smells."

Liv looked over Shakti's shoulder at the magazine, noticing the time. "Come on, my little one, time to head home to get to bed. It's a big day at your summer arts program tomorrow."

"Don't you want me to show Auntie the dresses I like?"

"Oh, for sure, go ahead."

Shakti scooted down and brought the big glossy magazine over to the table. "I like these two dresses best." She pointed to the ones on the 'be a princess' pages as opposed to the sex goddess pages. The gowns with big poufy sleeves and huge skirts.

"Oh, they're nice," was what Elyse said, but she knew she wouldn't be caught dead or alive in a dress like those.

As Elyse gave Liv a goodbye hug at the door, she looked back at Cory devouring enchiladas, beans and rice and chugging his beer. *I want this too.* Elyse followed Liv's gaze, then looked at her and rolled her eyes as if to say, 'what can I do?' "I'll call this week then."

Later that night, Eric called, sounding apologetic. Liv mentioned her visit to Elyse, satisfied to introduce her friend into conversation with him, but stopping short about putting out the word 'wedding.' Better when it was closer. Eric suggested that she come over next Friday night, remembering that Mimi would be on duty with the kids.

He's paying attention, thought Liv. She almost broached the topic of her work week, but then held back. Most of what Liv cared about in the world was likely not a fruitful topic between them. But hey, she thought, all relationships are built on compromise.

Her Sunday left her with an hour alone before bed. Nothing worth watching on TV to divert her, so she reverted to her old habit of pulling out her journal and writing. She hadn't really processed her sense of the impossibility that Elyse would not marry Cory. Shakti inadvertently had baited Liv in the car ride home talking more about the dresses and how she liked the ones in Cinderella. Liv still was furious with her mom for buying the Cinderella cartoon video for Shakti last Christmas. She probably watched it once a week, including yesterday. *I hate the Cinderella story!* And now Shakti was infected with the belief that at some time, some man was going to save her. Save her from poverty, save her from anonymity, save her into wealth and happiness forever after. 'What a bucket of crap,' was all Liv could think. She needed to try hiding the video again, better yet find something to replace it.

Was that what was going on for Elyse, looking for the happy-ever-after? Liv didn't think so. Elyse knew she could make it in her own right. No, it was likely about having kids who had both a mother and a father. Liv didn't argue with that one bit, accepting that a good birth father who stayed around was a huge asset in life. But beyond the biological urge to reproduce, what was that feeling, that sense of approval, when she looked at Elyse lean into Cory for a hug? Was she accepting the inevitability of it? What was this 'woman needs man' thing really about? She felt the power of its received wisdom, of how she too succumbed to it. Was it a desire to merge that went beyond one's rational knowledge that merger could mean disagreeable, even undesirable changes to one's life? Was it the provider partner thing? 'You make babies, me get food' - but in no way assuring a partner in the actual work of children. Why did women over and over again compromise their views, their time, and their lives to marry a less than full and substantial partner in raising a family? Couldn't they see what was coming? Was it hope, optimism, that over time the man would change? Likely the latter. That women believe the fathering trait will materialize as events unfold, that most men don't get into fatherhood until it's on their lap, saying, "Daddy, ball." Basketball, football, soft balls, large balls, small balls, it seemed to be what guys got into. Their balls.

Liv paused, her thought dribbling off. She rose and pulled down *The Four-Fold Way*. Here it was, already summer. *What's the message for summer?* She flipped to the 'way of the visionary.' *Interesting, a time to get a vision of the future.* "Tell the truth without blame or judgment." How odd. Liv didn't see the connection at first between being truthful and envisioning the future. Then she recalled something from the news about launching a satellite into space and the whole thing about trajectory being critical: the need for perfection in both the coordinates of where you start from, and where you want to go. She tried to apply it to herself. If I were to say envision getting married, married to a let's say good enough man for me and father for Shakti, then I must tell the truth about where I'm starting from. She went back to her journal: what are the truths about my current situation? She wrote down the obvious ones about herself: her age, her personality type, her work, her daughter. What else? Good looking. Can be sexy. Financially self-sufficient. Shakti is a delightful child. That she, Liv, was not exactly a fun person to be around, too introverted for most tastes, overly reflective – one guy said she seemed hollow, didn't show enough emotion. Liked to see the big picture of things. Not a leader. She liked that the book said you must tell the truth "without blame or judgment." It's just what is.

What else is? She put down Eric's name. Handsome, fun, seems self-sufficient financially. Someone I have an easy connection to. Possible community support of relationship from Bro and Mimi. *NOT MY TYPE. What does that mean? Be more specific.* Not intellectual. Does not appear to be interested in cultural issues or psychology of people. FUN. Remember, no judgment about that. Likely a good sexual partner. Appears to be okay with kids. Lacking awareness about whom and what I work with. Not interested in people with difficult lives? Other girlfriends? Shallow? Was that too judgmental?

Her writing started to flow. *Is the idea of him and me so different from Elyse and Cory? Of course, they're both super smart and doing important things like changing life for Seattle people, not repairing the boats of the wealthy. But, but if I take their issue, that he's not giving Elyse the time for their stuff that Elyse wants, he's not dealing with the details of merging, and he may not in the future deal with half the workload of children – and Elyse's hope has to be she can change him – is that really not what happens in most marriages? You see the difference, even the warning flags, but the pull, the attraction arising from one's own cravings formed and shaped by societal imperatives, like Shakti beginning to integrate the Cinderella principle, the sheer force of the longing to make a union happen in face of obstacles, really is my own situation with Eric categorically different? A different set of issues creates differences between us. But if I wanted him, would those differences matter? If I told the truth, wouldn't I love to relax into his arms? To be held and comforted? To learn to have fun? What's to blame or judge about that? We'd have issues like everyone has issues. I've seen it with Ryan and Mimi: she loves the theater so much, but he wants me to go to plays with her and spare him. She only tolerates the boats and the trips that Ryan loves. Why would Eric and I have to be any different? Any better?*

Rather than inducing sleepiness as usually occurred with her journaling, her body became more full-blooded, pulsing with desire. *I need to kiss him. I need to know his body against mine.* Maybe there was a vison, a version of life to be had with him, as mismatched in minds as Liv thought they were.

She determined to be as alluring as she could be on Friday night.

Thursday, July 5

Given the intervening holiday, it wasn't until Thursday after eight when Elyse called. "Hey sister. How was your 4th?"

"Not bad. Ryan found a good place at Waterworks Park to watch the fireworks. The kids had a ball. How's it going?"

Elyse was coming off being furious Cory's firm had taken on a new case that was chewing up his evenings this week. Some poor guy, Laotian, had just lost his job and wasn't getting his final pay. Turned out that happened a lot at this big landscaping firm that handled large suburban estates. But Elyse checked herself from starting the conversation with a tirade.

At work it had been a good week. She was about six months into a new job as a City Council staffer. As the newbie, she needed to deal with a lot of constituent complaints, the everyday stuff of life where people get teed off by potholes on their streets not being fixed, or the lack of speed bumps to control neighborhood traffic. The woman today was unhappy with the way the power company billed and the guy yesterday was upset that the pound still hadn't dealt with the barking dog next door to him. It was all the consequences of high density urban living and how people manage to annoy each other and expect the city to fix it. This flood of dissatisfaction forced Elyse to spend hours learning about departments and contacts within the city, whom you call about what. And it had taken her interpersonal skills to a new practice level, honing her acknowledgement techniques and fortifying her patience by cultivating a sense of detachment from the human drama, not uncaring, but intermixed with humor and good will. She appreciated the work as a training ground for both learning to deal with voters in a campaign should she run for Council herself, in her forties say, but also getting to know the ins and outs of a multiplicity of issues that infuriated pockets of people. For they never heard from happy citizens.

"Okay, so what would you do with a man who's upset because a sex perpetrator has moved near the playground where his daughter who attends a private school goes to play?"

"Obviously he has money, so just find an even more private school that has its own enclosed playground. Play to his fortress mentality."

"Yes, that did cross my mind. But he wanted the city to put a cop on duty there during lunch times. Not going to happen. I told him it's really a school issue and maybe they need to pay for extra help at the park in addition to those who already supervise lunch time. He wasn't satisfied. The call ended badly." Elyse paused. "How's your week been going?"

Liv was frazzled after her workday. "I'm all focused on the microcredit program launch. It's a separate nonprofit, Washington Community Alliance for Self-Help, they call it Washington CASH, that runs the program, but I've been dealing with the logistics of night time facility usage, security, and some of the marketing to people who use our center already. I don't mind that, basically just talking to women about the program. I love the idea of it, so that part's fine. But logistics, I hate that! I may wind up setting up the tables and chairs myself just because there's no one else around at seven to do it. Is this what I went to school for?"

"Got it. Yeah, but stuff like that goes with the job. I get to do all the copying for the Council meetings, along with this other guy who's also new. Anyway, how's Miss Shakti?"

"She's in bed on time tonight. Had a big day at summer camp. With the nicer weather, there's more outdoor time. She really gets into the games, a bit of a feisty character at times from what they tell me. Maybe she's evolving from her princess stage."

"What's your weekend look like?" Elyse wanted to plan something of her own since Cory basically filled his calendar with work commitments and climbing. "We need to get on with the dress thing, you know."

"As it turns out, Eric called and asked me over for Friday to help him decide on paint." Liv smiled at her end. "I bought a new lipstick."

"Oh my god! Ms. 'natural is my thing' is going to spruce up her lips! What color, pray tell me, are your delicious lips to be?"

"Usual peachy color I've bought since college, but this time with gloss."

"What got you enthused about making a play? I thought you were going to wait till the wedding was closer?"

"A couple of things. Ryan was talking at dinner the other night about how Eric might be away for several weeks on a work thing. I got thinking I might just fade into the deep background if I didn't do something soon. Plus..."

"Plus, your body can't hold the tension anymore?"

"Maybe. Not really. It's more what I was thinking about."

"How like you."

"I know. But I started thinking last Sunday night about the whole thing of how we really just want to get married. It seems to be what a lot of women want, at least what you and I seem to want, and yet we know that marriages are far from perfect. There will always be issues. So, you just have to accept that, right?"

"You're saying I need to accept Cory's lack of time as a given going in?"

"Yes. And, if Eric turned out to be good father material and I enjoyed being with him, I'd have to accept that he's not going to be into the interests I have, some of the things I care about."

Elyse was torn between the acceptance message Liv was feeding her and her instantaneous rejection at hearing it. And sadness. "I hate it when you say we have to settle for less than what we want. Remember my horse dream? I rear up and say NO!"

"But Elyse, there's so much stuff we don't have control over. Like take my grandparents, losing control of their lives. It happens to everyone. I got in this big to-do with my mom last weekend about Dad and Grandpa being able to use the living room as a real place where they could hang out and watch the TV they enjoy. Mom was hanging on to this vision of some perfect living room. It was silly to me. But I think she felt like if she could control that room, then she still had some control over life, even though Grandma's dying."

"And so?"

"I'm just saying you and I do the same things. I wound up getting bent out of shape about Shakti staying up too late. They all looked at me like I was a control freak."

"But my issues are about things Cory and I have supposedly agreed to, getting married and having a family. If he's agreed, then doesn't he have to put some effort into making it happen? I'm not trying to control him, I just want him to act committed to what he says he wants."

"You don't see it as a control drama? A battle of the wills over how you spend your time?"

Elyse was quiet. "I don't know. Maybe." She didn't like this angle on her behavior. "Anyway, so Eric. What are you thinking? Are you really attracted even though you haven't said that?"

"I'm definitely attracted. I mean I can feel it in my body. And he seems to have some interest in me despite the girlfriend."

Or in addition to the girlfriend. He could be a real player. "How will you control the situation at his place? Things could move fast. Is that what you want?"

"Not really." Liv was clear she didn't want to end up in that bed where so many had been seduced before. "I'll drive myself over. I won't drink much. If he's going away – even if he's not – I want to leave him with a taste, but not the full meal deal. And I want to taste, before I get in too deep."

"Sounds good. You can tell me all about it when we go dress shopping. Saturday or Sunday?"

"I need to talk to my mom about what works for her this weekend. I'll call you back."

"Okay, ciao." Elyse put her cell down and just sat, still resentful and sad about the idea that she was making too many compromises. Her thoughts rambled along. *If Cory can simply announce that so much time must be given over to work, or to climbing, shouldn't I be controlling my own time better? Making my own pronouncements? Or better, just doing it? I wonder how he'd like it if when he comes home from a late night at work, and he comes to bed, I pretend to be asleep already?* That's manipulation, she supposed, only making our lives together into a kind of game as to who gets what. And she figured it would just turn on her, because then instead of finally enjoying coming together, she'd have stopped that from happening. Still, she needed to get his attention and her complaints weren't cutting it. She moved on to the idea of having a real 'sit down and let's talk' session when Liv called back.

"Okay, I have it lined up so Mimi and Ryan will go over Saturday to Redmond at lunch with Shakti and then I can show up at dinner and keep the kids, so they get a night out."

"Thanks. It'll be fun. Plus, we can talk more about this thing with Cory and his time. I've got some ideas."

"What?"

"Well, maybe instead of just my little complaints that probably sound like whining to him, maybe we need to make time to sit down and really talk it through?"

"What's wrong with that? Sounds like the right thing to do."

"It's just that outside of work I've never had to do that, to get out in the open what's not working. I mean, even at work, like that time with one of my reports at the city, I'm just not good about confronting people about their behavior."

"Really? That's easy. Just pretend Cory is me."

"Ha-ha."

"I'm just saying, we're always honest. Why can't you tap into that with him?" Liv noticed the longer silence at Elyse's end. "What? Are you afraid he won't love the blunt, no-holds-barred, confrontational you? Have you been hiding your true personality?"

"Not exactly, it's just that we've not had issues before the engagement and moving in. We had our separate lives. Now that we're living together, it feels...maybe I feel, maybe it's my own expectation, that in fact I *should* be doing more, because stuff like the wedding planning, well it all comes about because he asked me to marry him. But then I resent it."

Liv suspected that Elyse was getting closer to something important now. "Doesn't it make sense, Elyse, that when two people change their lives to start living together, they would each bring some set of expectations into it? Cory likely unconsciously expects his life is the basis of your life together, two become one, and some atavistic dominance thing comes into play. And you're expecting a real partnership, where he makes compromises?"

"We haven't talked about any of that."

"So?"

"So, okay, I'll get him to sit down and talk with me about our expectations of each other in marriage."

They were both quiet. Liv was wondering what expectations she might have beneath the surface about what a husband and father should be. *Maybe I've been setting them too high?*

"Liv?"

"Okay, see you Saturday. Shall we do a girls' lunch out before we bury ourselves in fluffy dresses?"

"My treat. Come at 12:30."

Friday July 6

Liv applied the high gloss lipstick, stood back and smiled. She didn't like what she saw and wiped it off. She reached for her old favorite. Better. The high gloss was just too out there. He might see it as a direct invitation rather than a subtle suggestion. The push-up bra was enough. She examined her profile: out, in, slim enough. She'd tried different tops, but again settled on black as looking sexier. Heels with her jeans? Not her look. Sandals were more her, and at least her toes looked sexy with their frosted orange nails.

She'd worried that he'd forget, but he called at lunch to clarify when she could make it: did she want dinner? He was right there at the docks and could pick up fresh fish. They agreed on seven, with him doing something simple. She'd bring a salad.

As she drove over to his place, her mind was like a Mobius strip that made her travel in an infinity loop lacking any final destination. Rule #1 was to always have a getaway plan, so control of a car was good. But there was a sense of submission that threw her back on herself, like she was making it too easy for him by going to his place. Of course, she needed to see his paint colors. An underlying nervousness grew stronger. I've put way too much energy into how I look was her self-criticism. A different inner voice praised experimentation, getting out to intentionally gauge her sexual interest in Eric, which had been titillating mid-week. Now it seemed a mistake that would make her say and do stupid things.

She inhaled deeply, knocking on the wood of the screen door. The main door was wide open. He appeared from the kitchen and gave a wave half-way to the door. "You caught me just as I was getting the baked potatoes slathered up with olive oil."

"Sounds good. Here's the salad."

"Perfect." As Liv stepped in, Eric looked her in the eyes and was tempted to kiss her cheek. But he just looked, noticing her lipstick. Nice. He hadn't recalled her using it before. "Let's put the salad in the fridge and then look at the paint in this light."

Eric had painted big swaths of several colors, which all looked too dark to her. Turning her body like a camera swiveling around in arcs, she took in the light in the living room with its white primed walls, and the darkness the colors caused in the dining room. "Forget specific color for a minute, do you like the light or the dark? Or the idea of having one room be much lighter than the other?"

"Since I've been living with the contrast all week, I've noticed I like walking into the light of the living room. It's happier. But the accent is cool."

"The dark is more formal – is that what you want?"

Eric looked down at his old jeans and standard blue work shirt. "I'm not a real formal guy. I like bright, happy. And I'm into the colors of the ocean."

Liv switched over to comparing colors. As she stepped first farther and then closer, she found herself drawn to the blue-green shade.

"Stop. Turn towards me."

Liv, surprised by Eric's direction, swiveled to face him. "That color is yours. You should wear something that color."

"Yeah, it attracts me. Maybe you should find the lightest shade of this and do all but one of the walls in cream, and then use this on an accent wall."

"Which wall would that be?"

"The one with the credenza. You could put a nice picture or large photo above it, something nautical."

"Let me get this right: I should paint the rooms, so they look good with you?" He couldn't resist starting to play with her.

Liv smiled lowering her eyes. "I guess you've found a fatal flaw in my judgment. I'll always lean towards what I like for myself. But honestly, I was trying to pick what would look good with the kitchen color and the navy sofa."

"Right." Eric moved toward her a bit, noticing how her body contracted. *She's nervous.* "Hey, what do you want to drink? I've got beer and both red and white wine. I didn't know what you like."

"White, I like white."

"Sure. As I hone my culinary skills, I'm learning that white with fish is said to be better." Personally, he liked beer with everything. But he'd go with her choice tonight. "Want to sit out back while the potatoes finish? Probably fifteen minutes more and then I'll do the fish."

Being outdoors relieved Liv's uneasiness. She figured, *nothing will happen here on the deck, and nothing will happen* during dinner. Eric once again showed his talent for easy conversation, starting with his work. He'd calculated that making a few complimentary remarks about her brother would open things up, and his assessment hit the mark. He wanted to learn more about that lapse where Ryan wasn't with the family, and was looking for a thread to pull. Liv started going on about what she liked about Ryan and Mimi and it wasn't long before she let slip that it made such a difference to her to have them in her life.

"It wasn't always like that?"

He's probing. She sipped the wine, reflecting, what the hell, it's not like some awful family secret. Except it sort of was for her mom. *How do I keep this simple?* "No, we didn't grow up together. Only in the last several years since Shakti's birth, have we had much to do with each other." Her attempt to sound offhand signaled that she was guarding some family secret.

Was there a prior marriage and divorce on her mom's part? Why risk annoying her? He pivoted to the latest development at work, a 'special assignment' as they were jokingly calling it. "This weird thing happened this week. One of our wealthy customers, and I do mean wealthy, a hi-tech millionaire, he comes in. Which is unusual because ordinarily we go out to his yacht, which has to be one of the biggest boats at Shilshole. We go out to do service jobs there."

"Why'd he come in then?" Liv already knew what this was about but wanted to play dumb.

"Get this, he's looking to do a three-week trip up to and around Vancouver Island. Which is a trip I'd love to do. And turns out he wanted Ryan or one of us to join the crew for the trip, sort of an extra insurance policy in case anything goes wrong."

"I doubt Ryan would do it."

"Exactly, so Ryan calls me over because I've worked on the yacht before and the guy was satisfied with my work. And he says, 'What about Eric?'"

"That was bold of my brother. I mean it put both of you on the spot rather than asking you separately."

"Yeah, Ryan can be direct that way – maybe you know? Anyway, my face lit up and Deepak, that's the guy, the owner, smiled too and said, 'Just whom I was thinking of!'"

"Are you going to do it?"

"Ninety percent sure. Ryan and Deepak went off to talk money. There has to be enough in it to pay my salary plus something extra for me being away for three weeks, plus the cost of hiring a fill-in mechanic for part of the time at the business, plus Ryan making a small commission."

"Seems like a lot for an extra crew man."

"I know, but this guy has so much money he doesn't care."

"Except, what will you have to do? I mean, if nothing goes wrong, won't you just be there drinking beers with everyone else?"

"Excuse me, no! Heck no, I'm going to look to help in as many ways as I can and endear myself to the captain and Deepak. Hell, this could be a great way to see the world with the rich and famous."

"Sorry, I didn't mean…"

"Hey, I'm just playing with you. You're right, there may be a bit of downtime." Eric considered. "Do you want to see the boat? It's an eye-popper."

"You mean now?"

"After dinner? We could hop on my motorcycle and be there in no time. It'll still be light till nine or so." He could see she needed time to decide, so he rose and went in to cook the fish and bring out the food.

She followed him in to help, attracted to the idea of getting away from his place, yet still afraid of a longer ride on the motorcycle. She liked the way he kept inviting her into his life. And my God, a ride out to the bay on a beautiful summer night? She'd be ashamed to say no.

Over dinner Eric asked if she was still concerned about the safety issue.

"I am, not really for myself. It's just because of Shakti."

"I get that. You've got responsibilities. But honestly, I'm really a safe driver and haven't had an accident since the very beginning when I was seventeen."

Liv was grateful to move into stories of his adolescence during dinner, and listened with interest to his emotional capacity for processing the loss of his mother, and the harsh circumstances with his dad. As they carried their plates back into the kitchen, she decided. "You know, it would be great to go out to the bay tonight, really fun!"

Eric grinned, appreciating how easy it was to be around her. But then he always liked the early stages of romance before women made it heavy. Heavy and annoying the way things were right now with Kirsten. She'd called Thursday wanting him to join her and some friends for a movie tonight. She was really miffed when all he said was that he had a work thing and couldn't. As she interrogated him, he'd invented the need to meet with Deepak tonight to discuss the trip. Then began the questions about the trip. Hearing that Eric would be away for three weeks, her voice took on an edge he hadn't heard before: "So you're telling me, just as we move into the best time of the summer, you're going to disappear on me?" That put him on the defensive which he understood well from past relationships was an indicator that it was time to break up. He'd talked about the bonus pay and the chance to sail around Vancouver Island. She wanted to know how many women would be on board, imagining a line-up of slender girls in bikinis. That projection made her do herself in, as she lost it for the first time with him. "Well, I hope you have fun sailing and screwing your way around the island with the filthy rich." Knowing she'd blown it, she muttered an apology and he took the opportunity to quickly end the call. Yep, Eric thought, by the time I'm back, Kirsten will be history. And with Liv's arms around his torso headed out to the bay, he knew whom he'd be coming back to.

  The yacht blew Liv's mind. Mostly she managed her life to forget or ignore how rich people lived. The yacht was tied up at the farthest out pier and took up its full length. Eric started pointing, spilling out stats about the superyacht: a hundred and fifty feet long, six cabins. She saw three levels of windowed space and he detailed how he and the crew would be bunking down at the lowest level where there were discrete portholes, but that the space in the main living room on the first level with the huge picture windows was just like being inside a real house, only way better appointed and furnished than anything he'd ever lived in. Guest cabins were more upfront and on the second level, a smaller tier to this colossal floating boutique resort. And then the top deck was where the captain ruled under the massive sonar discs. He pointed out the front space were jet skis were stored and continued to stress the amenities of life onboard. The more he went on, the more depressed she became. The women in the microcredit class with their artisan jams, handmade jewelry, or house-cleaning businesses would likely be thrilled to get out on a little motor boat. Or simply to have a pleasant apartment on land.

She felt her thoughts bringing her down. Eric could tell something had shifted inside her. "Hey, why so glum? I know, you're sad I'm going away, and you won't get any more motorcycle rides until I'm back." He poked her with his elbow.

She laughed, and her spirits brightened. Sure, the wealthy have a lot, but she was going to get to watch the same sunset from here as they do.

Eric grabbed her hand. "Let's walk down to the beach. It's so gorgeous here tonight."

The first real touch of his hand to hers. That turned her mind off fast and brought her full bodily attention to him, the size of his hand around hers, the strength she felt, the pure joy of a beach at sunset with a nice guy. He'd flooded her with positive energy through that simple handhold.

He sensed a change in her as they approached the sandy beach. They kicked off their sandals to experience the pleasure of the cool grains shifting under their feet and between their toes as they walked. He didn't like to talk much when he was enjoying nature - which was another thing about Kirsten that was annoying: she never shut up. But Liv, she was a quiet one.

Near the beach's end, they sat on the sand and gazed out. He'd dropped her hand and she relaxed moving the sand between her fingers. The air renewed her. A perfect moment. Finally, she spoke. "When will you be taking off?"

"Next Friday morning. Deepak's estimating shy of a three-week voyage based on good weather and no problems."

"Will you be back for Sea Fair then?" She wasn't at all fond of the event with its obnoxious hydroplane races. But the Blue Angels were awesome, and she knew they'd all be out on Ryan's boat.

"I'll look at the calendar. We're probably back by then. Why? Are you going to be the Sea Fair Queen?"

He did have a way of making her smile. "I was just thinking we'd all be out on the family boat. Hardly a yacht, but I'm sure you could join us." Liv remembered the girlfriend. "I know that's a busy time with friends though, and you must know a lot of people doing fun things that weekend."

"Yes, they should make me Sea Fair King, I'm so popular. Not. It just depends on this gig with the yacht. If I'm back, sure it would be great to join you guys." He stood up, brushed the sand from his jeans, and put his hand out to her. The sun had set but the afterglow created a spectrum from deep orange to deep blue above the Olympic Mountains across the bay. She stretched her arm out to place her hand in his, looking directly into his eyes. Simply, effortlessly, he pulled her straight to him and wrapped his other arm around her waist. That smile, she thought, as his lips came closer to hers: it's ridiculously white. He closed his mouth around hers, surprising in the strength of contact he made. She hadn't been held like this in ages, the way he made her seem fragile as though he would crush her in his embrace. Her lips were unsure how to respond, but then he released her slowly. "I've been wanting to do that all night."

She tried to gauge his sincerity: did this guy really like her or was it just what the romance of the moment required? *Never mind.* She smiled, threw her head back a bit, and took his hand.

They were quiet on the loud ride back. Pulling up in his driveway, she was clear that her path would be to her car. She needed time to digest the appetizer he'd offered her.

Eric knew not to push. Better to have her think about the kiss for several weeks and then welcome him home. As he walked Liv the few steps to her car, his calculating mind turned off, slipping back into his basic sensual self. "Your turn to kiss me now."

She felt challenged. She wasn't up to a great kiss just yet. She didn't want to compete with some girl he'd be seeing tomorrow. Angling her face and eyes to him, with a twinkle visible even at night, her sexy side glance found a companion in her wide smile. "Ask me again when you get back." She pecked him on the cheek and made her exit. He just stood there laughing and shaking his head.

In Elyse's more seasoned relationship, romance had dropped a notch or two. Having decided to talk seriously with Cory about expectations, she wanted to do it as soon as possible. The fact that he dragged in at seven, following almost a twelve-hour day, held no sway. She wanted this talk and could restrain herself only until they'd broken out ice cream for dessert. "There's stuff I'd really like to talk to you about tonight."

Cory grimaced. He was beat. The unusually high July heat had made his two trips to the courthouse sweaty ones. And the motions in his anti-discrimination cases were vigorously opposed and defeated. On his walk home, intentionally slow to decompress, his thoughts turned to his dad. He still missed their weekly calls, and his dad's determination and spirited engagement with life. A lawyer in Boston, he'd worked as diligently and professionally as a human being could, inspiring Cory to do the same. A man of long hours, was what his mother said. Whatever Cory and his brother missed out on paternal influence during the week, at least one part of the weekends was reserved for the boys. Usually in nature. Those experiences eventually led to Cory's first trip to the Pacific Northwest to climb Mt. Rainier while he was in college. Hooked, he came back for law school to make a life where hard work could be matched by hard play: rock climbing, winter snowshoeing, wilderness hikes, sailing. An intense legal intellect combined with a healthy, muscular body were attributes that Elyse knew from the start were in a league above the couch-potato sports type she'd dated in the past. She once confided in Liv, he makes me try to be the best person I can be. Cory's attraction to Elyse had been quick, strong, and eager, with their first love-making in a deserted Volunteer Park after midnight on their second date. While she wasn't the outdoors girl he thought he'd choose, her fiery integrity complimented his Robin Hood brand of law. Trying to explain to his conservative Boston Brahmin mother why he was committed to a life across the continent with the daughter of Mexican farm laborers, he settled on repeating, 'I like talking to her. I want to talk to her the rest of my life.'

 Except tonight. Tonight, he was running on empty when her invitation came. "Really? I just want to relax, cuddled up with you on the couch watching something inane." Taking in her serious demeanor, he offered, "What about this weekend?"

 "I'm dress shopping with Liv starting at lunch tomorrow but that's all I've got planned. Are you going to be home in the morning?"

 "No, I think I'll go in early, so I can have all of Sunday off. The weather might cooperate, and we could take off somewhere."

 Elyse debated: wait and risk the almost inevitable waylaying of a planned conversation or strike now, even if he was tired. "That sounds great, but I at least need to get a few things out now - how's that? And then we can take it up on Sunday?"

Cory had learned by now that when Elyse wanted to launch into something, well, she would launch. "What's bugging you?" He already intuited that this would undoubtedly be about his behavior.

She looked around. Stay at the little table across from each other? Sit on the couch side by side? Table seemed better, so she might see his face as he responded. She set down the ice cream dishes. "Here's the thing. I'm thinking we may have different expectations of what being married will mean, and that we should just get them out in the open and make sure they match up."

Oh, doubts about our getting married. Interesting. Cory reverted to his legalistic questioning skills to get the facts out first. "Okay, so tell me why you're thinking this." Her past complaints were already assembling in his mind like a choral group taking the stage.

She didn't appreciate that question, wanting to avoid being a complainant. "It doesn't matter. What matters is that I want to know we're both coming at marriage as a real partnership."

"What do you mean by that?"

"Partnership? I thought that was a good term to use for a legal mind." She had. Plus, she'd recalled all that male/female writing of Riane Eisler about partnership in *The Chalice and the Blade*. Bringing more shared commitments to this merger.

"Yeah, but applying it to marriage? It could mean something different to each person. Take financial stuff. Some partners, take my law partnership, we basically all do the same thing, get clients and handle lawsuits for them. But Kelby is managing partner right now and takes on administrative duties for which he gets paid differently."

Elyse did not want to talk about his law firm. "Let's get off the partnership word then if that's too murky. Maybe I should just cut to the chase and say what I expect and want." She took a deep breath. "I love you. A lot. More than I've loved anyone. You're a truly fine human being. I want to be married to you and have you father my children. I want our lives to really mesh well together, where we're supportive of each other in all the ways we should be."

He sat back and continued holding her gaze. "Elyse, you know that's what I want too."

Restless energy that was invested in her concerns made her leave the table, place her dish in the sink, and take a new position, standing before him with her arms crossed. "It all sounds great when we say it. But..."

"But what?"

"I need to get beyond the flowery stuff we say, and know what it really will be like, the day to day, the taking care of kids."

"How can we possibly know that now?"

"We can't. But I have an expectation of what I want it to be, and I bet you have a latent expectation also."

"I do? Like what?"

She didn't know whether to talk about what she wanted first or what she thought he expected. "I want a marriage where my career is as important as yours, regardless of who's earning the most money. I want a marriage where there's a lot of give and take to help each other out, where when we decide to do something together then we're both helping make that happen. And when we have kids, I want a husband and father who's engaged, involved with the kids from the start."

Cory gave her his full attention, sizing up the emotional forces stressing her. Her most recent complaints about him - whining was how it registered - were that he was working too much, had no time for wedding planning, and played with his climbing buddies more than her. He was well aware she wanted more of his time. The challenge was how to respond, to reframe this. Time for kids years from now? Sure. Time for lesser priorities, or priorities of hers at any given minute? It would always depend. His law practice would always be demanding. He liked that, how it challenged him to be his best. *Climbing? God, a guy should be able to relax with friends. I can't give up the outdoors.*

Her eyes at first didn't leave his face. Then, she looked down, twisted around and ran water over the dirty dishes, reluctantly turning back. "What are you thinking?"

Be cautious. "Look, I'm totally with you about our careers, each is as important as the other's. Regardless of me earning more, that doesn't change how I think about it. But take planning the trip after the wedding to Hawaii, you just have more time to do that right now than I do."

"Not if you weren't spending weekends out with the guys."

Damn, she wants me to cut back on my friends. "But you care more about this than I do. Doesn't that come into the equation somehow? You care more about the wedding being nice and the trip and where we stay. Elyse, heaven for me is a tent in nature and being with someone I like. Beyond that? Make it the way you want."

"You don't care what your mom and brother think about the event we put together? It's fine with you if they think I'm some Hispanic chick from a migrant background who doesn't know how to put on a wedding suitable for Harvard types like them? Don't you want our public commitment to make them think well of us together?"

Jesus. Now my family. He'd always been an outlier, and it didn't matter what they thought. "I want you to have the wedding you want. However it comes out." He rose and came to her, embracing her in a bear hug. "If you make it so it's you, I'll love it. And I don't give a rat's ass about what my family thinks."

She let him hold her. "You say that now. But they're the in-laws I have to deal with."

"Elyse, just stop it."

She let her arms unfold and rested her head on his chest and shoulder. "What about the kids? Am I always going to be the one doing everything for them and you'll be missing in action?"

"I promise, when it comes to our beautiful, wonderful, adorable children, all ten of them that my Hispanic migrant woman will keep popping out, I promise to help. I'll take them camping." She couldn't help smiling. How could she not? But then she struggled to get out of his grip. How could she let him think the issue of their expectations was resolved? But he held her tightly and brought his head to hers. "I love you, especially when you're feisty."

Saturday, July 7

Elyse decided they should eat in for Saturday lunch to save money and have dessert out after shopping. "I'm dying to hear about last night! Was Eric so enticed by your lipstick, that he flung you on the floor and smothered you in kisses?"

"Hardly. Although there was one, long, hard kiss."

"Hurray! I think. What happened?"

"We went out to Shilshole and walked the beach. Honestly, it was so beautiful out there, definitely a night for romance."

"And?"

"And he kissed me on the beach."

"Score one for lipstick!"

"Elyse, it was hardly that."

"I know. So? Are we interested? Wildly excited?"

"Interested. But skeptical. He must be such a player."

"That turns you off?"

"Sure. I hate to compete. But I'm willing to play it out more."

"Because?"

"Because I'm noticing how light-hearted he is, and how that balances me out, sort of picks me up when I start to get too serious."

Elyse's tone moved from bantering to serious. "That actually sounds good. What's next? Another date next week?"

"No, I won't see him this week, as he's leaving town Friday to crew on a yacht for three weeks. A trip around Vancouver Island."

"You mean he's out-of-pocket for basically a month?"

"Yep. Likely back for Sea Fair though."

"How did it end, the evening I mean?"

"Upbeat. I owe him a kiss back."

Elyse put her hands on her hips. "Well done!"

"What about you? Anything fun last night?"

"Agh - after a while, but first I started that conversation with Cory we'd talked about, about expectations, mostly my expectations...I did get those out, except they were really general, so superficially he could either 1) agree to them, 2) duck them, or 3) respond humorously."

"Any headway?"

"Probably only in that I started the conversation. You know what's weird though, maybe not weird, just strange that I'm seeing this now. But it seems like we're going to be having this conversation the rest of our lives. Like I'll get wound up over him not doing enough, and I'll assert my position, and then he'll mollify me. And when all is said and done, there really won't be any meaningful progress. This little drama will become part of our marriage dynamic, played over and over."

"Maybe that's the way it is for everybody? Anyway, are you positive you didn't make any in-roads?"

"I don't call it a real solution when I still wind up with it being my job to make the wedding and trip the way I want it, because I have more time now and care about it more than he does."

"Is that so terrible?"

"No, just lonely."

"You've got me, girlfriend. I'll help you."

Elyse almost smiled. "I know. And I appreciate that, but I didn't get his involvement, I came up empty handed."

"Look, you are going to marry Cory. No doubts there. You are going to have a wedding and trip that is planned one hundred percent by you. That's the way it is. Resistance is futile. Just go with it."

That brought a pout to rival one of Shakti's. "You're right. But I lost."

Liv's eyes caught fire. "Just quit it! How can you say you lost, when you've got a great guy to marry who really loves you and in some way, shape or form, will turn out to be a good father?"

"Excuse me!"

"Enough okay. Let's just go out and have fun planning your wedding and getting the dresses. If you can't pull together one heck of a fiesta for your wedding that everyone will love, you're not my best friend. Come on, Elyse, get with the program."

The first stops at the bridal shops filled with dresses bursting from the racks with their poofs of billowy white tulle, clouds of chiffon, and huge skirts, all tended by their ever-so-into-your-wedding retail sales ladies, left them both slightly nauseated. As they exited from the second one, Elyse had by then tried on three or four at each shop. "God, I'm exhausted. I could never be a model."

Liv tried on a bridesmaid dress in each shop and though less tired, was equally out of her element. "You're supposed to be excited about this. Seeing yourself looking beautiful in all these magazine gowns."

Part of the problem was that they didn't carry each gown in every size. Some of the fluffier ones had been too big for even Elyse's globular breasts, while the sleeker ones had not shown all her ins and outs to their best advantage either. "Let's have something to eat. I'm slightly depressed. One of those old-fashioned soda shops with ice cream floats would be really good right now."

The choices nearby in downtown Seattle, however, meant they ended up dismayed at a funky café having Italian sodas and cookies. "I know. Let's just try Macy's fancy dress area and see if we get some different ideas." Liv wanted simple.

Elyse was sucking her soda through a straw and stopped abruptly. "Hey, at my place you said, 'a fiesta wedding.' It just struck me: what if I really play up the Hispanic thing? I'm already talking to a couple of bands and leaning toward the salsa one. I know my family would like it, but I've been worried about Cory's family and trying to please them, like with a band that plays sixties tunes. But maybe I should just go for a fiesta wedding?"

Liv's eyes lit up. "I'm liking it. Liking it a lot. And you're such a good dancer, and Cory's okay for a guy. God, it would really be fun!"

Elyse's eyes were sparking as a big grin took over. "Okay, so if I do a fiesta wedding – just think, even the invitations could look fiesta-ish! – what does that say about dresses?"

"Let's go find out!" About a half hour later, just as they were ready to give up on Macy's, Liv found the dress she wanted. "Bingo! Look at this one, Elyse." It was a bright orange party dress that had one wide shoulder strap that expanded down at an angle across the chest, leaving the other shoulder bare. The front edge of the dress across the chest had a ruffle over an otherwise smooth chiffon-covered sheath. The hem of the dress echoed the line of the strap moving from above the knee on the strap side to mid-calf on the strapless side, again with the same ruffle.

"Go for it! Quick try it on!"

When Liv floated out, even with her sandaled feet, they knew they were on to the look they wanted. "Take off your sandals and step on your tip-toes."

With that distraction gone, Liv looked in the mirror and started to shift her hips and dance.

Elyse squealed, "Yes! Yes! That's it. What other colors do they have?"

They attacked the aisle where the dress had come from and found turquoise and lime versions. "Triple bingo," laughed Liv. "What if Selena got the orange, Tessa the lime, and me the blue?"

"Or you in the lime? God, they all would look great on you."

"Call Selena. See if you can get sizes and color preferences from her and then your sister-in-law." Elyse reached Tessa who thought orange would be fun. She was close in size to Elyse, so she modeled that one. "I love this dress. How can I get this in white or beige?"

As Liv tried on the turquoise and then the lime, they both frolicked in front of the mirrors. These dresses were perfect for shoulder shimmies. They were sexy without going over the top. Selena called back in about twenty minutes and told them to put one of each color on hold for her in her size. She'd come by tomorrow and try them on.

Meanwhile, Liv suggested, "What if you took the orange one to a seamstress and had her make up one in white or cream for you, only with more ruffles to it, especially at the bottom?"

Elyse stared at her. "I'm seeing it, actually with substantial ruffles like a flamenco dancer's outfit, where I could hitch up the long side to my hand or the waist of the dress for dancing. It would be so Spanish and beautiful and so much fun to dance in!"

"I'm definitely getting the picture. I love it for all of us. I can hear the music and see us!"

"Me, too!"

"What about in church, are you doing a church?"

"I'm still debating between outdoors and a church. My mom wants a church."

"Would you do a veil? A hat? Flowers in your hair, like a big gardenia?"

"What else is Spanish?"

"Lace? Like a lace shawl on your head and covering your shoulders in church?"

Elyse closed her eyes. "Something about it all makes me see red and black too, but that doesn't fit."

"The guys are in black and white. Maybe they could have red ties or cummerbunds?"

Elyse squished her nose. "Not sure. But back to the lace, the shawl concept. I like that. Maybe a real seamstress knows how to find that stuff."

"Shall we check out shoes before we go just to get some ideas?"

Walking past the tables of dress shoes, they realized that as much as they were drawn to high-heeled stilettos for the look, there'd be hell to pay dancing in them. They left shoes to another day.

Before Liv took off to Redmond, they'd exchanged ideas on all the other ways to make this a fiesta wedding from the invitations to the décor to the food. "We have to offer mojitos." But they knew the standard food fare wouldn't connect well, so brainstormed ideas. "You're not going to do real Mexican or Tex-Mex food though, right? I mean like beans and rice kind of stuff?" Liv thought it had to be more upscale than that.

"What about chicken mole?"

"Might work, but you know it really depends on the caterer you can use."

"You're right. I'll talk to the Mountaineers Club and see if we can get some fiesta flavor into the food."

As they parted, Elyse was so enthused. "Liv, you've saved me. I've finally got the right spirit about this. I feel a thousand percent better about the wedding. Maybe we should go to Mexico for our trip instead of Hawaii?"

Liv got into her car content she'd helped her best friend plan a fun wedding, *What was not to like about a fiesta wedding? It's going to be perfect!* More importantly, she'd help to keep Elyse on the right track with her marriage to Cory. She'd said it: it would be a life-long conversation, true of all marriages. And Liv felt sure Elyse had found an exceptional person in Cory to engage in that on-going life dialogue.

Thursday, July 26

Finally, it worked out for Elyse and Liv to meet up with David and Jonathan, their friends from the Sudan. Years ago, in her early days with the Rescue Committee, Liv first met them when they arrived at SeaTac airport from New York. A week earlier, they'd still been in the Kakuma refugee camp in Kenya, where they'd grown up in that camp's deprived conditions, following years in an Ethiopian camp. In 1987, they'd been growing up in the south of Sudan as normal children did, helping with the cattle and goats, caring for younger brothers and sisters, and learning the ways of their herdsmen Dinka people. They'd never been in a city. They were twelve and ten the day when their lives were destroyed.

While Liv still worked at the Tukwila resettlement office, David and his friends used to stop by with their questions, make conversation, and play with Shakti. They all had family they missed, little sisters and brothers, dead or never found. As the guys got interested in girls, often Somali or Ethiopian, Liv began coaching them on appropriate behaviors. Like the time she suggested bringing a stuffed animal to a girl for her birthday and David walked in with a three-foot panda bear he'd picked up cheap somewhere. He would sit and just talk with Liv sometimes when things weren't busy. His conversation often turned sad. He'd share memories of the horrors of the treks as well as stories from the camps. No Pollyanna, Liv would hold the silence of his memories, until one or the other found a practical or humorous transition.

Liv shared the lost boy stories with Elyse, which led to them meeting up with the Jonathan and David to have a cheap dinner out now and then. Which led to making them dinners, teaching them how to cook American dishes. Jonathan, the funny one, really wanted to learn to cook, and to have his own small grocery store. David, among the brightest of all the lost boys, set his sights on law school early on. The four shared fond memories of the botched fried chicken attempt – for all her bossiness in that effort, it was Liv who burned it; and Elyse's successful instruction on how to make her family's special enchiladas (the trick was in choosing the right chilis.) The two young women had been at times mother, sister, coach, and friend, while Shakti had become their little sister.

Tonight, they were driving down to Rainier Beach, where the two guys still shared a place, and where Jonathan had opened a food and sundry store. Liv was mad at herself for letting so much time go by since seeing these two special people, and through them, staying connected with a community of survivors she loved. Elyse's reaction was, "It happens. We all get busy. But let me tell you what Cory learned about David." Once Cory had arrived in her life, he'd met David and Jonathan too, and taken a keen interest in helping David with his law school aspirations. David went to Seattle U Law School's part-time program which enabled him to work while he studied. After a long haul, David was going to finish by summer's end. "Cory says he's actually graduating with honors. That blows my mind, to not even know English well till you're twenty and go on to finish law school here. That guy is super smart."

"Is he interviewing for jobs?"

"He's been working part-time at a legal aid outfit, and they want him full time. But I don't know if he's even going to go that route. Cory says David still wants to go back to Sudan, maybe Chad, and try and learn what happened to his mother and sister."

"He's always talked about that." Liv's mind flashed back to one of the first conversations she'd had with him alone, watching the tears well up in his eyes. "Maybe it's time. With the law degree, he could get into a good position somewhere in East Africa."

"It's still not good there, you know. Despite the peace agreement, there's all that fighting in Darfur. I worry that it will be dangerous."

"If he's mostly looking in the camps, that shouldn't be too dangerous."

"Yeah, but doesn't he have to drive around to get there? I mean from what you see in movies, there's armed crazies all over, sticking up people."

"Let's bring it up then," Liv suggested, realizing she really didn't know much.

They arrived at Jonathan's storefront. He'd taken it over from an elderly man for whom he'd worked a few years and who was retiring. The old guy had really taken to Jonathan and was letting him buy out the inventory and lease at a discount over time. There was a fresh coat of paint above the window on the wood: 'Jonny's Spot' in pink lettering against a dark background.

On the windows were painted words letting folks know they could find a variety of African specialty goods inside, sweets like halva, and a couple of flatbreads. Jonathan kept up the old guy's basic inventory, but sought to attract new customers looking for items from countries home to the diverse population occupying Rainier Valley. Liv wondered aloud if they were going to eat here in a back room, but Elyse, chortling at her friend's dismay, responded, "No, we're just meeting here. They're taking us to their favorite local dive."

As they entered Jonathan was waiting on a customer but shot them a broad smile. "Right there!"

Liv and Elyse began to check out the shelves while Jonathan closed up, and then to consider his first effort at a deli counter. "What is this stuff?" Elyse had less experience with east African food than Liv did, who'd tasted samples brought to her when she worked in Tukwila.

"Oh, that's akara made from black eyed peas, and this is garri made from cassava – kind of gross no?" Its thick white consistency did not look appealing to western eyes. "This is pretty good, it's a sweet bread that I remember liking." There were also simple children's toys on one shelf, mancala board games, a few stuffed animals, hand drums, and some hacky sacks.

"My dear ladies, how do you like my store?" Jonathan's laugh was a joyous one.

Liv spoke first. "It's amazing. I can't get over that you finally have what you wanted. I'm so happy for you!"

"Yeah, but where's the enchilada sauce?" was Elyse's follow-up.

"That's when I expand into next door. Hey, it's time we go over to the place where we're meeting David."

"Can we walk?"

"No, it's farther down Rainier Avenue."

They piled into Elyse's car and were at a place called *South of the Equator* in five minutes. "What is this? You're taking us to a Latin restaurant?" Elyse mocked a shocked expression.

"Wait till you see the menu." Jonathan just continued laughing. He was always like that. Happy. He never forgot the camps and the token food they were given. His developing paunch made him proud.

The restaurant's fusion of ethnic meals was matched visually by odd and weird items on the walls: lizard skins from

Mexico, street signs from Peru and Brazil, and baskets from India. The African décor consisted of exotic bird feathers and pieces of tribal costumes. Toning it all down were grey Formica tables and metal legged chairs on decades-old black and white linoleum pockmarked with bare spots. Liv exchanged looks with Elyse. "I guess he really did mean a dive."

Jonathan noticed their dismay and put his arms out to each of their shoulders. "Ladies, ladies. Just wait. Looks are deceiving. The food is fan-tas-tic!"

Elyse stared back at him refusing to let her own laugh out. "I need convincing."

By the time they ordered their first drinks from a selection of southern continental beers, David walked in. He'd been parked on a side street nearby for quite a while, seizing the rare opportunity for down time, closing his eyes, and loosening the tension in his shoulders. The internal open space invited old memories in, usually not a healthy use of time, and mostly he avoided it. But as his future was now re-directed toward the place those memories were formed, his resistance was ebbing. Perhaps the only way forward included accepting the past.

Dut and Jok were out with their dads and the herd of cows, that day when the raid blew the boys' lives into fragments, a day seared forever into their psyches, yet from an incident that left the sun not much further along in the sky. They were not that far from their tents, while Dut's mom was at the well with his sister, Amer. Jok's mom was working outside near her tent, making extra food for the upcoming autumn celebration. Jok, who'd been singing to himself while bent over to look at a calf's leg, had sensed the rumbling in the earth first and looked up to search for his father. The assault for Dut arrived as an ominous, growing, whirring sound above that caused him to jerk his head up. Then the gates of hell opened, as government helicopters and Janjaweed tribal men on camels and horses descended upon their village, an explosion of sound from rapid-fire machine guns above spraying the village, and rifles cracking as the riders thundered behind. Dut's father pointed to run towards the well when a robed desert tribesman's shot halted and felled him. Too frightened to move, Dut hid among the long-horned herd as they were being mowed down. He fell to the ground near one, pretending to be dead. Later, he crawled to one of the children's dugouts nearby, one of their play areas where Jok had already taken refuge. His dad had run toward his wife near the tent and Jok had seen him fall in an elongated stretch of his body towards her. Jok hadn't seen what happened to his mother and younger sisters. The well where Dut's mother, sister, and other women had been gathered was in the distance. The boys were too scared to move to begin their search.

There had been talk for weeks among their clan as news of other Janjaweed attacks filtered in, but those had been farther north. Nonetheless, walking to and from this well every day, the women had discussed what they would do if their village was attacked. They'd heard that sometimes women and children were shot, while others were seized and taken by the riders only to be raped later. Their best option was to run in all different directions from the well until they reached cover and then to keep moving, moving stealthily. Some would likely be pursued, but others hopefully would not be found hiding in the bush.

Much later after the attack, as the sun was setting, Dut and Jok crawled from their hiding spot back towards the village. As they crawled, one would see a prone body, a friend's mother or father, then the other would gasp as they found one of their own friends. Their tears were flowing hard and they struggled to hold back their sobs, but they had to know for sure what had happened to their families. That night, they both stayed beside their father's bodies. At dawn, having slept little, they rose with the stench invading their nostrils, the vultures circling overhead. Standing, they saw the slaughter. So many dead bodies. Jok moved slowly toward his tent and then recognized his mother's and sisters' clothing, his mother lying face down with her arms flung out as she'd run to meet her husband. His sisters were still hand in hand as they'd been running after their mother. Jok's weeping began and knew no end. Dut bent down beside him. "Come with me, I have to find my mother and Amer. I think they were at the well. Come with me. We need to stay together." Jok looked up through his tears and slowly stood. Deeply afraid, he took Dut's hand, as they moved first slowly, then more quickly on the way to the well. They stopped when they saw more bodies. Three lay just a few feet from the well and three more were strewn apart in the surrounding area. Dut was immobilized by the fear of discovering his loved ones. He tried to recall which robe his mother wore that morning, was it orange or red? Brown for Amer? While he feared moving any closer, he had to know.

Dut and Jok continued to hold hands as they approached the well. Jok thought of his playmate Amer. So pretty, so fun. Surely, she made it somehow. The flies were buzzing around the bodies and the smell was sickening. Together they looked at the women's faces, each caught in fear or anguish, but none Dut's mother. When he came to the last body, the one farthest away, it was his mother's sister. But where were her children? He hadn't seen them back in the village.

The two boys slowly turned their gazes in a circle at all the brush surrounding them. They began to call. "It's Dut. It's Jok. We're alive. Where are you? Where are you?" They each penetrated outlying areas of the brush calling aloud. Dut found two children, a boy and girl of four or five years old that he knew belonged to one of the dead women at the well. Jok found three others, also younger children belonging to families of people he'd seen dead. They gathered at the edge of the brush. A few were old enough that they wouldn't take Dut's or Jok's word that their parents were dead. They had to be shown. Mostly they all stayed in the brush together.

Dut and Jok were the oldest and intuited they should move; they saw no point in remaining among those slaughtered. Each had been to neighboring villages with their fathers. They could only hope that those people were okay and would help them. They made themselves go back to their tents to gather food. The next morning, they filled as many water carriers as their young troupe could carry and headed that day into the rising sun towards another village.

They reached it as people there, again mostly young and numb from the attack on their village, were packing up to leave. Thus, the children joined the stream of refugees that would walk hundreds of miles to Ethiopia first, and later to Kenya, for a journey of a thousand miles. With only the clothes on their backs, and dependent for the most part on food from villages they passed through, they became malnourished and diseased. An incredibly dangerous and death-ridden walk, it killed half the children along the way. Crossing rivers, if crocodiles didn't attack them, they might drown. Lions or hyenas pulled apart stragglers, while soldiers killed or abducted them to become child soldiers. Unrelenting fears were a constant companion. Some just gave up and died.

In Ethiopia, they survived for four years until ordered out. So, they walked to Kenya. In the north, the Kakuma refugee camp received them, mostly boys who'd made it. The girls who had survived were put in the families of existing refugees to protect them; yet losing orphan status would ultimately preclude them years later from resettlement elsewhere.

After nine years in the camps, Dut and Jok, now superficially Christianized by their fellow Dinka and Nuer youth and called David and Jonathan, were chosen for resettlement due to their ages. They were old enough to be viewed as capable of handling the immense challenges that lay ahead: being resettled out of the desert and nomadic life they'd first known, then the scrabble existence of the camps, into not only more urban environments, but outside their eastern African culture into highly mechanized, dense cities in foreign countries where the English they'd been learning would have to dramatically improve. And where they would need to adapt to new ways of living with technologies beyond belief among people who had no cultural or ethnic connection with them or Sudan. The most resettlement agencies could offer was to send them in small groups, provide housing and aid, and then keep sending more to the same area in order to build a new community for them.

The two 'boys,' David and Jonathan, already in their mid-twenties, were among the pioneers resettled in 2001 to Seattle before 9/11 brought a hiatus to the program for several years. More than 3500 had been brought to this country by then, a minority of the 20,000 Nuer and Dinka boys displaced and/or orphaned during the Second Sudanese Civil War, and a tiny fraction of the 2.5 million tragically affected by the fighting over oil and mineral resources. They'd picked up some English in the camps, and there was a bit more formal indoctrination to western culture and speaking English as aid organizations sent in volunteers to begin to ease the transition. In the camp in Ethiopia, David met his first white person and wondered how such a pale creature could survive. When his group arrived in Seattle, they were getting accustomed to being surrounded by all kinds of strange looking people. Liv was among the Rescue Committee greeters when they stepped off the plane.

By then, the term 'lost boys of Sudan' was becoming known in refugee circles, as though they'd survived under the leadership of Peter Pan and the fairy dust of Tinker Bell. Liv hadn't known what to expect, but imagined she'd be greeting these incredibly sad looking young men, ages eighteen to mid-twenties, emerging from customs looking completely out of it.

No way had she foreseen the likes of David and Jonathan. They and most of the group of six guys and one girl were all flashing these beaming smiles as they came out of customs with their in-transit guardians from New York. They're beautiful, was her first thought. A few as tall and lanky as David was, looking like they belonged on an NBA basketball team. Their ebony bodies were lean, with an accompanying grace or artistry about them, like a Giacometti sculpture. And the biggest shock to her was that they were so alive, so vibrant, cracking jokes as they looked around, punching each other lightly in jest. Well, why not? They were out of the dead-end camps and being fed strange but okay food in volumes that amazed them, and being helped to understand each step of the way by some very kind people. After what they'd been through in their lives, this was a way out of sorrow and danger. And they had each other.

David felt a close bond with Liv from early on as she'd listen quietly to his stories from the camps. She had this weird interest in trying to visit a refugee camp in person, to experience it even for a few days, as though she wanted to travel back in time and experience his life with him. While he wasn't overly fond of foreign do-gooders in the camps – some had a backstory that explained what was in it for them – he did not judge Liv harshly. He knew her desire to feel as a refugee did come from a genuine interest in empathizing. She'd always been exceptionally kind to him. Early on he'd imbued her with angelic qualities of care and compassion.

Liv saw him first, her heart speeding up. He'd just come from work and was still in professional clothes – had she ever seen him before like that? Maybe. But tonight, with his creased black slacks, dark purple long-sleeved shirt with the cuffs rolled up, his confident gait as he walked toward their table, it all combined to make him appear as an international globe-trotting professional. Actually, she thought, that's what he was now. He was grinning, his white teeth illuminating one of the blackest faces you'd find in the world. His perfectly oval head was topped by a cap of hair, and all his features were in perfect balance with each other. His forehead was wide and smooth, free of the ritualistic scars that would have been made, had his adolescent journey not been interrupted by the genocidal violence inflicted on his life. Once Liv's mother saw him at a refugee fundraising event and said he reminded her of a black Harry Belafonte, which made everyone screw up their faces at her, as she lamely tried to explain, "Yes, I know, but Belafonte looks mulatto compared to David." Not her mother's finest moment.

Jonathan rose, looking rounder, flabbier, and more jocular. His eyes sparkled at seeing his friend, while David's only ever got as far as conveying sober humor. They grabbed hands and slapped each other on their backs. "Hey Bro! Man, aren't you looking sharp!"

The guys were all laughs. David looked Jonathan up and down in a pronounced manner. "You need to clean up your act, Jonny," with reference to the latter's cut-offs.

"Hey, you work in a store with my clientele, you need to be a man of the people, not some high-brow type."

David turned toward Liv who was next to him. "And you, my angel, aren't you looking fine, really fine! You get prettier all the time."

Liv couldn't help but feel special around him: always he called her his angel. That had started all the way back at the beginning as they learned more English. They'd shown up in the resettlement office and told her that they decided in class that she was an angel. She'd been quizzical, so David explained. "You met us at the airport. You brought us here. You taught us how to use the stove. You got us things we needed. You are our special angel!"

That was sweet, but it got funnier the first time she'd taken them with her to meet Elyse. When she heard them say that Liv was their angel, she looked at them with hands on her hips. "So, what does that make me, the devil?" That made them howl, even though Elyse didn't think it was THAT funny. But always then, they were the angel and the devil. "So..." came her voice, as she pointed to herself, "...and me, where's my greeting?"

David spoke first: "And you...you be the devil woman!"

By the time they got their first beers, toasted "Jonny's

Spot," and put in their orders for African food on Jonathan's advice - "The other stuff is frozen, the cook's African" - Elyse launched the conversation aiming it at David. "Cory tells me you're almost done with law school. That's so amazing."

"Yes, it's very hard to believe that I've come this far, even for me who studied all those long hours."

Liv loved hearing his smooth voice and the proper articulation that formed his words, so school-learned. "You've worked so hard. Always. And your parents must have had some great genes in the verbal skill area. Remember, you told me once what a good storyteller your mom was. She'd be so proud of you David." Liv realized a little late that perhaps her remark would make him sad.

But instead he found the recognition supportive. "I know. I think about it a lot. I've decided that when I'm finished, the first thing I want to do is to get back to Sudan, maybe try Chad, and see what I can learn about her and my sister."

"I thought the International Red Cross already tried to find her?"

"They searched the camp lists as best they could from the late eighties into the nineties, but my mother may have moved on, settled someplace new, come back to South Sudan, who knows. And Amer may have married."

"How could you ever find her trail? It's so old. I don't mean to be pessimistic but...and meanwhile isn't it still dangerous?"

David looked down, and then back at her. "It's a very long shot. But everything about my life has been that way. Anyway, I don't want to be moving around just on my own. I'm trying to go and have a job. My international law professor has been very helpful. He sees a lot of different angles to this."

"Like what?"

"Like whether I could get a job with the UN or the International Court as a beginning investigator of war crimes in the area. How best to connect with the politics in South Sudan now, with people trying to form their own government for South Sudan. Whether there's something I could do with one of the international aid groups there. It's complicated by all the tribal issues between the Dinka and the Nuer. And then the Darfur horrors continue to make it dangerous."

"We were talking about that. Doesn't that make traveling around looking for your family pretty dangerous?"

"It could be. I'll just have to evaluate the situation once I'm in that area."

Liv flinched internally with the thought of David in danger again. No one would choose David's life story, but his ability to rise and reclaim himself was so magnificent. What a giant of a man. And what a tiny bird she was, perching on his shoulder and wishing he'd take her along for the ride. In the next breath, her mind slipped into the familiar territory of diminishment, once again recognizing that her life would never have the global flavor, adventure, or challenges she'd hoped to have years ago. No, she'd made her bed so to speak in keeping Shakti, and had to be content with her role and work as a supportive, kind counselor and problem-solver, who helped incredible people learn to turn on stoves and access systems in the US, and find work; or more recently, how to start a business making sauces or cleaning house.

While Liv sank into reflection, Elyse kept the conversation going about the timing for David's departure, eventually switching the topic to her wedding. "You guys need to bring dates okay? The music will be really fun – do you remember your salsa steps?" The guys sat back in their chairs and smiled. "So, who are you going to bring to my wedding?"

Jonathan smiled coyly. "Well, if you must know I may be approaching a wedding date myself!"

"You're kidding! Who is she?"

"She's from Ethiopia, a really good cook. Evelyn is her name."

David chimed in, "She is so lovely too, and really a nice, nice girl. As well as a divine cook - she could charm the gods with her cooking!"

"And what about you, David?" Whom will you bring?"

"I don't know. I haven't thought about it."

Liv felt relieved on two counts. If she didn't have a date, at least she might have a good friend to hang with. And her crush on David got a shot of fresh energy as his answer implied that he'd continued his well-known focus on school and not made time for anyone. Not that her crush had ever became actionable. Early on Elyse and she made a pact, the 'code' they called it, which they'd never broken: we do not get involved with any of Liv's 'clients.' There had been the lost boys, the Meskhetian Turks, and an endless stream of Somalis. But once, when Elyse started flirting with a Sudanese guy, Liv spoke to her afterwards about how every person coming through the Rescue Committee was damaged. And that neither one of them should deal lightly with that situation. For sure, her clients needed friendly supporters, sisterly kindness, even motherly love, but they did not need flirty American girls delivering mixed messages or playing games with them as they moved uncertainly into and through a myriad of new customs. Hence, the pact: Liv's clients were out of bounds. That had worked well, creating an ennobling glow to their outreach efforts, warming their hearts, and making them both feel that in small ways they made the global diaspora just a little more bearable for a few people.

"Why don't you give Selena a call and come with her? Last we spoke, she wasn't sure if she'd bring a date."

"Yeah, okay. I think I have her phone number. I should catch up with her anyway."

No sooner had Liv spoken, then she regretted it: why shouldn't I seize the opportunity and ask David myself? *The pact no longer applies. He's no longer a refugee to be protected, he's an independent success story.* She felt irked that she still had to focus on asking Eric. Eric who was fun but who left her hungry for a mind. Damn, she felt she'd missed a chance to be with David in a different way. *Except he's leaving for God knows how long, so what would be the point of that? No point.*

Over a satisfying dinner, they all enjoyed each other's company until Liv noticed how late it was. "We should go." As they parted company outside the restaurant, Liv lingered an extra minute near David. "I'm so happy for what you've accomplished. But slightly worried about you going off. You'll stay in touch, won't you? Let me know when you're going."

"I will." David looked down at her face, his eyes more serious.

Liv looked up, surprised by a gaze that drilled into her soul. "What?"

"Don't worry. I won't leave without your angel blessing. I'll want that for my next thousand miles in Africa."

Liv didn't break eye contact, as though a message was being sent, one that moved her, excited her. Scared her. She leaned into his mid-chest, a full head shorter than him, and gave her habitual sisterly hug. "Okay, I'll hold you to that."

In the car going home, Elyse rattled on, then grew quiet.

Darkness concealed a sadness passing across Liv's face. She said as matter-of-factly as she could, "David looked at me in a way I don't understand. Does he think he's going back into danger and might be killed or something? It was like a veil was pulled aside, a shield removed, as though I was really seeing inside him in a way I never have before. Don't laugh… but it was like catching a glimpse of his soul."

Elyse was quiet. "Liv, don't you know? Honestly, don't you get it?"

"Get what?"

"That's not the first time he's looked at you like that." Elyse was debating what to say. *What's the point?* David had always been clear he was only available for friendship, work, and school. And now he was leaving. But maybe that made it a good time to speak the truth as the pact reached its sunset. "Look, the guy's always had a crush on you, from the first. I've seen it times when you didn't notice. But we had the pact and that made sense. And basically, the man is not available."

Liv, alert, lips parted as though awaiting an inner vibration to release, turned to look at Elyse's profile. "I didn't know."

"Well, now you do. And if nothing else, the next time you're glum about nobody wanting you, take some comfort in knowing that a really amazing human being cares a lot for you."

Liv's eyes became watery. "Thank you. I guess." In a silent ten minutes that had little precedent in their relationship, they arrived at Liv's car where she'd parked it near Elyse's apartment. Liv got out, but then turned back and bent down to look at her friend. "What do I do now?"

"You do exactly what you planned to do. You ask Eric to be your date to my wedding." Elyse bent sideways towards the door looking up at Liv. "And maybe it's time you got more intimate with him…" emphasis was added by a wicked smile, "…and figure out if there's something real there with a person who has no plans to leave Seattle."

Liv just looked at her. "Yeah. Bye."

Sunday, July 29

Over two weeks into the sailing trip, Eric was continuing to experience an uncomfortable reversal of north/south roles. The superyacht's passengers included Deepak, his traditional and pleasant wife Mehta, and their eighteen-year-old daughter Lakshmi. She'd caught Eric's eye as soon as she boarded and flashed him a smile. Oh, oh, he'd thought, here comes trouble. Deepak's business colleague and his Indian wife, flaunting enough jewelry to buy another small yacht, also boarded in Seattle. The crew included the Captain, Lars, an old Seattle hand with over thirty years' experience in these waters. He served under a regular contract with the owner to maintain and sail the yacht. So far, Lars had sailed it with a small crew to Hawaii and Tahiti. There were plans for trips to the Mediterranean and perhaps South Africa. Lars, having become acquainted with Eric's skill set during prior repair jobs, was pleased he was joining them for this trip, calling him 'our insurance policy.' There was also an all-around assistant for Deepak who appeared to handle business-related matters for him and his colleague, taking notes at regular early morning meetings in the cabin, and executing a variety of management tasks related to the cyber-security anti-terrorism company they ran. There was also a chef, Maurice, and a laborer, Al, who helped with the meal prep behind the scenes, made beds, cleaned bathrooms, and did anything else he was told to do.

Following their first half-day sail and night spent moored in Victoria Harbor, they were joined by Deepak's brother Raj who'd flown into Vancouver on a private jet to join them. Raj was the east coast partner in the business and gave off an air of superiority that immediately ticked off Eric. Deepak and the others were courteous to the staff which cultivated a comradery, like hey, we're all people and we all have different jobs to do. But Raj was the polar opposite. He'd directed Eric to carry on substantial luggage without even greeting him as a crew member. It wasn't just Eric either. Lars had sailed with Raj on board before and gave advice to the rest of the crew that morning in the mess. "He's an extremely important guy, he's Deepak's brother, and no matter how rude the guy is, just keep your cool."

And then there was Raj's wife, Linda. Very American Linda, who obviously was the thirtyish trophy wife to the fifty-five-year-old, paunch-bellied Raj. When Eric was bringing her bags on board, she watched his every move. Now he really knew trouble was on board.

The last two weeks had gone well enough though. Decent weather. No major repair issues that Eric couldn't handle, which brought kudos from Lars and Deepak. And some excellent opportunities to learn more from Lars about the best in yachting technology. As Eric had assessed from the get-go, the daughter kept trying to attract him. As they'd stop in shallow bays, like that detour to Princess Louisa Inlet on the other shore to take a swim, she'd inevitably find some reason to bring her bikini-clad body across Eric's path. Always that Lolita look with the lowered sunglasses. But he knew how to both be pleasant with her superficially, while frustrating her obviously calculated moves. He didn't need or want trouble from her.

The real problem for him was Raj. Not many days into the trip, Eric was chewing on the situation he found himself in. The rich guys in charge were all Indians, 'colored' his dad would have called them, and the crew, 'servants' was the word coming up for Eric, were white. Without being able to articulate it that well, Eric was sensing that his world had gone topsy-turvy. Raj was always ordering Al around, with his 'bring me that drink, get me a snack.' And never a thank you. He never acknowledged the amazing culinary feats of Maurice. And Eric? Well, Eric was invisible. He didn't exist in Raj's world. Eric had never experienced such non-personhood in a group of men before.

Which was why the really big trouble came in the form of Linda, her hot body, and insinuating looks. He knew the first night when she passed him on her way to dinner in the cabin, that she was gunning for him. She made sure he had to pause to go around her size D breasts and take in her seductive scent, her dark eyes probing his, the inviting smile. She never spoke to him, not that first week. But her interest was clear.

Eric was not about to get fired in the middle of nowhere. But he knew he wanted to fuck her hard to let that Raj son-of-a-bitch know that money wasn't everything. At night in his bunk below the level of the guests' hotel-like cabins, he'd feel his anger against Raj and want to penetrate Linda and release it in her. When he tried to take his mind off them, he'd return to nagging questions about this artificial world he was stuck in, with the dark guys on top and the white guys below deck. When his thoughts turned to Liv, he wondered who the father of her child was. He imagined how Liv had likely met a hi-tech guy in Seattle who'd then gone home to India to an arranged marriage. Why hadn't she just gotten an abortion, why let herself get stuck with a kid, and a dark one at that? He couldn't make sense of it.

At times, he'd get categorical about it: I'm never going to get myself in this situation again with these Indian Sambos. And why would he get involved with Liv who had Shakti in tow? Shakti. What kind of name was that anyway? Not that Liv wasn't sweet. He liked her well enough, how it felt being around her, like he was in charge and had a talent for bringing her out of her doldrums. But the kid? Now that he'd been with these Indians, the whole Liv situation conflated into a much larger muck of racial prejudice that lived inside him.

Last night, they'd crossed over the Straits of Juan de Fuca and anchored off Dungeness Spit. Five miles of sand spit where on a hot day a few even braved the waters. Nice area. Eric motored one group ashore for a picnic while Al handled the others in the second zodiac. Eric waited to see who was in which craft before he avoided the one with Raj. He was relieved to get back for lunch and have time to lay out on the boat for a few hours without any of the Indians. He'd just pretend for a couple of hours this baby was his. Even the captain was going ashore with Maurice and Al to help with the four-course picnic. With all the back and forth, Eric hadn't noticed that Linda had stayed on board until he heard her voice above him, as he lay prone on the deck chair.

"Hi, good looking."

As he shielded his eyes to open them into the sun, there she was above him, black shades, big hat, skimpy black bikini, bulging breasts. He rose slowly. "Can I row you over to the picnic?"

She threw her head back and laughed. "God, no way do I want to deal with all that sand. I'd much rather be on the boat."

"Don't you want to eat?"

"No, I've been eating too much. I need to watch my figure." She paused, putting her hand on her hip, turning one knee out, and lifting her chest. "Do you like my figure?"

He hated that she was playing with him. Next thing she'd coax an erection out of him. Good thing he had baggy trunks on. He knew he needed to ignore her comment. "Well, I can get you a drink if you need one."

"Sure, find me a diet coke. With ice and a squeeze of lime."

As he walked toward the mess, he was relieved to get away from her. But by the time he returned, having taken as long as he could, she'd come down a deck, positioned herself lying tummy down, bikini strap unhooked, and the bottom hitched up like a thong.

Shit. "Okay here you go. Let me know if I can do anything else. I'm just going to go up to the bridge and check a few things."

She turned slightly on her side, revealing a substantial part of her breast, and gave him a 'come hither' look.

He turned and climbed the ladder up to the cabin at the very top of the yacht. *Damn. Unbelievable.* He knew all the reasons he needed to keep his cool. Heck, if he made the wrong move, he'd lose his job. No way.

A half hour later, just as he was starting to snooze on the leather padded bench in the cabin, he heard her again. Closer. *Maybe she'll leave me alone if she sees me sleeping.*

"Hey, are you sleeping?" She was right there at the opening to the bridge.

Eric opened his eyes. "Not anymore." He swiveled up to face her.

She moved into the space pretending to look at the instrument panel and then turned. "I'm tired of playing games with you. We probably have another hour before they're back."

He pretended to look puzzled, anxiety rising, like he was being attacked, and it was time for fight or flight.

"You know what I mean." Her face looked different, rid of flirtatious smiles and insinuating eyes. "Look, you can keep ignoring me and when Raj comes back I'll tell him you made unwanted advances…" and now she smiled again in a menacing way, "…or you can give me what I want, and Raj will never know. What's it going to be?" With that she came towards him, stood in front of him where he was seated, reached behind her and undid her bikini strap, letting her top fall.

Eric rose, raw emotion flooding him. Later, he'd recall it as the angriest moment in his life. Ever. He looked straight at her.

Had it not been exactly what Linda wanted, what followed had the force and logistics of a rape. He did everything he knew how to do to her aside from outright hitting her. No orifice ignored, positions rapidly altered in muscular moves, no plump, tender surfaces ungrasped. When he was done, he shoved her on the leather bench, while he slid down to sit on the wood-planked floor. Both were breathing hard. He turned and saw a bruise on her arm and another near her hip. "How are you going to hide that?"

She looked down at her body. "I have my ways." As he raised his eyes, he felt hers trying to lock on to him. No way. He lifted himself up, pulled up his trunks and left her lying there. Turning towards her to lower himself down the steps, he stared at her. "You'd better not breathe a word of this to your husband, or I swear I'll drown you."

Her lips parted and something like a cackle came out. "Don't worry, Mr. Viking. I got what I needed. And who knows what could happen on our next trip together."

He wanted to lunge back and punch her. Instead, he jumped backwards down to the next level and took a dive into the frigid sea. When he immediately got out, he headed for the shower below to pull himself together. In short order, he got in the zodiac and motored to shore. Fast. He needed to work the adrenalin out of his system. He slowed near shore, waved to the group, and seeing they weren't ready to leave yet, just anchored the boat. He felt violated, despite having indulged in aggressive manhandling. His mind was going in circles. He hated everything about what had happened, most of all her. He hated the sense of being forced to perform. He hated the violence he had felt moving through him into her. He hated her husband's power that had maneuvered Eric into thinking he had no choices but those she gave him.

The rest of that day he kept waiting to be confronted. Instead, when he found himself alone with Lars at night taking in the stars, his soft voice spoke firmly. "You're not the first, and you won't be the last." Eric swiveled quickly to look at Lars. "It's really the only part of the job I can't stand, the time when those two are around."

"So, nobody's going to come down on me?"
"Nope. That's not what she wants."

Eric felt tension start to leave his body. He stretched out his arms and legs. "Thanks."

Lars laughed. "Been there. Done that. That's why I always like to have some new blood on board when she's going to be around."

Shock registered in Eric's eyes, while dismay played on his lips. "God, it makes me feel like some black on a plantation. Like a hired slave."

Lars rose and looked down at him, still with humor in his eyes. "You'll get over it." With that he went below.

Thursday August 2

A few days later, after another stop in Victoria, they were back docking at Shilshole. Deepak called all the crew up and out to the sun deck. Raj was standing there. "As some of you know, my brother likes to give the tip for all your great efforts." With that, Raj gave Deepak a set of envelopes that he handed out, smiling and genuinely expressing his thanks for a smooth, enjoyable trip.

Once Eric was in the parking lot with Al, they opened their envelopes. "Nice, very nice," was Al's reaction to his $500 tip.

Eric looked at his check. A thousand bucks. He considered tearing it up, but shoved it in his jean pocket instead. All he could think was that he hated Indians. He hated these rich sons-of-a-bitches with all their money and yachts and trophy wives. He still felt dirty from the experience.

Ryan had dropped him off at the outset, and said he'd pick him up, so Eric called over to the shop. It was almost noon. "Hey, I'm back. Can you come now?"

"Sure, give me twenty or so."

When Ryan arrived, he was all smiles. "Got a call from Deepak thanking us. Really pleased with the way things went. Congratulations!"

Eric's look turned sour. "I'll never be doing that again."

"Hey, what happened? I imagined you having a decent time of it, seeing the island. Lars is a great guy. Deepak's nice. Fun to be on a yacht?"

Eric debated what to say as Ryan decided they should grab seafood for lunch at one of the cheaper restaurants out this way. His choice was one with an outdoor picnic table at a place where the locks opened to the bay. "C'mon Eric, open up. Why was this a bad deal for you? I should know."

That was enough of a push for Eric to begin to vent. "You're right, there was a lot that made it a decent gig. But have you ever met Deepak's brother, Raj? From back east?"

"Oh Raj. Yeah. Well, I just met him once on the dock, last year I guess. Not a simpatico guy, if that's what you're getting at."

"The guy is like a slave owner. Everybody's waiting on him. And did you meet his wife? Anyway, we're all invisible to the guy and he throws that paunch of his around – and those gold chains always hanging - and then at the end, he, well not he, Deepak, hands out these checks from him. Deepak probably did it because Big Mr. Raj didn't even know our names. God, I hated being on that boat with him!"

Ryan listened intently watching Eric's expressions. "Sorry. I didn't know."

Eric wanted to tell someone about Linda too, but he didn't dare let Ryan in on what happened. "Yeah, and his wife's a real piece of work too. I would never go on a gig with them again." Eric was warming up to getting things off his chest. "And honestly, I just came away not wanting to have anything more to do with these rich, hi-tech Sambos." Ryan was quiet. Eric ordered another beer. The sun was beating down. "How's the business been?"

"Good, really good. Our fill-in mechanic made me want you back though."

Eric appreciated hearing that. He was well into his second beer and beginning to relax for the first time in days. Away from those Indians. Away from women parading their bodies. Away from the excesses of wealth. Out at a good old picnic table picking away at Dungeness crabs. His boss liked him. And Eric was getting a chance to vent. "Hey, how's the family? How's Liv?"

Ryan smiled, aware of the slowly brewing relationship between the two. But he was clear: it bore no relationship to work or business. He could easily imagine Eric or Liv deciding it was a no-go. No side-taking for sure. But Ryan knew Mimi would continue her matchmaking and wanted his help at times. "Family's fine. Hey, we're going for Sea Fair Sunday on the boat – want to join us? It's not the yacht of course," he chuckled. "Look, here come the Blue Angels now to practice!" Suddenly their ears were deafened as the jets flew over on their way down from Whidbey Island for the afternoon practice session. They looked up and could see the markings on the planes. "I even saw the pilot's face one time. God, they're awesome."

It was dawning on Eric now that he had Liv to deal with. It befuddled him, the whole Shakti thing, especially now that he hated Indians. "Can I ask you something about your sister without being out-of-line? I mean, I like her, she's a nice girl – woman. But I don't get her and Shakti. How did she become a mom to a part-Indian girl? If it's none of my business, just say so."

Ryan's first reaction was, "You should ask her." He deliberated. "It's not like any of us know too much about it anyway."

"Was it some hi-tech guy here in Seattle who's since gone back to India? She told me he's out of the picture."

"No, it didn't happen that way. She went to India for a couple of months her senior year in college. And she came back pregnant. The father might not even know, I don't know what the status of that is. Mimi might know."

"Didn't she consider having an abortion?"

Ryan was not about to get into their family saga. "Let's just say she thought about it and about giving the baby up. And obviously didn't." Ryan debated adding more but felt protective of Liv's choices. "And let's also just say that everyone in the family supported her choices." Ryan took a final swig of his beer and set the bottle down firmly. "Let's go. I think you deserve the rest of the afternoon off. I'll drop you at your place."

As Eric opened the truck door and stepped down to his driveway, he turned and leaned back into the cab. "The Sunday thing, what time are you taking off?"

"It gets crowded out there. We'll shoot for nine at the latest. See you then. You know where the boat is."

"Yep. Thanks."

The prior week's perturbation around David had dissipated rather quickly given the undeniable reality of his leaving later in the year, and the inner assessment patterned in her brain that it was a hopeless cause. The three weeks while Eric was away were full and satisfying for Liv. The weekend routine of providing caregiver relief for her mom and Aunt El was bringing her into the fore of her family's life, not as the disappointing daughter she knew she'd been with her unwanted pregnancy, but now as a reliable source of family support. Not only was she 'on duty' as her mom was starting to call it, but Liv actually brought good energy with her into the home: ready to listen to Grandma's old stories as she might rally to tell them, or to willingly sit with her to watch a chic flic, holding her hand. Then, as Grandma tired and returned to bed to sleep, Liv spent time in the living room with Grandpa watching the History channel or war flics, sometimes turning the TV off to just sit and talk, and slip sideways into how he was coping with the days that dragged and the petty annoyances of sharing a home. Liv of course always brought Shakti and sometimes Little Jeff, a pairing which brought steady amusement and new tales to share of misdeeds and endearing remarks from the mouths of children. Liv even managed a heart-to-heart each weekend with her mom about her progress in dealing with the stress of balancing her parents' needs against the unflagging demands of work - while pre-processing her grief as Katherine tended to do.

 At work, the microcredit class was concluding its sessions on business regulations, financial accounting, and marketing. Liv sat in on every class the first time around, so she could assess the value of the program. A truly upbeat experience unfolded, as she observed the fifteen women in the class struggle and help each other with the complexities of running a small business. Liv pronounced the program successful to her work colleagues in staff meetings. She was planning the graduation celebration in a way that would enable the Center to tout the women's accomplishments in its materials. Photos of smiling grads with their product and service marketing materials, along with quotes expressing gratitude, would be useful to fundraisers seeking potential donors. Pete, the founder of Washington CASH, was also pleased with this batch of fledgling business women and anxious to increase funding so they could do this program quarterly. Liv was clearly the owner of the program for the Center, having helped birth it; she felt immensely satisfied.

 She was learning the value of personal story in capturing attention for a program. Two of the class participants, Michelle and Leslie, agreed to be interviewed and have their photos taken. Liv was schooled in how this could contribute to a more compelling article in the Center's publications, providing subjective feedback in addition to more objective measures of the program's performance.

 Michelle managed to show up before class this week to have the interview, arranging for her mom to come early for babysitting. Her business was home-made barbeque sauces that had been in her family for generations. She'd loved the marketing session of the class that engaged her in thinking about all the historical, local, and health aspects of her product. Creating the logo and label brought intense concentration on applying the marketing advice they'd received - followed by gleeful outbursts during the breaks as she shared ideas with her new colleagues. During the interview, Liv got into the depth of family history in the sauces and the pride in Michelle's family about her going forward with a product for the local markets. Her aunt and mom were going to help run the kitchen, mass producing the sauces, while one of her cousins was totally into producing the labels for the jars. "This program has been really great, affecting my whole family. Some of it, like the accounting parts have been new to me..." Michelle's regular job was cleaning toilets in big downtown office buildings "...but I honestly think I can do this. I can make myself into a business woman and change the future for my kids."

Liv had her pull out some of her kids' school shots from her wallet and lay them out on the classroom table. "Wouldn't it really be amazing, Michelle, if that happens? How your children would think about what they could become, following in your footsteps? There's so much good that can come from this program, don't you think?"

"I do, I really do, especially now that I know some of the other women in the program, and what their hopes and dreams are." Michelle leaned forward across the table. "You've been doing all the interviewing, but I've got a question for you."

"What's that?"

"Well, don't take this wrong, but you look like a girl who's had things pretty good all your life. Why are you hanging out here at this Center with all of us? I mean I get it when the staff is former clients, which works well. But why are you here? There are plenty of other jobs you could have. You have a full college education, right?"

"Yes, that's right."

"I don't mean to be overly personal, but like I said, I'm just wondering."

Liv hadn't really thought about it in a long time. It went back to high school when she started learning about all the incredibly difficult ways other people had to live. "Hard to say. Once I woke up to my own sheltered bubble and began to learn what other people go through...there was no going back, I guess. I couldn't live with myself if I wasn't trying to make things a little better for a few people."

Michelle sat back again. "That's nice. Real nice." By now other women were arriving for the class and shouting their hellos to Michelle. She moved to get up and greet them, and then swiveled back. "You're a do-gooder, that's what you are. My family makes fun of do-gooders – but next time they do, I'll tell them about you, that I know one who means it." And then she blended into the noisy group, leaving Liv with the sense that she'd had both a poke in her ribs and a pat on her back.

Later it made Liv wonder yet again about more schooling for herself. She'd seen an article a while back that was critical of people in well-paying jobs managing poverty programs. The point being, why not just give the money directly to those who need it, and not support a whole nonprofit management industry. That perspective disconcerted Liv, as she contemplated growing in the profession. Both the Marketing and Communications Master's at UW, and the Nonprofit Leadership certificate program at Seattle U, had accepted her. But she was clearer now about putting off starting anything until next year, a euphemism for waiting until after Grandma died. If Liv wanted, she could start the cheaper alternative at UW in January, but entry to the Seattle U cohort program would have to be postponed a full year.

She was leaning towards marketing and communications for another reason: her interest was being sparked by news accounts of social entrepreneurs. Might that be a pathway towards something truly groundbreaking? The idea of creating an innovative business that created some jobs for people while solving a social problem appealed to her. Although Elyse accused her of ignoring the fact that none of the microcredit training elicited any desire in Liv to start her own business, and 'since when had she come up with any innovative ideas?' Liv reflected that maybe she needed to consider further schooling more deeply: whom was she trying to serve? And could she do it more effectively in the nonprofit sector or in a socially oriented business? Or was there a both/and approach?

Sunday August 5

As Liv rode in Ryan's car to the Sea Fair boat excursion that Sunday, her thoughts placed her at the top of her game: I'm a good mom with an adorable daughter. I'm embedded totally in my family and I'm helping others with my own good work. Life is full of possibilities. And today she'd be picking up the thread with Eric. She'd imagined that next kiss, how it might happen, and what might follow. Her bloom was fresh. And it was time to move on the wedding invitation, since the event was only five weeks away.

Ryan stopped for morning coffees and Liv picked up one for Eric. She'd put on her peach one-piece, high-cut leg, scoop-necked swimsuit, covered by black running shorts, plus a flowy long-sleeved shirt if she needed sun protection. Plenty of sunscreen on hand too, as well as her big brimmed floppy hat. Shakti looked adorable in her pink bikini. What was not to love about them?

When they arrived, Eric was on the dock, standing there staring out at the boat, wondering why he hadn't called Ryan and begged off. Especially now that he was almost done with the wall painting. He just wanted to finish that and relax. When he painted yesterday to loud metal music, he'd gotten away from the haunting images of what happened with Linda on the yacht. Sometimes he loathed himself for letting go the way he had – he'd never been so violent before in handling a woman. Sure, there had been times in Alaska when he'd gotten a little rough with native girls. But hadn't it been what they wanted? The episode with Linda though made him ashamed of himself, like he'd raped her. Other times, as he replayed her words and saw the attitude on her face, he felt taken advantage of, used to satisfy her need, not his. Almost as if he'd been the victim. The contrary views of the incident generated opposing emotions that in their complexity were beyond his capacity to resolve. They kept circling and bumping into each other until he just wanted to screw his head off and put it on a shelf. Threading through, into, and around this upsetting confusion of judgments generating shame and anger, were images of the yacht, and the others, most of all Raj. He wanted to wipe himself clean of this slime, or punch him in his fat gut, and never think again about the rich bastard. But Raj and Deepak were hard to get rid of, as Eric felt the need to address new doubts nagging him: the fear that hi-tech was where it's at, that he, Eric, was being left behind, a lousy mechanic making peanuts. *You're thirty years old and where are you headed?*

He really should have cancelled. Now he had to spend yet another day on the water wondering how he fit in. He couldn't recall what he'd liked about Liv. And then there was her Indian kid.

Eric watched them all tumbling out of Ryan's SUV, each carrying and hugging all manner of baskets to make the day's outing more complete. He walked over to them, and Liv handed him a cup of coffee with a big smile emerging from under her charming hat. She could tell he was under a cloud. "Hey, cheer up! You're among friends."

Eric focused on her, not ready to smile yet. "Sorry, had a rough night and not awake yet. Thanks for the coffee, it'll help."

Rough night translated to Liv as something with his girlfriend. After all, he hadn't seen her either in at least three weeks. But maybe a rough night opened potential for her?

In fact, Eric had arrived home to several messages on his answering machine. He'd purposely left his cell at home during the gig. "Hey Eric. It's me. Call me when you're back." "Eric, hi, Kirsten here. I'm going to this Sea Fair party – why don't you join me." The thought of Kirsten had no appeal. He hadn't called her back, resurrecting his past reasons about the need to break things off. And, while unacknowledged, there was this subliminal lack of desire not only for Kirsten, but for any woman.

Once they all boarded the boat, stowed most of the food except for bagels and fruit, and got the kids into life vests, Eric helped push off as Ryan engaged the motor. They were headed over to anchor off a private housing beach area, Laurelhurst, where Ryan had a client throwing a party on his boat. While they didn't tie up together, as a homeowner the client gave permission for Ryan's family to use the beach area.

Mimi and Liv were happy not to be tied up to the log boom for the hydroplane race as they used to do in years gone by. What a scene! Too much drinking. Too loud. Fun of course to be right under the main flyway of the Blue Angels for their performance over the race area, but it was just too crazy.

Shakti was anxious to get to the beach. Too confined in the life vest, she was excited to use the new blue pail and shovel beach kit Grandma had given her. She was determined to build a castle. Mimi and Liv figured best to wear the kids out in the morning, have lunch and watch the planes, and then let them nap, at least Jeff. Liv hoped the combination of sun and sand plus a little swimming lesson from Ryan would also knock Shakti out for a while. Meanwhile, Mimi was trying to give Liv and Eric time alone.

By eleven, that happened. Eric had been politely present, but hardly himself. Liv thought it best to give him space. As she turned from waving the others off in the dinghy, he sat sprawled in one of the cockpit corner seats, eyes closed, working on a coke. She had to admit, the virility of his deep bronze tan and bleached-out hair attracted her. But he'd been off-putting, so she took the cue. "I'm going forward to stretch out and get some rays."

"Okay," came his flat voice. *Time to myself. No acting.* He'd tried to be nice to the kids. Usually he enjoyed kids for a while, but not today. Low, he felt low. And he'd been thinking as they motored over here, that with his ten years on him, Ryan had both a boat and a business. *What have I got? Well, the house. But he has one too. Damn, we're being left behind by these tech guys.*

This negative thinking was new to him. He'd never much noticed, let alone been bothered, by material wealth. He ran his hand through his hair, wanting to pull out of this mood. He stood, stretched, grabbed another coke, and went forward to where Liv was lying. "You need sunscreen on your back? It looks like you burn easily."

She opened her eyes under the visor she now had on. "I guess I better." She sat up, enthused he'd come to her. Eric slathered her back in a most polite way; yet, for her, his strong, hands on her back, creamy with lotion, were seductive. "Thanks, I can do the rest." She flipped over looking back at the beach. The lake wasn't nearly as choppy here as down by the log boom. The boat was swiveling slowly in response to light winds. "So how was your big trip? Was it great going around Vancouver Island?"

Eric flipped on his stomach, thinking, how do I change the topic? "Yeah, the best part was seeing the whole thing, experiencing the difference of the two sides of the island, one side a channel sheltered by the mountains, the other exposed to all the rough water of the sea. I love seeing the world from the water."

He paused. "Like now, there's all this life out there on land, but out here, we're removed from all that activity. It's peaceful. But the sea can be wild, like the day on the ocean side that was super windy with crazy cross-currents. Troubled seas they call it."

"Troubled seas. I like that phrase."

Good, so let's just be quiet now.

Liv was quiet but felt awkward with the silence. He didn't seem to want to talk, but she did. Couldn't he at least ask her a question? "You know, you don't seem yourself today. Is there something wrong?"

He opened his eyes and looked at her. "What do you mean?"

"There's a cloud hanging over you, pushing you down. That's not how I think of you - depressed." She smiled. "Not that I know you that well, it's just you've been so upbeat and light-hearted the other times we've been together."

He rested his chin on his arms folded on the towel in front of him. *What am I supposed to say?*

She followed up quickly. "I'm sorry if that made you uncomfortable. It's just that last time we saw each other I was the one who started to get down looking at the yacht and you brought me back to a happier spot."

"I did?" She nodded her head, thinking maybe he doesn't even remember. How could she back out of this now? But then his internal engine finally started up. "Remind me. What about the yacht was getting to you?'

"Oh, I'm just not used to the lives of the rich. I mean it's not like my folks were poor or anything close to it. They're well off, both in IT. Mom has a good management job at Microsoft and my dad's a consultant." She heard herself talking too fast and too much but didn't stop. "I think I was pretty affluent growing up. But now I work with people who are having a hard time making ends meet. And the difference, the disparity between what they have and what those people on the yacht have, I mean, it's huge." She sat up and redid her hairband. She looked so appealing trying to control the vagrant wisps of hair surrounding her face that already bore a slight sun glow.

He realized afresh just how pretty she was. "What was it I did to cheer you up?" He did remember the kiss.

"You teased me and distracted me, like I do to Shakti too. You took my mind off something depressing and helped me get back into the beach and the sunset and the sand." *And then you kissed me.*

"Thanks. Let's just say I'm not at my best today. You know, I have some of those same ideas coming off weeks with..." He stopped short of using a derogatory term for Indians. "...with that group of wealthy folks." His playfulness surfaced. "So how are you going to tease me and distract me?"

Liv sensed she'd reconnected with him. "Yeah, I guess our family boat doesn't quite cut it after what you're used to."

"No way, it's not that. I left that yacht disgusted. Your family boat is just fine."

"Well, let's enjoy it then!"

"Okay, how about you get me a beer?"

"Sure."

He pushed himself up while he watched her slim and appealingly pear-shaped body maneuver back to the cockpit. Shaking his head, he stood up and moved over to the boat's edge, then lay down to reach over the edge to get cold water to splash on his head. He was half in, half out of the boat when Liv returned. Seized by a spirit of play, she started toward him to push him in. But he rolled over, grabbed a stanchion, and laughed. "You do that, and you're going in with me." And with that the dark cloud vanished, as he righted himself, grabbing her arm. He took them both overboard so fast she didn't know what happened. The water was freezing. He bobbed up quickly, still holding her arm and pulled her close.

"I'll freeze to death!" came her sputters. She let him swim them both over to the ladder at the boat's stern. She climbed out first and began diving in beach bags for a towel, shivering and laughing with alternate breaths. He grabbed a towel too, patted himself dry, and grinned. "Now, that was fun!"

She traded accusatory remarks with him, until mollified, they sat next to each other in the cockpit and cuddled. She turned and looked at him. "You know you left town and I still owe you something."

He pretended to look serious for a moment. "Really? Now what could that be?"

She put her lips to his in a tender frosty kiss that deepened into a warmer, soothing balm.

When Mimi, Ryan and the kids returned, the spirit onboard was decidedly different than when they'd left. As Liv and

Eric busied themselves laying out the food below, Mimi and Ryan exchanged looks acknowledging the change.

They ate. And then out of the blue, startling them all, the jets buzzed them, momentarily terrifying the kids. Jeff screamed and cried, while Mimi shielded his ears. Shakti held her ears but then broke free from Liv. Back in her vest, she scrambled out towards the bow, causing Liv and Eric to follow her. She stood there watching the planes' every move. As one passed over she cried, "Mommy, Mommy, he smiled at me. I saw him!"

Liv and even Eric laughed, negative thoughts of the Indians left overboard for now. He picked Shakti up so she could be even closer. "Try to touch the wing this time."

Shakti looked him in the eye. In a surprisingly sober voice, she replied, "That wouldn't be safe." Thinking more, she touched his face, her tiny caramel fingers not too far in shade from his tan cheek. "But someday, maybe I'll fly that plane."

He liked the feel of her little body and boosted her up on his shoulder with Liv's help. "I can touch the sky! Look at me, everybody!" Indeed, anyone looking would have seen an ostensibly happy family.

When the show was over, they finished grazing on the plentiful spread. The kids both decided lying down in the V-shaped berth was fun. As Liv and Mimi packed stuff up in the galley, she quietly asked Liv if she'd invited Eric to Elyse's wedding yet.

"Hey, it took me a while just to cheer him up. Don't rush me."

By the time the kids woke up, the adults were sunned out. Mimi was ready to head home. No objections being voiced, they were back at the dock by four.

Liv caught up on Eric's progress with the painting. He invited her to come back to see it with him. She felt a tinge of sun stroke and nausea and declined, asking if it would work out for the coming Friday.

"It may be all done by then, and you'll lose your final say on the accent color."

"So be it. I just feel off now." They left it that she'd come by next Friday.

As they parted ways at the dock, he came close, touched her arm, and put his lips to her ear. "Thanks for putting the wind back in my sails."

Friday, August 10

Eric felt tense about Liv coming over. His violent encounter with Linda haunted him in a new way: that morning in bed, he imagined taking Liv in the same way. He'd had an adrenalin rush that merged into ejaculation. Later, confronting himself in the bathroom mirror, he felt scared – by himself and how he might upend his rational plan for fitting in with Ryan, his business, and his family.

While Liv drove to Eric's place to have dinner and view the results of the great painting project, her clear objective was to ask him to the wedding. She was trying to accept Elyse's advice that he presented a real possibility for something longer term, albeit one that still needed a fair amount of investigating. How did he feel about her? Could she stand to live with someone with whom she had so little in common? How did he feel about Shakti? Simultaneously, she longed in that moment to turn and go see David instead, and not 'settle for' less than what her heart craved. She was mad at herself that she only seemed to want the impossible. *Get grounded. Accept what's real.*

Ironically, it put the two of them in the same mindset as they came together: put on the best face you can and try to make the most of this. They shared a quick peck on the cheek as Liv entered. She quickly disengaged, putting down her shoulder bag to move into the full impact of the transformed space. Golden oak floors, a light feeling all over with darker accents in the rooms provided by the navy leather sofa, the wood dining set, and of course, the teal accent wall, now bearing quite a lovely large framed photo of a sailboat.

"Wow." She slowly turned in a circle. "I love it." Looking at Eric then with eager eyes, "Don't you?"

He walked toward her smiling. "Of course, I do!" He gently put his hand in the curve of her back. "And now come see this." He guided her through the kitchen out to his back deck.

She knew walking through the back door something had changed dramatically. The yard spread farther and was more open, still with light this lovely Seattle summer eve. "What? What happened?"

"With my extra money from the sailing gig, I had a crew take down that towering tree at the back that was going to fall onto my roof one of these days." He moved her around the corner of the house to see a huge stack of wood, musing about rehabilitating his defunct fireplace next. They walked to the yard's center. "Check out this rockery back here holding up my neighbor's property. I hardly knew it was there."

Liv was already envisioning the garden you could make back here, now that there might be enough sun for vegetables. And then some lovely plants between the rocks. "It's really, really nice. There's a lot you could do with this. I think it probably increases the value of this place, don't you?"

"Yeah. I'm pretty satisfied with what I've accomplished around here." He second-guessed himself about flirting, but then fell into his usual easy pattern. "Ever since I met you, my property value's gone up."

She broke into a smile. "Well, no one's ever told me I've had that effect before."

They stood continuing to look around. Liv imagined what a nice yard for children it would make. "So, what's for dinner tonight?"

"I thought we'd just go out for burgers, okay?"

"Sure." Liv wondered whether to bring up the motorcycle and decided to show her openness to it. "Are we going on the bike again?"

"Aha, I knew it! It's in your blood now."

At the pub he chose, they sat outside. Liv noticed how she was enjoying the evening, while Eric was contemplating the fact she'd worn high heels with her tight jeans and an elasticized strapless tube top under a sleeveless semi-sheer cover-up. She is definitely trying, he thought. *She wants me.* That realization brought two further unacknowledged sensibilities: one was complacency that he would get his tonight, that his easy pattern of flirtation would lead to pleasant love-making. The other was an undercoat of adrenalin, subconsciously reminiscent of this morning: I wonder how she likes it, soft with lots of foreplay, or intense and a bit rough. Kirsten had liked that. The excitement in his body arose as though a Pavlovian bell had gone off causing a hormonal response affecting his vital organs.

As their conversation moved easily from his work week back to the house, to her life with her family members, she consciously excluded references to her work unless he specifically asked, and of course offered nothing about books, world affairs, or criticisms of pop culture. As she bit into the giant greasy burger in front of her enjoying the flavor, she had it in the balcony of her mind to find the opening for the 'ask.' It arrived as she introduced Elyse into the conversation, mentioning their night out last week with some friends in a Rainier Beach dive, and how the food there just couldn't compare to these great fries.

"I never go down there. It's pretty run down."

"Oh, it's a mix. But anyway, I think you'd like my friend Elyse. She always calls a spade a spade, and she's funny. We've been friends forever, well, since freshman year in college."

"What does she do?"

"She works for a city council member, so she knows a lot about how the city works, how to get things done."

"Sounds like a good person to know."

"Funny you say that, because I'd love for you to meet her at her wedding coming up next month." There, she had it out.

Eric pulled back in his chair, tipping on its back legs, putting down the remaining bite of his burger. "So, is this you asking me out on a date to go to someone's wedding?"

Liv had to laugh. "Yes, you've caught me in the act. Look, I'm standing up for the wedding, it's going to be a great fiesta party with dancing – Elyse is Hispanic – and I need a date." *Did that come out right?*

In a way it did. Eric enjoyed the disarming honesty of it. No suck-up pretense. But he knew he could work it. "Oh, so all this be-nice-to-Eric stuff has just been a cover for getting a date to the prom. I get it. And here I thought you really dug me."

He succeeded in making her blush a bit, as she sought to protest. Except she wasn't sure what to say, because she didn't want to say she really liked him. *Do I?* At least she wouldn't say it before he did. And after all, in a way he nailed it. Nailed her. She went with the latter. "Hmm, there it is. I need a date. But I do clean up nicely..." at which point she dropped her open shirt down her shoulders, turned her head slightly, and smiled a coy smile at him. "And the dancing will be so much fun. And you don't even have to pick me up. Just show up at the Mountaineers Club on Queen Anne."

He was laughing now too. "Oh, well, let me check my social calendar." Noticing his attraction to her in that moment, he saw no reason not to. "Hey, most likely I'll go with you. After all you've increased my property value. It's the least I can do."

Their light tone continued as she shared the date and time, affirmed that Ryan, Mimi, and her parents would be there too, and kept emphasizing how much fun it would be. When the cycle pulled up his driveway, Liv wasn't sure at all what would develop next.

He put away the helmets and looked at her, standing in the driveway near her car. "Well, come on," his arm beckoning her inward. "We're not going to be the best dancers out there that night unless we practice. We might as well work on our salsa moves." With that he put his hand in hers and Liv, in her light-hearted mood now, did a sexy salsa move toward him.

Eric in fact had quite a lot of salsa music, and with some beers and chips on the tables, they began. Liv had learned at the feet of a master, that being Elyse. Eric was less adept although energetically into moving his hips and arms. Liv, knowing the moves better, coached him on a couple of trickier hammerlocks and embraces. They'd stop between songs to swig beer, and then take up again. She was imagining how well her bridesmaid dress was going to work. And once she took off her shirt fully revealing her nicely tanned shoulders, slim arms and narrow waist, Eric was imagining pulling her top down and taking her breasts in his hands.

After about a half hour of fast songs, Eric made sure a disc with a mix of slower music came up. As they danced their first slow dance, he started making his moves ever so deliberately, pulling her closer, and gripping her waist firmly.

Liv was – well – having fun. The dancing made her happy. The beers and repartee had removed thoughts of another's eyes, as she saw how her very good-looking date would be fun on the dance floor. And now the firmness of his grasp felt delicious. It had been a long time since she'd danced at all, and even longer since she felt this lit up dancing. Having a whole month before the wedding to enjoy this level of intimacy was a delicious possibility.

"You know you owe me something."

She pulled back slightly to see his teasing eyes. "Oh, that." She nested even closer, lifted her face to his, kept eye contact for a prolonged moment, and then tilted her head slightly to bring her lips to his. Ever so slowly, then ever so fully, then opening to receive his French kiss. The kiss lasted. Liv slowly pulled back, looked him in the eyes again, and said in her best Lauren Bacall deepest voice, "There, now we're even."

He pulled her back closer. "Not if I start over." It had come to him to take her on the sofa. He took her leg in one hand and she responded wrapping the other around him. He laid her down gently on the couch. Prolonged kissing led to her tube top down and his shirt off, bodies rubbing, until the awkwardness of their jeans coming down. Then reconnecting with her eyes, holding her head, he slid into her as though he belonged in her inner space. And she welcomed him, muscle embracing muscle. For Liv, it was better than she'd experienced in years, more masterful and yet more fun. For Eric, it was as natural as could be to indulge his well-worn patterns and knack for experimentation which came from years of sensitivity training with all types of women. With no awareness of it, nonetheless, there was a healing quality to their coming together that affirmed a healthy Eric, an Eric who didn't need to be rough or violent to feel good about the act. As they lay in the dark quietly afterwards, not talking as the soft music played on, he felt more content with himself, certainly since his encounter with Linda, and more at peace than he had with Kirsten.

Liv lie there. *This is real. Good.* She too felt content in the moment where 'me woman, you man' was all that mattered. *Maybe life is this simple?* But then a jarring image of David confronted her. *Don't go there.* There being a labyrinth of complexity that was confounding. *That's not real and this is.* She began to lecture herself using Elyse's voice: just because you've made your life difficult in the past, you don't have to do that again. An arrow of fear pierced her heart, fear of spending another seven years without a man in her life. She snuggled even closer to Eric.

August days

What followed was a month of ups and downs of summer love. Liv shared enough with Mimi and her mom to generate a great conspiracy of female calculations aimed at creating a free Saturday or Sunday now and then for Liv to date Eric. Ryan let them take the boat one day and spend the night over in Port Madison. Anchored away from others, they enjoyed the evening stars and rocked the boat with their love making. There were pizza and movie dates.

This time, it was Mimi and Ryan's turn for a three-day get-away to Vancouver. Katherine came over for a break herself to help with the kids, leaving Liv alone with them only that Sunday. She roped Eric in to taking them all on a Discovery Park picnic, with a partial agenda of taking in his comforts and discomforts with child care.

At first, in setting up the picnic site not far afield from the playground area, he put some effort into playing with Shakti and Jeff, chasing them, helping Jeff on the slide while she watched over Shakti on the climbing gym. But after their mid-day feeding frenzy with the overflowing picnic basket that Liv and her mom packed, and then some necessary but short-lived rests on the blankets, Shakti was ready for more. "I want to go down to the water."

Eric balked at that, knowing that it was quite a climb down, and then a challenge going back up. He tried to reason with Shakti. But she wasn't about to budge from her need for an activity. That's what they did at daycare after all, after lunch and quick naps. And it was in her head to get close to all that water they had viewed from the cliff. The adults tried waiting it out and providing distractions, but Shakti had made up her mind and turned into a rather pouty unpleasant child. So, they packed up the picnic residue in the car, and started the substantial and steep hike down the bluff. The need to help Jeff while keeping up with Shakti resulted in Eric carrying him most of the way. Which was fine, till Eric tripped on a tree root and dropped Jeff. As Liv tended to them, stopping Jeff's tears, more from surprise than injury, she looked at Eric, hoping to inject perhaps some humor and a sense of common endeavor to their hike: "And you know, we'll eventually have to come up all this." Her smile was not returned.

For Eric, the kids were okay for a while, but by now he was grumpy himself at how bossy Shakti was, and how she'd gotten her way with Liv. He wished he was on his motorcycle or sitting with a beer on his back deck listening to music and reading his new boat magazine. Liv noticed the mood change as his usual easy smile morphed into a face of resignation. While the time at the rocky water's edge was fun and engrossing for the kids, Eric wore the pout now. The long hike back up the south bluff was intimidating to her as well given his mood. "Why did you let Shakti convince you to come down here? Do you really think she's going to make it back up without me carrying her and you carrying Jeff?"

Liv was nonplussed. Then she spied the paved road coming down to the lighthouse. "How about one of us goes and gets the car and drives it down here?" Her eyes were soft and pleading, knowing she was stretching his patience and good will.

Eric considered, thinking of the climb up, and then brightened a bit. "Sure, I'll go get the car." He moved away quickly back toward the path, feeling relieved to be getting away from them. When he dropped them off eventually back at Liv's house, he turned down Liv's invitation to dinner. His quick parting conveyed exasperation.

When Mimi and Ryan returned about an hour later, and after all the catching up and putting kids to bed, Liv and Mimi sat on the upstairs deck sipping wine and looking out towards the sunset. "How did it go today with Eric being around the kids?"

"He does small doses well. He put out good energy for an hour or so. And then, it's like, 'I'm done.' So today he got aggravated with Shakti's command and control behavior."

Mimi thought to herself, yeah, well, we're all done after about an hour. But then as a parent you need to keep going. It's just the way it is. "Well, that's an issue, even for all of us. That girl is going to develop into a really difficult teen if we don't redirect her into more collaborative behaviors."

Liv took no offense. She, Mimi and Katherine had been discussing this for weeks now, and what new responses they all needed to adopt. "Right." Liv looked out at the sunset. "You know, after we got back, I started asking myself, so what is it that Shakti needs a father for at this point? Why can't Eric and I just enjoy whatever, and leave Shakti out of the equation? Really, how do you talk about what fathers do for seven-year old girls?"

Mimi was staring at Liv, feeling pressed to think about what she just took for granted. "I've had three days off, am savoring my wine, and you want me to say something profound about fatherhood?"

Liv lightened up. "Sorry." Ryan came out on the deck to join them, beer in hand. "Are we trading Eric stories?" Ryan mostly tried to stay out of their calculations and conniving. He liked Eric well enough, valuing him as an employee, even more now as Eric had ideas about expanding the business to include more technological aspects, improving their capacity on the sonar equipment side. But Eric and Liv? Ryan knew his sister well enough to know she had an intellectual depth to her that Eric could never match, and a concern for the vulnerable in her nonprofit work that Eric didn't value.

"No, we're discussing fatherhood. And Liv wants to know how a father would contribute to Shakti's upbringing at this point in time."

"Oh." Ryan had clear opinions about that, fresh from a prior weekend's babysitting with Shakti. "She needs taming."

"Taming? Are you saying my child is a wild animal?"

"No, but she has the potential to grow from a spoiled child into an unpleasant teen."

"Okay, so how would a father tame a wild girl?"

Ryan settled into a deck chair. "I can only say what I would do. She has a very strong mind and she really believes that what she wants is what has to happen. Call it bossy. That's not going to go over well as she grows up. And she's going to make chopped meat out of you," thinking better of resorting to an Indian image of crumbled tofu. "A father…" Ryan leaned forward toward Liv, "…a father in her case has to put boundaries on that, be firm in a way maybe you can't be. Mean 'no' when he says it but be willing to show her another point of view. Bring her along. Not to bring in an overused term, but she's got to learn to be a team player. I'd get her in team sports and coach her. I'd be firm but loving." Ryan paused, his advice coming as slowly as it took each star to appear while the dusk deepened into a night sky. "What's coming up for me, Liv, is that a father would be just as committed to the long-term nurturing and raising of a human being as you are. A dad would give you a partner in that very long effort. You wouldn't be alone. You'd have someone to talk with about what approach to take to issues and discipline, to everything. You're carrying a heavy load, Sis. And those teen years could be full of troubles, really a nightmare if you don't create more of what I've heard you call 'a holding container' for her."

The women were considering each phrase and not eager to interrupt this kind of guidance from Ryan. Eventually Mimi's brain kicked in. "I think it's also, like if you've got your male partner, and the girl sees how you two behave, then she has, at least potentially, a role model for how she should behave with men. Like, do you each treat each other with respect? Respect each other's feelings? I mean it doesn't even have to be a man, it could be a gay household, but I think the same applies. First the child is watching you, and the relationship between you and your partner is developing, and then the child is watching how you get on, or don't, with other people. Isn't that part of a father's contribution?"

Ryan was into this conversation, wanting Liv to realize all that his presence in Shakti's life was contributing. "There's also the self-esteem issue, a man praising her efforts, not putting her down – or her mother either, like Mimi was saying." He downed some more beer. "God, this is all so analytical! Really, isn't it just what is supposed to be, that a kid has both a mom and a dad? That's the way nature wants it."

This provoked Liv, hearing a slight to her life style. "Nature produces all types of fathers in the wild kingdom, some who stay around and some who don't. I'm just trying to focus on the specific situation I have with Shakti right now."

He glanced over at them. "Is this all about sizing up Eric as possible father material?" Ryan knew this was coming as he'd frequently overheard the women's conversations this past month geared toward giving Liv more time with Eric.

"Well, you work with the guy, what do you think about him? For that matter, me and him and Shakti?"

Ryan sat back, as though a shield came up between them. "Doesn't matter a bit what I think. You have to answer those questions."

Mimi roused herself. "What did Shakti think of Eric today? That's important. Did she say anything?"

Liv revisited internally the bedtime conversation she'd had an hour ago with Shakti. Liv had already processed over dinner how it was her own fault that she let Shakti's insistence on going down to the water override better judgment. Liv hadn't wanted to have a scene at the field, and had given in, regretting it later. Now she was dismayed with herself that she hadn't exercised appropriate firmness in Eric's company. Shakti didn't take long to steer the bedtime conversation back to the afternoon. "Mommy, is Eric a daddy possibility? Is that why we were all together on the picnic? Do you like him, Mommy?" While Liv was composing a response, Shakti didn't wait, impatient to state her views. "I don't know if I like him. At first, he was okay, sort of nice, but then he got mad at us."

"Why do you think he was mad at us?"

"Because of the way he looked at me."

"When?"

"Down on the rocks by the water. He didn't look happy. And he stared at me like he was angry."

"Well sweetie, it really wasn't such a great idea to have brought you both all the way down from the cliff to the beach. We didn't think it through very well. It would have been better to trust my first judgment on that and not go."

"But I liked it there."

"Yes, but then poor Eric had to walk all the way back to the parking lot by himself to come and get us. You wouldn't have made it up the hill on your own, you'd gotten tired, remember?"

Shakti was quiet. "You didn't answer me about whether he might be a daddy."

"I don't know. I like him and sometimes I have fun with him."

"But not today. Did I ruin it, Mommy?'

"No. It takes people time to get to know each other and see what's really good about them. If we do anything else with Eric, I want you to let me decide things, okay? And I want you to go along with what I say, no being pouty and making a scene. Because then you might see some things about Eric you like, and he'd see you being the sweet girl I know you can be."

"You love me even when I'm bad."

"Yes. But that comes later, after knowing the good."

Mimi watched Liv processing, then grew impatient. "Liv? Earth to Liv? What did Shakti say about Eric?"

"Sorry. She noticed that he was mad about the situation at the end."

"Was he?" Ryan's interest sparked, having observed Eric's rough edges on a couple of occasions.

"Yes, although understandably so." Liv explained what happened.

Ryan found he couldn't resist. "That tells you something there though. If it was me, and I was really into you – or let's say Mimi – and she was a single mom, and this is the first big time out with her and her kid, while we were out together, I would do my utmost to show I could handle whatever came up. I'd figure I'd sort it out when I was alone, think about the balance of it all, but I wouldn't do anything to alienate the kid."

"So, what are you saying, Bro – put it out there."

"I'm saying, maybe he's..." Ryan looked at Mimi at this point, then moved his gaze directly to counter Liv's piercing look, "...maybe he's not totally in love with you. Yet."

Mimi kicked him lightly. Liv looked down and then sat back again staring at the sky. "Yeah, well, that goes both ways."

Monday, September 3

Labor Day, before Elyse's 'big fiesta wedding' as they referred to it, Liv had time to get back from Redmond for a four pm meet up with Eric. She didn't like plans with him that were just about 'figuring out where to fuck' which was what Elyse called dates just for the sex of it. Liv proposed the Arboretum since she passed it every time she drove back across the 520 bridge from Redmond. Years ago, really a life time ago, she had walked there to contemplate the news that she was pregnant. She'd still been living with Devin, but had returned from her internship in India to learn she was carrying Rama's child.

Now as she drove into the parking lot by the Arboretum Center, it brought back poignant memories of herself, twenty-one and about to make hard decisions, ultimately the one to raise Shakti. Which landed her where she was, trying to assess the viability of Eric as a potential mate and father.

He was there already. She saw his motorcycle first. He'd been walking around the place which he'd never been to before, a little surprised, first at how difficult it was to go west to east in Seattle, and then how he'd gotten to be this old and never been here before. Trees and plants weren't big in his life, but as he'd driven along Lake Washington Boulevard and up through the park, he felt awed. Seeing Liv pull up, he waved across the parking lot. As she stepped out, he opened the car door farther and put his arm to her waist as he kissed her. "This place is huge. Great idea to come here." He was supremely happy it was just the two of them and that the kid was not along. After last weekend's baby-sitting gig at Discovery Park, he remembered why he was still a bachelor. With no warm, fuzzy familial memories to draw upon, coming cold at taking care of two kids initially enthused him with its playfulness, then became boring, and lastly aggravated him as Miss Bossy Pants called the shots. He'd resolved: no more kid dates. Liv was a nice enough girlfriend for now, they had a good thing going, but he knew it would end once she began to pull him towards being daddy-like.

Liv grabbed a ratty blanket in the car. "Let's walk out to Foster Island. We can be at the lake's edge there." As Eric enjoyed himself keeping up a commentary on the surroundings, Liv recalled times here with Devin, when they'd walk all the way from their apartment near Seattle U for a day of reading and playing among the thousands of trees. Devin would teach her as they walked, sharing aspects of forestry once he had his Earth Stewards job. And then there was that day she walked here by herself, a six-week old fetus inside.

"Why so quiet? I'm talking to the air."

"Sorry, I used to spend time here in college and a lot of memories are coming up."

Eric's attention perked up. He had yet to find the right time to ask her about Shakti's dad. He still wanted to know more details on what happened years ago. Not that it really mattered, he told himself. But still, he wanted to know about the Indian guy. "This may sound odd coming from me, but what are those memories? Tell me something about yourself when you were in college."

Liv turned to gauge his facial expression and decide whether he meant it. He appeared serious enough. *He wants to know more about me, which she assessed as a good thing. Maybe we could trade memories and get a little more depth in the relationship?* "Only if you tell me something back, okay?"

"Fair enough. But you go first."

Liv spied a semi-shaded place near the edge of the field to lay out the blanket. Eric brought out a bottle of cheap white wine from his backpack, along with cheese and crackers. Once settled, plastic glass in hand, Liv's eyes rested on the water and then lifted to take in the sky. She recalled her mantra from back then: *my heart is as open as the sky.* "Still want me to share?"

"Yeah, I do."

"Okay. The last time I was here, standing right over there, over six years ago, I had just learned I was pregnant. I was afraid, not knowing what to do. Elyse, my wedding friend – which by the way we should talk about logistics for the event next Saturday – anyway, Elyse had just talked to me about getting an abortion, but I wasn't at all sure I wanted that."

Although Eric already knew from Ryan that Liv had met the dad in India, he played dumb. "So, you'd met this guy here and what? You didn't really like him? You did like him?" In a smaller voice, "Were you raped?"

As Eric spoke, Liv's face took on a puzzled expression, forgetting that he didn't have all the pieces of information about her life. "Oh no, none of those things." She saw she needed to take the plunge she'd avoided with every man she'd been with since having Shakti. "I went to India on a college internship."

"How did that work?" His lack of college experience made him feel deprived for a moment. Usually his persona of good cheer and fun times masked any pain about missing out on that, but ever since being around those techies on the yacht, doubts had been coming up about his own lack of accomplishments.

"You work it out with professors to study something and write papers on your experiences as an intern, what you learned, and you get credit for it. I went for ten weeks to India to study, actually to study a lot of things about their culture and society, and how people lived."

"How do you just drop into some other place like that? I mean does somebody sponsor you? Did you know someone?"

"I knew this girl who was working for a sustainable agriculture nonprofit..." Eric's face squished up a bit showing his not being sure about what that was, "...just think organic farming – anyway, she got me the placement." Eric's quizzical look challenged Liv about how much to say. She wanted to leave the Devin piece out of all this, how Arita had been here first with Earth Stewards, and then gotten Liv into the nonprofit in Mumbai. "It's complicated. But the point is, I was there in India, in Mumbai and then in a village. And Shakti's father was a guy, a manager, at the nonprofit."

"You had a fling with him?"

Liv felt her spine prickle up as though she were a porcupine. "I never thought of it as a fling. It was just something that..." She didn't know what to say.

"That felt right?"

"That wanted to happen. That's all I want to say about it. Except I have no regrets. It was special."

Eric was seated, arms around his slightly sprawled knees, looking out at the lake. He put the plastic cup of wine to his lips wishing it was a beer instead. So, she had something special with this Indian guy. Free choice. No regrets. It bothered him that she didn't feel bad about it. The image of Raj and Linda came up. "I'm curious, was the guy wealthy?"

Liv frowned. "I have no idea. That wasn't at all part of the picture. Why do you even ask?"

"No reason really. Just trying to understand why things happen." He laid back on his elbows. "So why did you decide against an abortion? Religious reasons? Your family's Catholic?"

"No. Religion wasn't part of my decision. It really came down to..." *what do I say to this guy?* "...it came down to loving what was growing inside me. I didn't want to kill it, kill her. I mean, the result of what happened, what seemed right, was for Shakti to come into existence. Who was I to stop that?"

Weird. Who is she, that she did what she did, screwing some Indian, and then keeping the kid like the kid needed to be born? Really weird. And now the kid is spoiled and verging on obnoxious. "If that's how you felt, well, it's not that I get it. And I don't mean to make you mad, but Shakti is going to be running your life even more if you don't start getting better control over her."

What? Did he just change the subject after I bared my soul, no acknowledgement of me revealing more of my life to him? He might as well have touched a match to her. She turned away to contain herself. *Who was he to talk like that?*

They sat quietly pretending to watch a dog play fetch in front of them. Eric realized he needed to rescue the moment. "I guess it's my turn to come up with a memory now?"

Frankly, Liv could have cared less in her wounded state. "Whatever."

He reached over and pulled her down next to him. "Seven summers ago, I was up in Bristol Bay. Has your brother ever told you stories from up there?"

"A few."

"For me, that first summer, it felt as strange to be in Alaska out on fishing boats, working non-stop, as it must have felt strange to you to be in India." With that, he started to tell his favorite coming of age stories as the young kid out with older, more experienced guys who found plenty of ways to give him a hard time while also pulling him into their special community of risk-takers.

Liv shelved her disgruntlement and began to lighten up as they returned to the parking lot to head over to his place. Just then, her cell phone rang. It was Elyse, so she took it. "You're not going to believe this. Cory's had an accident. Can you come see me?"

"What kind of accident? Is he okay?"

"He's fine." Liv could hear frustration and anger in Elyse's voice which sounded at odds with the situation. "He screwed up while repelling down some fucking cliff and hurt his leg. When can you come?"

Liv looked at Eric. She found she had little interest in going to his place. "Given what you're saying, I'll come now." She watched Eric's face drop and his body turn away in exasperation.

"Thanks."

"Eric, that was Elyse. Cory, the guy she's marrying next week, has been injured. I need to go see her. I'm really sorry."

Eric turned back to face her. "What happened to him?"

"Something about falling from a cliff."

"Man! Okay. Yeah sure. Give me a call when you get home and let me know."

"Thanks for understanding." She put her hands on his face and gave him a perfunctory kiss.

When Elyse opened the door, her red nose and smeared make-up confirmed a grim situation.

"Tell me. Let's sit down. Tell me what's happened to Cory."

Elyse didn't feel like sitting down at all. Her body was holding and then setting free nervous energy as she spoke. "This is sooo stupid. I can't believe this happened."

"What? Just tell me the basics."

Elyse moved from standing in front of where Liv sat in a chair, to the kitchen counter to sip water, back to the table to lean on it, spewing out the story. "The guys, the climbing crew, decided to give him a bachelor party yesterday. It involved an overnight camping trip. That's all Cory and I knew. And Steve promised me there were no women involved. They were taking him off somewhere to do something he always said he wanted to do but hadn't."

"Like what?"

"Now I know it was rappelling off the side of a cliff up near Mt. Baker. Apparently, the time they'd tried it a few years ago, Cory hadn't been with them, so he'd always lamented the fact he'd missed that trip and kept wanting them to do it again."

"Keep going, did he hurt himself rappelling?"

"Not at first. Saturday, they had a late start, so it was afternoon before they did their first rappels. They did fine. And had a blast over the campfire that night. Then they all decided to have a go at it again this morning before heading back. They were feeling their oats and getting more aggressive about it. You know how they push off and jump out from the cliff as they descend? Well, near the bottom Cory was trying for one more big push off, but then when he came back into the cliff, his foot went into a crevice and got twisted badly."

"Did he fall to the ground from there?"

"No, he held on for dear life to the rope. Those on the ground below watching his descent heard him cry out. They coached him down the last twenty feet or so."

"And now, where is he?"

"He called about an hour ago – and then I called you – from Lake Stevens Hospital, up not far from where 405 and I-5 intersect. There's something wrong with his foot or ankle. Cory hadn't wanted to get stuck in some hospital up in Bellingham or Everett. They'd driven till they saw the Lake Stevens hospital sign and he decided it was close enough and getting late, so he should go to the ER there. They're doing some X-rays and he'll call me when he knows more."

"Who's with him?"

"They had two cars that went up, but now it's just him and Steve. Steve's promised to stay with him and bring him home."

"You don't think they'll put him in the hospital overnight?"

"It doesn't sound like it. It was a slow hike out from the rock climbing area, although a short one fortunately. Cory say it's just too painful to put weight on his right foot now. He used a branch or something as a walking stick to hop out. He's hoping it's just a fracture, but it's possible the ankle is broken."

Liv visualized the situation. "He'll be okay Elyse. He's not hurt badly. I can see how upset you are, but he'll be fine."

Elyse stuck her face out in the ugly expression she made when she was most upset, mouth terse, and eyes on fire. "Liv! We're getting married next Saturday! The fiesta wedding? Dancing? And the romantic honeymoon to Hawaii where we planned swimming, walking the beach, all kinds of activities?"

Elyse crossed her arms, her eyes like slits now, and turned and stared at the wall.

"Oh God." *Would Cory even be able to walk down the aisle without crutches? Would he have a boot on? Shit.* She saw the vision of the wedding Elyse and she shared fade away. *Maybe it won't be that bad?* "Elyse, calm down. You don't know yet what condition he'll be in next Saturday. It may not be that bad, maybe just a sprain. He could be mostly over it, even completely over it by Saturday. Just wait and calm down. Focus on Cory and what he's going through."

Elyse finally sat down and put her head in her hands, smearing them down her face slowly. "You're right. I'm overreacting."

Liv leaned over and gave her a one-armed hug. "How long since he called?"

"Maybe an hour. Hour and fifteen tops."

"You know how long it takes to get out of an ER. You've probably got at least another hour before you hear anything. Grab your cell and let's go out and get some comfort food."

"I'm not hungry."

"How about a beer? Have you got some chips too?"

Liv rose and found fortifications. They didn't talk much while they munched. Elyse turned on the TV just to pass the time. By seven, Liv needed to be going. The call came then. "Where are you? And what's the diagnosis?" Liv watched Elyse's features grow sad. "When will you be back here?" Elyse took a deep breath and resignation settled on her face as though a black veil had been lowered. "Okay. Love you. Bye."

"Tell me."

"They're on their way back, not too far." Elyse tilted her head back and released a huge sigh of exasperation. "His ankle is broken, and he needs to keep weight off it for at least a couple of weeks. And he's got a boot on." Elyse looked straight at Liv. "And it's supposed to stay on for at least two weeks, maybe more."

"Shit. How did he sound?"

"He was really down. He kept saying he was sorry. His voice cracked like it does when he's really upset. He's thinking the same stuff I am about the wedding."

"I feel so bad for you guys."

Elyse was still, then stood up to gather her energy. "There's no postponing it. Place is rented. His mom and brother have airline tickets to come. We just finished paying for the trip."

"You're right, there's no sense in not going ahead." Liv debated saying more. "Maybe…maybe it's a metaphor-like thing about marriage, through sickness and health and all that."

Elyse stared at her like she was nuts.

"Do you want me to wait until he's back? Mimi was thinking she'd have to put Shakti to bed anyway, that I'd be over at Eric's."

"Sorry about that."

"No big deal. I think we may both be wondering if this little fling has any more life left in it."

"He's still coming to the wedding though?"

"Oh sure. But he begged off the rehearsal dinner like I told you already."

They each returned to their own inner dialogues, Liv wondering if she really ought to try harder, to give Eric more time. She did need help with Shakti. Elyse was contemplating why this had happened to Cory, why after all the plans she'd made, a wild move on his part had spoiled it all. "So, you think there's some life lesson I'm supposed to learn from this? From having my best laid plans punctured?"

Liv drew her own attention back to that question, feeling like she herself had been living a somewhat punctured life plan. "That's life really, isn't it? Who said, 'life is what happens when you're busy making plans?'"

"John Lennon."

"Maybe this is all about taming the inner wild thing in you? You wanting to be in control. You expecting a certain life with Cory, and him not doing everything you want, at least not all the time."

"My wedding is some lesson?"

"Or a last red flag before you go over the cliff?" Liv chirped a laugh, but then quieted her humor. "Sorry, you know I don't think of it like that."

"Want to bet that's what the climbing crew were teasing him about with this whole rappelling thing? Going backwards over the cliff, trusting in the rope and the pitons holding you?"

"I think that's it. Prepare for danger, a whole new experience. And whoops, you get fractured along the way. And now you're fractured too, Elyse." Liv was definitely into using metaphor to create a wedding myth for them.

"God!" Elyse was starting to laugh outright now.

The door opened, and Cory hobbled in on crutches. He looked exhausted but made a sheepish smile at Elyse. "I'm so sorry, baby." Steve was coming in behind him having driven Cory back.

Liv caught Steve's glance at her. "Hi."

"Hi." Seven years had passed since they'd last seen each other. Steve had been and still was Devin's best friend. Devin, who'd loved Liv since high school, Devin whom she'd lost her virginity to, Devin whom she'd lived with during college. Devin, whom she betrayed in India. And Devin, who as far as she knew, didn't know of Shakti's existence. Steve's entry was like sticking her head under a cold shower and abruptly waking up to the wedding that would reveal all. Steve would be at the rehearsal dinner with her and Shakti, and then Devin would see them at the wedding. Time had come to pay the price for keeping silence and never telling Devin the full story of their break-up. For sure, the wedding was seeming much less fun in the happening of it than when the dresses were chosen. The silliness of their girlfriend experiences was morphing into real life confrontations. Liv shifted her gaze to Elyse and Cory.

She saw how Elyse moved quickly to support Cory and give him a kiss. Liv seriously wondered what would come out of Elyse's mouth, hoping that their own conversation had helped. Elyse put one crutch down and was huddled holding Cory under his arm, looking up at him. As they focused on each other, palpable love showed in their faces.

Elyse was working on what to say, holding her words as a test of herself. She struggled between some parental tone – "You cocky guys, jumping off cliffs backward, what the hell!" – to a victimized tone – "You know you won't be able to dance worth a shit at our wedding now" – to what ultimately triumphed, the voice of an apprentice loving wife: "Are you in pain? How do you feel? Are you hungry?"

Liv relaxed. *Elyse passed the test. Good for her.* Even Elyse's next glance at Steve accompanied by her necessary venting wasn't too awful. "You guys! I could wring your necks. Thanks for ruining my wedding." Steve looked down, unsure what to say, feeling the pain too. "Oh, lighten up. I just needed to say that. Thanks for staying with him and bringing him back. Really."

Steve looked at her. "We all feel bad about this. We just got a little cocky at the end with our last rappels."

Liv moved to get the guys some beers, while Elyse ordered a pizza from downstairs in their apartment building. Liv wanted to disappear from Steve's presence. "Well, I should be going home."

"Thanks for being here," accompanied Elyse's hug. "And tell that Shakti girl, she needs to be on her very best behavior for the wedding."

Steve wondered who that was but said nothing.

"I will. I'm finding my calling in taming wild creatures."

Shutting the door after Liv, Elyse was still smiling. As she moved to the sofa where Cory and Steve were seated side by side, she thought Steve looked a bit stunned. Steve's curiosity was heightened since arriving, seeing Liv for the first time in so long, and then her reference to an unknown player in the wedding. "It's a long time since you two saw each other."

"I know. She looks the same, better I guess. What was that about, what you said to Liv, the wild creature thing?"

Elyse had known this moment was coming and debated how much to say. Direct communication seemed the best approach. "That was about Liv's daughter, Shakti. She's the flower girl and a bit of a wild child." Bombs away, thought Elyse, watching Steve's eyes grow more alert as his neck and shoulders shifted. His lower lip dropped a bit while a furrow in his brow deepened. "I wasn't sure if Cory had told you." She knew damn well he hadn't.

"Really? Liv has a kid? It never occurred to me that Liv had married already and had a baby." He shook his head quickly. "Surprise! I mean I thought she'd be like all the rest of us, still not married. But a kid too? Wow. So, when did she marry? Whom did she marry?"

"She's not married." *Go ahead, let it all come out. It will save Liv having to deal with it.* "She got pregnant and decided to keep the baby." Just lay it out. Then he can call Devin with accurate information and then it will all be taken care of before the wedding. One potential bad scene diffused. "And no, it's not Devin's baby." Cory was more alert now, wondering how far Elyse would go.

Given the day Steve had so far with Cory and the guys, the accident, the ER scene, no food since breakfast really, and now hearing all this, he didn't know what to say. He wanted to ask about the father, but knew it was none of his business.

"Look, this is all going to be visible to you at the wedding. Shakti is half-Indian. Liv got pregnant senior year when she went to India on that internship. And..." well, why not? "...and that's why she broke off with Devin."

Cory was taken aback that Elyse had told all. He kept shifting to look at Steve. Steve's face scrunched up more, as the answer to the seven-year-old mystery settled in. "Why didn't she just tell him?"

"You, or really Devin if he wants to at this point, will have to ask her that. Me, her mom and dad, Ryan, people told her to, but she kept putting it off, waiting to know if she would keep the baby. And, when she did, by then she had other things on her mind and commanding her attention. She just let it go. That's my best explanation for it. But only she can speak to it. Maybe it was shame? I know at one point she thought it would hurt him less to leave it vague, and just say she'd changed."

Steve ran his hands through his greasy hair. "I can't believe this day."

Elyse and Cory looked at each other with the same response, but she spoke first. "Yeah, neither can we."

Friday, September 7

They gathered for the church rehearsal at Saint Anne's Catholic Church on Queen Anne hill with a progressive pastor whose arm Elyse had twisted. Cory was walking with a cane to keep weight off his black-booted right foot.

Liv arrived first with Shakti and assessed. "Makes me think you fought in a war. The cane is a good touch, conveys a certain dignity, don't you guys think? Much better than crutches."

Shakti ran to Elyse for a hug. "Auntie, Mommy talked to me for a long time. I really love you. I'm going to be a very good girl and do whatever you say."

Elyse bent down to her level, delighting in the enthusiasm coming from the child's huge round eyes. "And I love you! We're going to have a great time." Elyse noticed how a headband holding back Shakti's curls changed her look from a wild kid hiding in hair to a more sedate Shirley Temple type. "How do you like your flower girl dress?"

Elyse's mom in Yakima had found something with a Mexican flair while not being overly ethnic. The darling dress with ruffles and pink polka dots imprinted on orange taffeta looked smashing on Shakti. "Oh, Aunt Elyse, I love it! I can't wait to wear it."

Steve and the others were arriving. Selena, Elyse's mom and sister-in-law Tessa, Cory's mom Wynona, and his brother Ron and his wife from back East. Liv caught Steve staring at Shakti. Elyse had called her first thing Tuesday and let her know she'd told the bare bones story to Steve. Liv was relieved. If nothing else, this wedding saw them both come through for each other as they had so many times in the past. Just do it, thought Liv. "Steve, this is my daughter Shakti. Shakti, this is Steve. We went to the same college together."

Steve's eyes were hard arrow points looking at her. He'd gone home last Monday night and called Devin to update him on Cory's condition. Given their long crazy day, Steve had sworn to himself he wasn't going to get into the Liv thing with Devin that night. But then it just flowed out of his head through his mouth as though his brain was flooded. "You won't believe this."

Following Monday's revelations, Devin and Steve, partners in the same small environmental law practice, had daily exchanges on the subject as their paths continuously crisscrossed. The topic dominated their regular Thursday beer night out. "I still can't believe it. I mean it's not like life hasn't moved on for us all. Law school. Jobs. Girlfriends." Devin was referring to Steve's own recent engagement to Laurie, a stunning visual coupling with his tall, dark, still somewhat scruffy look made more man-ish by her willowy strawberry blonde Cate Blanchett look. And for his part, Devin was in pretty thick with a very smart and sexy Chinese-American girl named Eddi who styled hair. They'd met at her upscale salon when he was getting his hair styled before a big trial. It felt good as she played with his hair, and one thing led to another.

"I know. I was stunned when Elyse just hit me with it."

"It all makes sense now – I guess. How weird Liv had become. I didn't have a clue though. And it's just sat there with me, buried away. Things change, I've changed. But sometimes, the way a girl on the bus looks, or someone I pass in a store, makes me think of her. Little stuff comes out of the blue, and then it's there, this black hole of not knowing."

"Not anymore." Steve's mind flashed back to how she looked at Elyse's. "How are we going to act around her? It feels awkward to be near her."

"I can't imagine. I suppose it's awkward for her, too. She's not going to want to deal with either one of us, especially me. Should we just act like we don't know her? I mean, we really don't know her. Now I realize, I didn't know her back then. Why should I act like I know her now?"

"Absolutely, right on. At the party, we'll be at our table, she'll be at hers. We'll have our climbing buddies there. And Laurie and Eddi are knock-outs. It's just about not crossing paths and keeping our heads down when she's near."

"Or heads up having a great time with the people we're with!"

"Exactly."

Now Steve was being introduced to a striking little girl with Liv's hair, caramel skin, and a narrow face with very bright, surprisingly blue eyes. She was looking up at him. "You're very tall like Cory. Were you this tall in college?"

Steve cracked a smile. "Yes, I was."

He noticed Liv turning already towards Elyse's mother and feeling for Shakti's hand. But she managed to stay her ground for another few seconds. "I'm going to go to college someday."

"That's a great idea. See you later, I've got to go."

Later at the dinner held at Ivar's on the north side of Lake Union, Shakti whispered to Liv, "Mommy, I really like that tall man Steve. I think he's very handsome."

"Yes, he is."

"You know him from college. Could he be a daddy?"

Liv was startled. "Shakti, he didn't really like me in college very much. And look at that beautiful girl he's with. He's going to marry her."

"Oh. Why didn't he like you?"

"It's one of those long stories, Shakti. And it's not a story I want to tell."

Shakti pouted.

Liv observed how lively the dinner was, and especially how happy Elyse and Cory were. The boot wasn't such a big issue during the practice. Cory's mom appeared friendly enough, maybe a little straight-laced as Liv's mom would say. Elyse did seem uptight around her, projecting that Wynona would be happier if Cory was marrying an east coast type, not a Latina who would keep him far away from Boston.

Liv was just as glad Eric hadn't come. It gave time for her and Selena to catch up. "Were you surprised when David called to talk to you?"

"A little. It'd been months since we'd seen each other last."

"Are you excited to be with him tomorrow for the wedding?" Liv realized how juvenile this question sounded as soon as it left her mouth.

Selena turned and looked at her in a 'got-to-be-kidding' way. "You mean, am I excited to have a date to the prom?"

"Sorry. It's just that he's such a great guy. You two make a beautiful couple together."

"Because we're both black? Come on, Liv, you can do better than that. Why are you acting like this? You know he's not available, never has been. He's just way too reserved for me anyway. Are you projecting any of your own stuff on this?"

Liv was surprised by the confrontational nature of the response. She didn't know what to say. "I'm sorry. It's just..."

"Just what? What are you holding back that's messing with your mind?"

What's the point? Sure, she wished that David was going to be her date. But she needed to play out the Eric thing. Why even talk about it. "Not worth discussing."

Selena felt bad now. She'd intuited that there was an unspoken thing between Liv and David. Liv was just grasping at straws to talk about him. "Don't be a stranger at the party. Come and hang out with us. We'll have a great table with Jonathan and his fiancée there. We'll get some bridesmaid action going on the dance floor with our shimmies up top and our shakes down below!"

Saturday, September 8

Elyse and Cory opted for a photographer who was willing to forego the pre-wedding poses at the altar and deal with that after the ceremony. Elyse was clear: no way would Cory see her in her dress before she came down the aisle. She and Liv were in a tiny room off the back entry to the church doing final adjustments to Elyse's hair, while Shakti's eyes were bulging to record every detail. Mimi and Ryan had brought the kids to the church and would take them home from the party, leaving Eric to bring Liv home. Mimi was hoping for a turning point in their relationship today, that he'd be swept away by Liv's electrifying look in the lime dress, that he'd find himself falling for the darling flower girl, that suddenly he'd see himself waiting at the altar. And that Liv would be swept up in the emotion of the event and realize that with her best friend getting married, she should settle now.

Liv was mostly feeling sad. As she dressed and assessed herself in the mirror, she wondered, what is it? *Why am I alone?* Then, when she caught her first sight of Elyse looking so beautiful, Liv almost cried. She felt the loss of a friend. However much or in whatever ways they remained connected, life would never be the same again. Elyse would be a wife. Liv wanted tears of joy, but knew them to be tears of loss. She kept dabbing under her eyes with one of Grandma's old embroidered handkerchiefs to keep them from tearing up.

Thank God, Selena and Tessa were full of good cheer, buttressing Liv's spirits. And Elyse? She'd stayed with her mom and family at a motel the night before following the rehearsal dinner. She'd wanted some space to herself and had her own room. Oddly reflective for her. But she hadn't wanted to wake up on her wedding day in the same bed with Cory. And she'd wanted to face her demons, even though they were in retreat, one more time on her own terms. Cory not being able to salsa was not the end of the world. A slow dance here and there, him sort of standing still, would suffice. She would show she was a good sport. They would still have a lovely time in Hawaii, lying on the beach or being in bed. What would it be like to have days together? Hours in bed? After already living together for months? Would they wind up reading or watching movies? She was still bummed though about going to clubs in the evenings and not being able to dance.

By morning, she'd realized that spending the night alone was a bad idea. She'd drunk quite a bit at the rehearsal dinner and regressed beyond the immediate situation of Cory's foot to deeper questions about whether she was doing the right thing. She admired Liv, going it alone. Why am I walking into this trap? Today, she was slightly hung over, and popped some Excedrin to get rid of the headache. She drank too much coffee and felt jittery. Her mom was getting on her nerves with her good cheer.

Now it was Liv and her in the small room trying to get Elyse's hair to stay put, just so, and not have the lace shawl slide down. "Liv, I feel like a mess inside. I'm not sure who I am today. I wish Cory and I could just walk away together from all these people." She started to tear up.

Liv embraced her and held her. She reached into her mental basket that held humor and short-term positive thoughts. "Wedding days are overrated. They're strange. The important thing is not to let your eye make-up run. You'll get through this, and sun and sand and sea are on the other side." What else? "And damn it, I never got to do this, so do it for me."

That made Elyse laugh. They both looked at Shakti whose eyes had a ravenous character to them as she hungered to know how to be a grown-up girl. "Aren't you happy, Auntie? I thought weddings were happy?"

Elyse bent down. "They are happy. But they're a very big deal too for your whole life. And I'm full of many, many feelings and they're all running around inside me mixing me up."

"Like being all wound up?"

"Exactly."

"Well, Mommy tells me when I'm all wound up to sit quietly and take deep breaths."

Elyse looked at Liv. They joined their hands forming a circle and closed their eyes. Each took a deep breath. By the second one, they were synchronized. Then they returned to their normal breath, keeping their eyes shut. For Elyse, a calming came: make this a happy day that begins a long life with the man I love. For Liv, a moment of joy burst through: to be one with those she loved so much. As they slowly opened their eyes and hugged, Shakti looked from one to the other. "I feel like we're all one person."

"Are you ready, Shakti, to spread the flower petals down the aisle?"

"Oh yes, I'm very ready. I practiced again early this morning."

"Let's do it then!" Elyse stood, took one more look in the mirror. "I'm ready." When they opened the door, the photographer was there. They came close again, joining hands and making a divine photo. As though they were goddesses.

The church was reasonably full, Cory's family, climbing friends, and legal colleagues on the right, and Elyse's family, and girlfriends from years of working in Seattle on the left. Plus a few other college and high school friends sprinkled on both sides.

Elyse's sister-in-law Tessa came down the aisle first in the turquoise version of the dress, followed by Selena in orange. The bridesmaids carried white rose bouquets. Then came Shakti, with a serious demeanor, carefully dropping hot pink rose petals as she went. Liv followed closely behind her, smashing in the lime dress, so much so that even Katherine later told her, she'd never looked lovelier. Very womanly with the pale green lace head shawl complimenting her curly auburn hair, such a knock-out in the dress with one tan shoulder bare and the sloping neckline and hemline ruffles. The breathing together had helped. Liv was fully present, integrating the import of Elyse's wedding. She'd resolved not to look at people, thereby avoiding any possibility of seeing Devin, while perhaps smiling only to the left at her family.

As Shakti neared the front, she saw her Grandma Kathy and Grandpa Gary, and then Ryan and Mimi and Little Jeff, and then even her great grandparents who had insisted on making the effort to get out for the wedding ritual. Colleen was on oxygen with Jeff holding her hand tightly. Seeing everyone made Shakti break out into a big grin and lose her sense of protocol. She paused and strayed to the left where Mimi was holding Little Jeff back. Liv, without breaking step, reached Shakti, and bent and whispered in her ear, "Sweetie, you need to finish the walk up the aisle." Liv gave a slight touch to her arm to motion her forward. Shakti looked at her and then faced the front again, deliberately centering herself in the aisle, and taking an obvious deep breath, while she began again meticulously dropping more rose petals. The scene brought a chuckle from those watching, which caused

Liv to drop her guard, and smile. While moving her head back up, she caught the eyes of Steve's fiancée Laurie on the right who flashed a gleaming smile. And then, there he was, one row in front of Laurie. Devin, looking Liv straight in the eye. What she saw was a more mature looking man than she knew. A ripened fruit, a more virile face than she recalled. Attractive and less boyish.

Devin chose an aisle seat because despite knowing he should ignore Liv, as Steve and he'd agreed, what he really wanted was to confront her in some way, to force her to deal with him. He could not NOT have chosen an end seat in the pew. He needed to watch her come down the aisle.

As others were engaged in watching Shakti, or now doing half-turns to see the bride, only Katherine saw her daughter pause and seem to falter. Liv's face blanched and looked somber.

As Liv neared the altar, Cory, his brother Ron, and Steve were standing to the right. Her gaze passed over Cory's sweetly eager face to pause at Steve's. He was staring at her and then moved his eyes towards Devin.

Elyse, on her brother Hernan's arm, was stunning. As Liv watched her approach the altar, she saw her friend's eyes begin to moisten. Elyse's face shone with love focused on Cory, and her carriage conveyed what could only be labeled determination. She was transforming, stepping into the bridle, and ready to give her best effort. Liv felt her own tears start to come, not tears of joy as a stranger might suppose, but tears of jealousy. Elyse was making a marriage. She was at the altar, a place that had eluded Liv. And there, five rows away and staring at her, if she let herself look, was Devin. The man who had loved Liv most, who would have married her had all gone according to the unspoken plan in college. The loving partner she had pushed to the background when in India and discarded when she returned home. The loser in the decisions about her unwanted pregnancy.

With Shakti so close in the front row, Liv's choice was fully present. My karma. My reality today. Liv dabbed her eyes repeatedly. *I'm going to sob if I don't distract myself.* And with that she locked her attention on the exchange of rings and vows, on the quality of voices, anticipating each phrase. She was so grateful this was a short ceremony with no mass. *My next challenge is to look all fine and smiley as I walk back down the aisle with Ron.* She kept taking deep breaths to the point she started to feel dizzy from hyperventilating. *I can do this. I can do this.*

The bride and groom received a blessing and turned to kiss. Liv lowered her eyes, not wanting that moment of joinder to disrupt whatever equanimity she had managed. When she and Ron needed to come together, she turned quickly, intent on avoiding any further connection with Steve. At the first row, Shakti looked at her and struggled out of the pew to take her hand and walk out with her and Ron.

Devin's sustained state of low level shock at seeing Liv left him open-mouthed watching his best friend, his former love, and her Indian child come down the aisle. He was in no hurry to leave the church, and let others go ahead. He knew he should just focus on Cory and Steve in the receiving line outside the church – maybe nod to Liv's parents in the crowd. There would be photos now, both outside and inside the church. He counseled himself to simply shake Cory's hand and be on his way. And so he did. As he opened his car door and looked back at the church steps, a clear voice spoke to him: you have to hear me out, Liv. *You owe me that.*

Katherine pulled her daughter aside before she and Gary left to take her parents back to Ryan and Mimi's where they could all relax, and get Jeff and his sitter settled in. Then, without Colleen and Jeff, the rest would return for the party in a few hours. "You had a rough moment there."

"You mean with Shakti? It was okay."

"No, I mean seeing Devin. I could tell you were fighting tears at the altar. Were those happy tears for Elyse?"

"Not really." Liv knew she needed to be moving back towards the wedding group for the photo-taking. But she lingered in the release that came with her mom's understanding. "It was a shock to see Devin even though I expected it. It hit me hard."

"And were you standing at the altar wondering what might have been?"

Her mother's intuition and knowledge of her caught her off-guard. "How did you know?"

"Because I was feeling the same thing. You know I adore Shakti and always have and agree with the choices you made. But there's always the consequences to face. And you got a fresh dose of that today." Katherine also had in mind her own choice in giving up Ryan and how that thirty-year interval had left her sad. "It's just hard. I feel for you today, darling."

"Thanks, Mom. Really. It helps to know you know how hard today is for me."

Following an hour of photo taking with every possible combination of family members, bridesmaids, and groomsmen, and lots of duos of Elyse and Cory from the waist up in order to obliterate memories of his booted leg, the bridal party moved on to the Mountaineers Club on lower Queen Anne. They needed to check in with the caterer and finalize the setup of the table decorations and seating arrangements. Elyse's mom's friends in Yakima had spent hours on the décor: colorful center pieces composed of tiny rugs with pottery vases of colorful orange and yellow flowers, and larger wedding flags, or *papel picado*, strung across the ceiling on strings. The effect was definitely fiesta and made the otherwise worse-for-the-wear sixties ballroom of wood panels appear special. The room held thirty tables, provided a decent sized dance floor, and a small stage area for the band. Elyse and Cory had grouped clusters of friends together in sorting place cards. But now as Selena and Liv laid them out, she had the opportunity to ensure the furthest distance between the climbing crew's table on the right, and those of her family and mutual friends on the left. The table for Cory, Elyse, and their families was in front of the dance floor and stage, dramatically lit by colored cam lighting.

Once guests began to arrive at six, there would be forty minutes for appetizers of flautas and chicken taquitos, before a dinner of chicken mole or chili-honey glazed salmon. The wedding cake was *tres leches*. It hadn't been easy persuading the pre-approved caterer to adjust the standard options for them, but Cory made noises about discrimination, and the Club decided adding a Mexican fusion option to their list might be a good marketing idea.

Eric arrived on the early side, apprehensive about meeting more of Liv and Ryan's family and her friends, but looking forward to a great party. He felt odd wearing his old navy blue suit which saw the light of day once a year, if that. Thanks to Liv he sported a new gold and blue tie that she said emphasized his natural coloring. He was psyched to see her dress since she'd sounded excited about it the other night. He entered the room free of thoughts of where this relationship was and anticipating how great the two of them would look dancing salsa. He scanned the room and saw the bride in the distance, and then splashes of color moving around the room. As he zeroed in on Liv bent over to adjust a center piece, his pulse quickened. To his eyes she was the prettiest girl in the room. Aware of her slightly muscular tan bare legs in those lime-colored heels made him stand taller, pull back his shoulders, and move with confidence across the room to take possession of his date.

She looked up. "Eric. You're here!" She came close and kissed him on the cheek. "Let me introduce you to everyone."

Elyse had just turned around to view the room one more time. *Oh my god, he IS a Viking! No wonder Liv is unsure about this guy.* Elyse came forward in her best saunter, continuing to size him up while flashing yet another best bride smile. "Hi, you must be Eric." Unsure whether to shake hands or do nothing, she reverted to a Hispanic kiss on the cheek.

Up close, Eric realized how sumptuously pretty Elyse was also. He stood back to really take in their gowns. "You two look fabulous together. Those dresses are fantastic."

"Thank you! It took us a while to get the concept down. Eric, this is my..." Elyse was turning in Cory's direction, grinning broadly, "...this is MY HUSBAND. Wow! How amazing is that."

"Yes, WIFE," Cory replied as he moved over using his cane. "I'm Cory. Crippled for this event by my own cockiness."

"What happened, man?" Eric pretended he didn't know to make conversation.

Cory began filling Eric in on the specifics, while Elyse raised her eyebrows to Liv and mouthed, "He's gorgeous." Liv just smiled, glad she had him as her date tonight, especially given her low point earlier during the ceremony.

Guests began to arrive, so the wedding party self-organized an informal reception line by the large entryway. There would be more people coming than had attended the wedding, partners and spouses of their friends that they hadn't met before.

Liv managed to stand at the far end away from Steve, hoping she could simply drop off the line once her family arrived. She'd gotten Eric a beer to drink and pointed out their table. Heartened to see Ryan and Mimi in line next, Liv decided to peel off to the table with them, and later flag down her parents who'd done the last bit of tending to her grandparents' needs before they drove over. She was content that her mom and dad were finally meeting Eric. Katherine and Gary were bringing Shakti back with them for the meal, and then they would leave early with her, collect Colleen and Jeff, and all head over to Redmond for the night along with little Jeff. Katherine wanted to ensure that Liv, as well as Ryan and Mimi, could have a real adults' night out and be as late as they wanted.

When they arrived, and Eric readily made nice to Shakti complimenting her on her dress, Liv relaxed. Her parents were so eager for her to find a mate, they were super friendly to Eric and acted like they knew him already. Which relaxed him and brought out all his social graces. As the party settled down to the tables and dinner, the clinking of glasses came, and Steve rose at his table next to the rest of the bridal party. It was time for the big toast, and Ron as best man provided some humorous remarks on his brother. But Ron didn't really know him that well as an adult, so Steve was roped in to a supplemental toast. While he'd toyed with a roast of Cory, and couldn't resist an opening joke about his being a lame bridegroom, Steve mostly went with laudatory remarks. He praised Cory for his work, his character, and the quality of his friendships with many attending; for Elyse, he called out her feistiness, and her fidelity.

Watching him deliver his toast in a measured way, calculated to create humor and touch hearts, he impressed Liv. What had she had against the guy back when he was Devin's best friend in college? Likely a control drama she figured between her and him over how Dev spent his time. As Steve spoke, Liv's gaze moved to his fiancée Laurie. *Quite the smashing couple. Lucky her.* Next to Laurie was the Chinese girl that must be Devin's current girlfriend. *Sexy, very pretty.* And then Devin fortunately was the one with his back to her as she looked across the room. Her seating arrangement had worked out well.

The table conversation over dinner was lively. Liv noticed her parents were visibly impressed with Eric as he exhibited his easy grace in making small talk. His professional relationship with Ryan and his boat repair business, combined with her dad's interest in the family boat, made the male chatting more spirited and engaging than was often the case. Liv finally was enjoying the event. The wine helped. Shakti was quiet, noticing how dressed up everyone was and how fun the decorations were. For her, this was a first wedding event; her baby presence when Mimi and Ryan married didn't count. She sat between Liv and Katherine, who was determined to keep her granddaughter engaged and well behaved so that Liv and Eric could enjoy themselves.

Liv had placed Selena, David, Jonathan, and his fiancée Evelyn at the table next to hers, along with a couple of mutual friends of Elyse's and Selena's from some neighborhood nonprofits. Good social networking for Selena's own long-term aspirations. If Liv turned her body slightly she could look directly across Jonathan's back to David's face. She caught his eye and lingered looking at him. He mouthed something, but she couldn't make it out, and gestured by lifting her shoulders and looking quizzically back at him. He waved his hand as though to say 'later.'

Liv reached for her glass, found it empty and asked Eric to pour her more. "Who was that you're making faces with?" Eric had caught the exchange with David.

"He's an old friend from my days at the Rescue Committee. David's his name and this is Jonathan with his back to me. They're both from Sudan."

"Sudan?"

"Africa. Below Egypt."

"Well, I knew it was Africa just by looking at him."

Liv felt slightly uncomfortable with that remark although she wasn't sure why. "There's been a war going on there since the eighties and those guys are real survivors. As children, they walked a thousand miles to get to safety. They used to be called the 'lost boys of Sudan.'"

"So how come they're here at the wedding?"

Liv began to wonder why Eric was interested in them, as opposed to others in the room, but hey, this was the most she'd talked to Eric about her time with refugees, so why not see if he could get more interested. "I met them at the airport about six years ago as they arrived from the refugee camp. Part of my job in Tukwila was helping refugees get used to the way we do things here, everything from appliances and food and grocery shopping to cultural stuff. And they were such nice guys, they liked Shakti, so Elyse and I started having them over to our apartment to teach them cooking and how to deal with all kinds of school things, getting into college. We all became friends, along with Selena, the bridesmaid in the orange next to David. We had a lot of fun as a group in those days."

Eric took this all in, wondering if these guys were old boyfriends. At least if David was with Selena now that made sense. But he wondered what had gone on between David and Liv. It troubled him a bit. Slightly nervous now, Liv continued to drink wine as though it were a soft drink, while Eric moved on from the champagne and wine he didn't care for to drink beer.

As the dinner plates were being cleared, and the meal progressed towards the cutting of the cake, Eric spoke with Ryan about his sonar technology ideas, while Gary expressed interest also. Liv turned to Shakti, "Hey, turn around and see who's next to us."

Shakti complied, and her eyes lit up. "I remember him. It's David, right?" She waved at him. "Can we go talk to him, Mommy?"

"Sure, after the cake is cut and we have our pieces, and before you leave to go home."

Shakti frowned. "I don't want to leave. I like it here with all these people. And I want to dance."

"Maybe. If you're good, you can dance a little, but then you're on your way."

Later as they polished off their *tres leches* cake, Shakti poked Liv. "Mommy, now can we say hello to your friends?"

"Sure." With that, Liv pulled back her chair and leaned towards Eric. "Shakti wants to say hello to the guys behind us, so I'll just be a minute."

Eric nodded.

Shakti moved quickly, first to present herself to Jonathan and then to run around to David's side of the table. Each turned to embrace her and greet her with big smiles. Liv stood behind Selena's chair bending over to listen as she and David got an earful of Shakti's account of the events so far. "I almost goofed up going down the aisle, but Grandma says I did fine. And I love all the dresses, especially yours." She held a piece of her own ruffle up to Selena's orange dress. And I like this big party - I want to hear the music and dance. Will you dance with me?" she queried David.

"Of course, Miss Shakti. I'd love to."

Her eyes were twinkling. "When will they start, Mommy?'

"Soon. The band needs to finish setting up. The first dance will be slow, and only for Elyse and Cory."

To no one in particular, Shakti opined, "She's so beautiful. Aunt Elyse. I want to dance with her too."

"Given Cory's condition, you may have a good chance to do that."

"And then I want to dance with David, and Jonathan too. And that Steve, I really like him too."

"What about Eric, sweetie?" Selena thought she was being helpful.

"No, I'm not sure Eric likes me."

Liv rolled her eyes at Selena. Better to leave that one alone. They chatted a bit more. "Let's get back to our table, Shakti."

"No, I want to stay here. I want to sit on David's lap till the music starts. That way he has to dance with me first." She put her arms up towards him, and he lifted her on his knee.

Liv was in no mood to make anything an issue. "Okay, just remember, you get three dances, max four, and then home."

"But what about Ryan and Grandpa, don't I get to dance with them too?"

"We'll see," was the best Liv could respond at this point. "Talk to you all later," was generally directed to David's table, as she returned to her seat. Eric looked piqued. "What's up with Shakti?"

Liv poured more wine. "Oh, she's always liked the guys, David especially. She wants the first dance with him."

"She always gets her way," was Eric's reproach.

Liv turned and squinted her eyes. "Hey, path of least resistance tonight, okay?" With that, she returned to steadily sipping wine.

Soon the music started, the band playing the old Carpenters' tune, *It's Only Just Begun*, which even though dated was still what Elyse wanted for this special dance. As the bride and groom moved on to the parquet dance floor, Cory foregoing his cane to lean on her, Elyse looked playful. She'd drunk quite a bit already, which hadn't gone unnoticed by Cory's mom. Elyse seemed not to mind Cory's rather stationary situation, as they swayed with each other. Occasionally, she'd twirl outward under his lifted arm and then come in close again. They looked happy, in their own world. For the last stanza, Elyse moved off to bring her brother Hernan on to the floor, and Cory's mom Wynona came up to dance with him. The slow music continued into the next dance, and the lead couples did the split and multiply routine with Elyse dancing with Cory's brother, then with Steve, while Elyse's mom and sister each had their times with Cory.

The band then moved into a faster tune and Elyse and Cory sat down. Elyse spent the next half hour of moderately paced dancing in a calculated way, circulating in the room and picking partners she wanted to acknowledge. When Liv and Eric began dancing, she kept them to the far left on the parquet dance slab, hoping that Devin would stay on the other side. Shakti had her dances with David, Jonathan, and Elyse, and then Liv took her back to their table to get Ryan and then Gary. She intended to make sure that Shakti did not take off on her own to Steve and kept reminding her that soon she would have to go. While Liv was supervising, Eric danced with Mimi and then Liv's mom.

At the table, David approached Liv. "I was trying to tell you before how beautiful you look. I've never seen you so gorgeous."

Liv smiled widely. "Thanks for saying that. It's fun to be dressed up. You look smashing too, Mr. JD attorney."

"Shall we dance?"

The rhythm picked up a bit. Elyse had chosen almost all the music so that while some older folks were there at the beginning they could participate, but over time the pace and rhythm was to quicken as the young and salsa-gifted took over the floor and let loose their inhibitions. Interspersed now and then with an occasional slow song so Elyse could pull Cory to the floor.

A few years back, Liv and Elyse had taught the lost boys some salsa moves while the guys had taught them Sudanese tribal dance movements. It had always been a hoot. Once Elyse saw Liv out there with David, she pulled away from the table where she'd been sitting one out next to Cory, and asked Jonathan to dance. Over the course of the first song, the four reminded each other of some of their old culturally fused moves, and by the second fast song, their bodies were remembering for them how to move. Butt bumps, hand claps, broad two-footed stomping jumps and fluid sexy turns, the girls doing more complex foot work and shimmies while the guys spread their legs, bent their knees and moved rhythmically toward them. As Liv and Elyse performed their best salsa moves their heels added to the sexiness of it all. But then they kicked off their shoes, letting their bare feet with bright orange toenails more freely maneuver. They periodically swiveled to stick their bums out toward the vibrations of the guys' groins. The naked feet with their interlocking gyrating pelvises suggested an invitation into a bedroom where clothes would be shed – which must have been what Cory's mother was finding salacious as the four dancers moved into a whole-body performance that now commanded the attention of the rest of the dancers. People backed away to give the bride and her crew more room and egged them on with hoots, claps, and cheers. Elyse and Liv were having so much fun that Eric's sour expression went unnoticed. More noticed by some of their friends was Cory's noncommittal expression, Wynona's dropped open mouth and pained eyes, and his brother Ron's raised eyebrows. Devin had tried to avoid watching but his clueless girlfriend Eddi had pulled him closer to view the spectacle. When the song finally finished the foursome all hugged each other to the applause of the crowd.

Following this number, the band chose something slower and Liv moved back to David's table. "Selena, take this wild man off my hands!"

"I think you both need to sit down after that one! God, it did bring back the memories! Remember that party we all went to when the guys graduated from college!" That led to each trying to recall people and highlights from earlier times.

Eric? He'd gone to the rest room and expressed his frustration with a good piss. *Damn, all that practicing they had done to be the best salsa dancers on the floor, and she takes up with this jet-black dude.* Even Eric had been a tad shocked at some of Liv's moves. He wondered how the groom felt.

Entering the room again his eyes moved immediately to Liv sitting with the black bridesmaid and this David dude. They were laughing hard. Eric was affronted: what did she think he was here for? And where was the kid? He saw Liv's mom coming toward him. "That's enough of all you young people for us. We need to get this girl home before she gets any more ideas. I can only imagine how she'll be dancing at daycare this week! No doubt Liv will hear about it," she said in good humor. "Nice meeting you, Eric."

"Yes, great meeting both of you."

Gary shook Eric's hand. "Good talking. I hope you and Ryan get that sonar service expansion going. Technology is everything today." Gary slapped his arm. "Hope to see you around."

"Shakti, say goodbye to Eric and we'll touch base with your mom and be off."

Shakti stood almost shyly behind Katherine. "Bye, Eric."

"Bye." He followed them over to where Liv, Selena and David were still yakking it up. Liv rose for goodbyes and kissed Shakti goodnight. As her parents and Shakti left, Liv looked ebullient. "Hey, join us. We're remembering some fun times we've shared."

Eric wasn't smiling. "How about you and me dance for a change?"

Liv's wide-open smile evaporated as she quickly tuned in to his sullenness and irritation. She felt the tug of his being her date for this event and that it was time to shift gears. "Sure."

The music was slow enough for traditional close-up coupling. "Those were some moves you pulled out that last dance. You've never danced like that with me."

Liv laughed it off. "I didn't even know I remembered them. It's been years since we all partied together and taught each other moves."

Eric pulled her closer. He couldn't help it, anger rose in him. He put his cheek to hers. "So, you like them dark."

Just as she had relaxed in his arms, his words jolted her like a shock of electricity. She immediately put her hand to his chest and pushed back from him. "Excuse me! What did you just say?"

Eric was on the brink - and he couldn't resist. His feet stopped moving. He stared at her. "I'm just noticing you like your men dark."

Liv's eyes opened wide in disbelief, her forehead wrinkled in shock, as she forcibly pulled out of his grasp and took a step back. "What?" She stared at him and raised her hands as though to repel force. "Oh my God! You're a racist!"

His arm moved as though to hit her. But she pivoted quickly and half-ran from the room, towards the hall to the ladies' room. Eric pursued her. Selena and David were dancing near them and she saw, but did not hear, the incident. Knowing something untoward had occurred, she quickly followed Liv. When she went through the doorway, she saw Eric and Liv halfway down towards the restrooms. Eric was gripping Liv's arm and Liv was pulling away. Selena wasn't sure what to do but then Eric dropped Liv's arm, turned and walked past Selena up the stairs to the exit. How did such a handsome man look so ugly, was her reaction.

Liv went into the ladies' room, moved through the make-up area, and shut herself into a stall. She was shaking and holding herself. There was a bruise where he'd grasped her. She wrapped her arms around herself, her back against the door, then raised her hand to cover her mouth. *What was I thinking? How did I not notice? What a bastard!*

"Liv?" Selena's voice came over the stall door. "Liv, are you in there? What happened?"

Liv wasn't up to facing anyone. In a low voice she said, "I'm here. I just need some space."

"Do you want me to stay here?"

Liv's mind was racing. Mostly she wanted to know if Eric had left. "Could you go see if Eric has left? I don't want to see him again. Ever again."

"I'm pretty sure he did but I'll go out and check. Back in a minute."

Liv kept holding herself. Adrenalin was overwhelming her body. She wanted to be home. NOW. In her room. How could she get home fast? But did she need to be around for the garter and bouquet thing? How could she not stay till the end?

"He's nowhere to be seen. And I did see him walk up the stairs." Selena was unsure what to say or do next. With Liv so upset, she couldn't go back and try to have a good time. "Want to talk about it?"

How could she tell Selena she was dating a racist? "No, I just need some time to calm down. You go out, Selena. I'll settle down and be out in a while."

"Sure?"

"Sure."

Liv stayed in the stall for another ten minutes, listening to women come and go. At one point, she heard two women talking. "Did you see the look on his mother's face when Elyse was doing that wild dance?" Another voice softer: "Cory didn't look too happy either." "Well, a girl's got to have fun at her own wedding," came the response. Liv heard the door open and shut as they exited. *I need to be out there.* She opened the door and stood in front of the mirror. Her face looked tense, even haggard under the light. She needed to find Mimi and make sure she could leave with them. She splashed water on her face and patted it until the remaining moisture on her face provided a glow effect. *I need to stop drinking and pull myself together.*

She stepped out from the restroom, raised her head and saw someone standing half-way down the hallway with a drink in his hands. He turned. *Devin. Shit.* He filled the hallway space confronting her. After being pushed by his girlfriend to watch Elyse and Liv dancing, he'd grabbed a drink and to his date's surprise said he needed to step out for a moment. He'd gone outside to get his head straight. Somehow, he'd thought that he'd have a chance finally to face Liv. To do what? He didn't know. Make her ashamed for not having been truthful with him? Make her feel bad. Say something profound although his mind hadn't settled on what that was. He'd gone over lines like "Why didn't you tell me?" "You owed me the truth." "The truth would have been easier than not knowing." Although he wasn't so convinced about the latter, now that he knew the truth.

As he was returning to the room, he saw the other bridesmaid he didn't know. "Excuse me, do you know where Liv is?"

Selena wondered who this guy was, but oh well. "Actually, she's in the ladies' room right now. But she may be a while."

He decided to wait in the hallway. He knew his date Eddi was probably getting upset about him being missing so long. He'd explain later. Sweating under his suit coat he was racking his brain trying to decide what he was going to say to Liv. He opened a door and saw another party room, empty and dark. Maybe they could talk in there. Then, she was there. He confronted her full face. "Liv."

"Devin?" questioning his presence in her life at that moment.

"I'd like to talk to you. Can we go in this room?" He opened the door and she saw the empty space. Saying nothing, she moved slowly into the unlit space. He closed the door, but not completely so as to leave a shaft of light.

Really? On top of the Eric thing, am I now going to get the dressing down of my life? Instead of a fresh adrenaline rush, came resignation. *What a fuck-up I am! All he can do is make me confront what I know already. Let him have his say.*

"Liv, look at me."

She took a deep breath and turned to face him, but with her eyes still down.

"I said look at me."

She raised her gaze to see a face incredibly familiar, a face she'd loved for years. It looked in pain. Unsure. "What am I supposed to say? I assume Steve told you the basic information. What more do you want to know?"

"I don't know. I think why you never told me and just walked away. How could you be so mean, so unloving to me?"

Liv turned her head to peer into the dark space of the room where she wished she could disappear. "Look, I'm really upset about something else right now. It's hard for me to talk about anything, let alone about what I did all that time ago."

He didn't want to let her off the hook. He was between her and the door.

She tried to focus on him. "I know you deserved better than that. It was...I was so confused. I thought the truth would be too mean as you say. I was changing, and the changes resulted in me...not being faithful. Our relationship felt over, there was no going back." She could hear her voice growing harsher. "I mean, there was no way I could keep both the baby and you. Don't you get that?"

"I do. Ever since Steve told me about your little girl, I've thought about what my reaction would have been. I would have been so hurt, just in a different way. I wouldn't have wanted to be with you anymore. But didn't you owe me the truth?"

"But you just said it, either way you were going to be hurt. I thought at the time that what I did was the lesser of two evils. And my choices happened slowly. I might have given Shakti up. Who knows what I would have done then as a single woman again? Would I have tried to get back together with you none the wiser? I didn't think I would do that. But first I had to decide about her, and what I wanted my choice to be. And once I chose to keep her...for sure, there was no going back." Liv's heart was opening to him a bit watching his eyes watch her. She wanted to give him something. "It's not like I still didn't care about you, love you. But there was no good way to save it. There was love, but not the kind we used to share."

"I need to know; did you regret what happened in India?"

Liv couldn't bring herself to lie now any more than she

could have then. She knew this would hurt. But by confronting her, he had risked that. "No, I didn't. I've never regretted it. And I totally love my daughter."

His eyes closed slowly. She worried he would cry. He looked down, then at the door, then at her. "I guess I needed to hear that. That there was no mistake. No lost opportunity between us."

"I said it that day at Seattle Center, Dev. I changed. And there was no going back." Liv's demeanor softened again. "And I know I lost a lot. We might have had a really nice life together if I'd never gone to India. I feel that loss. Especially today, when my best friend is married now and stepping into a real family life with a husband. And I just found out my date is a racist. It feels pretty lonely right now." She wanted to touch him but knew her doing that wouldn't send the right message. "You're with a great girl from what I hear."

"She is a sweet person, very smart. I'm happy to be with her." He stared into Liv's eyes one more time. "I guess you taught me some important lessons. You taught me that you never really know a person. You taught me that my ideal is not obtainable. And that we all need to settle. Maybe you should settle for the racist, Liv. At least you know that about him now." He turned to leave, and then paused. "Thanks for talking to me. You didn't have to do that."

After Devin left, Liv left the door open a crack. She found a chair and sat down. *Unbelievable. Is this day really happening?* Her mind was stunned. Eventually she heard the music picking up again. *Elyse. She freaked out her mother-in-law. Maybe I should go sit with Cory.* She stood, straightened her back and rolled her shoulders. *Hell, what else could happen?*

As Liv moved into the pounding beat of the party, she saw the dance floor was overflowing with movement, as though a dance corps was putting on a stage show of totally choreographed moves, each executed slightly differently, but collectively creating a dynamic pulsating whole. She saw Cory sitting alone at the bridal table, sipping wine and watching the dancing, his expression more in keeping with viewing a funeral procession. As she neared him, she saw Elyse in the center of the floor with a Hispanic guy Liv didn't know, some friend's date or husband. Elyse was holding up the longer side of her gown to her waist to set her legs free, still barefoot, looking like all she needed was a red rose in her teeth. She was in the zone, her Latin dancing music frenzy zone. And there was Cory moping.

Liv slid into the chair next to him and followed his expression. He looked sad but smiled as he became aware of her. It was too loud to talk. Finally, the band took a fifteen-minute break. Elyse was completely flushed, her neck and arms all rosy. She came to the table to grab her glass of beer, sweaty, her hair disheveled. "Too bad your mom didn't stay around to see that performance."

Cory grimaced. "Elyse, don't you think you've had enough to drink?"

"Hell no! I may drink another six-pack at this rate. She laughed too hard, then became aware of Liv. "You don't look so hot, what's up? Where's that Viking of yours?"

Having assessed the growing gulf between the smashed bride and the judgmental groom, Liv saw the need for this to end. "Shouldn't you be doing the garter thing and the bouquet?"

"Oh, that's right. I forgot about that! Should I rig it so you catch it?"

"No, please don't. Aim for Steve and Laurie." Liv stood and moved closer to Elyse who was walking around the table downing the remains of other's drinks. "Elyse, stop it." Liv kept her voice low but strong. "Just stop it. You're starting to look ridiculous. And you're hurting Cory."

"Well, maybe he should have been thinking about dancing instead of rappelling down cliffs!"

"Elyse. Come with me. Right this minute." Liv hauled her off to the room she'd just been in with Devin.

"Liv, what the hell? What are we doing in here? Where's my beer? I want to dance some more."

Liv gently slapped her friend's face. "You stay put here. Don't you dare move." Liv moved quickly to gather water and coffee from the other room. By the time she returned, Elyse was crying. "Why did you hit me? My maid of honor? What's wrong with everybody? How come his mother walked out? Can't I have some fun on my own wedding day?"

Liv got Elyse drinking the water, keeping her own voice calm and direct, repeating simple instructions. "You're going to go out there and do the garter thing with Cory, and then toss the bouquet. And then you two are leaving. Understand? No more dancing. No more drinking. The others can stay for the last songs.

And then Selena and I will get this shut down. Got it? Here, have some coffee too." Liv wouldn't let Elyse leave until she stood up straight, pulled her hair into place and repeated what Liv had told her to do.

Cory threw the garter. Devin stepped aside, and Steve caught it. Elyse threw her bouquet and Laurie had no problem reaching for it. As Cory guided Elyse from the table, he whispered to Liv. "Thank you. I owe you big time." Selena and Liv and David along with Mimi and Ryan stayed through another half hour of slower music to shut the wedding down. As David and Selena left, Liv reminded him not to leave town without saying goodbye in person.

Liv would look back on Elyse's wedding as the worst day of her life. The wedding from hell. The day she got her comeuppance. It would be a long time before she felt like going to a wedding again. Relationships were fraught with complexities beyond her capacity. How could she date a guy for over a month, damn, even have sex with him, and not have figured out he was racist? Or had she misinterpreted Eric's remark somehow and she owed him an apology? That was easy: hell no! Why was she cruel to Devin years ago? Had she really ruined his ability to trust a woman? Would Elyse's deportment or lack thereof permanently shape her mother-in-law's view of her? More importantly, would Cory recall his wedding as spoiled by Elyse's behavior? Would Elyse rise to the challenges of being a wife and mother? So many unanswered questions from the fiesta wedding matched the mood of the paper flags drooping to the floor when they left the hall.

Sunday, September 9

The next day Liv needed to pick up Shakti and Jeff from her mom's. On the way over, her thoughts turned to her parents' having to handle getting both grandparents returned to Redmond with them, plus deal with the little ones. *How did the rest of their evening go?* Upon arrival, Katherine assured her that, all things considered, a big outing for Grandma, dealing with Shakti and Little Jeff, it hadn't been that bad. Grandpa had done his share. Little Jeff was asleep when they loaded him into the car and then Shakti too by the time they reached Redmond. It had mostly tired out Grandma to be away from her own space for so long and she was still in bed this afternoon.

"Mommy, I'm so glad you're here now. There are so many things I want to ask you!"

"Go for it."

"Can you teach me to dance like you and Tia Elyse did?" With that, Shakti put her hands on her knees and stuck her rump out and wiggled it.

Katherine looked cross. "Shakti, I hate that kind of dancing."

"Why, Grandma? They had so much fun. And everyone clapped their hands." She shifted her eyes back to Liv, "Can you?"

"I'll teach you a lot of dance moves when it's time for you to learn them."

"When's that?"

"When you're in high school."

Not the right answer as far as Shakti was concerned, resulting in her sticking out her tongue.

"What else, what other questions?"

"How come we don't see David and Jonathan more? I really like them."

"Actually, we may have David over for dinner before he leaves town. Would you like that?"

Shakti's smile was her answer. But then she turned serious. "Mommy, are and you Eric going to get married?"

"Nope, Eric and I won't be seeing each other anymore."

Shakti hugged her, obviously happy with that answer. Katherine's eyes opened farther, and she tilted her head in a question.

"You didn't like Eric, did you, sweetie?" Liv was holding Shakti closer.

"Not too much. He was pretty. But I didn't like his eyes."

Liv could see that her mom wanted to talk. "Shakti, can you start packing your green bag while I talk to Grandma?"

Katherine gave her further directions to make sure she had time with Liv. "Oh, and ask Grandpa to show you the dogs and cats game on the computer for a while, okay?"

"Oh, that game is so much fun! You know I want a pet, Mommy?"

"Yes, I know that. Off with you now."

As soon as Shakti was out of hearing distance, Katherine followed up. "What happened between you and Eric last night? I left thinking he was a nice guy and that you might be getting into a good relationship with him."

"I know, Mom. I guess I thought that at times too. But he surprised me with something he said, and I knew I couldn't tolerate being around him. Can we just not get into it, please?"

"It's disappointing is all."

"Yep. Yesterday was a disappointing and extremely difficult day for me."

Katherine was concerned that Liv's sustained and now renewed rejection of possible husbands went deeper. "Say more, please, I'm worried for you."

Liv had lain in bed awake last night going over the unlikely synchronicity that in the same hour she closed out her relationship with Eric, she had to make an accounting of her behavior to Devin whom she shut out so long ago. Really, how weird was that? And the Eric thing was generated, of course in part by drinking, but also by her having spent time at David's table, and yes, well, then the dirty dancing. She knew the truth but didn't want to speak it. Yes, she really wished David was available. She was attracted to him, cared for him, respected him completely, could talk to him about anything she cared about, AND he loved Shakti. "Maybe you should be worried, Mom. I should be worried about me too. Because the men I find most attractive are not available, and the available ones make me know I'm settling. Giving up."

"What did Eric do that upset you so much that now you're done with him?"

"Were you still there when Elyse and I revived our dance moves with David and Jonathan?"

"Oh yes! You should have seen the look on Cory's mom's face – ay yai yai! She went from shocked to angry and then she and the brother left with no goodbye to Elyse."

"Really? I heard someone say something about that."

"Believe me, people took note of the whole thing. Where did you girls learn all those gyrations? You should have seen Shakti's eyes taking it all in."

"Well, Eric took it in too. Shortly afterwards, he said: 'oh, so you like them dark.'" Liv screwed up her face and increased the volume: "Can you believe that jerk? His closet racism came out! And here I have a biracial daughter! What an asshole." Katherine understood perfectly now. Whatever excuses one could make for Eric's comment, it showed a side of him that her Liv would never tolerate. End of story. "He can take his Nordic good looks and go fuck the Valkyries for all I care." Liv stood and shook out her body as though she was ridding herself of any remaining skin cells she shared with him.

"And what about you and David? Isn't he leaving?"

"Yes, he's going away, not sure for how long. It depends on what job he takes. But for the foreseeable future…" Liv sighed here, "… he's gone. Period."

"What's there between you two?"

"Hell, if I know. I care about him. A lot. I'm attracted to him. He thinks I'm special. But his focus is one hundred percent on trying to find his mom and sister in Africa."

Katherine leaned back on the kitchen counter assessing. "This is a strange question, Liv, but do you really want a man in your life? I mean you never wanted to pursue Shakti's father. David is unavailable. You've found reasons to reject, what, maybe nine or ten guys over the years. "

"Honestly, I ask myself that question sometimes. Especially last night after I also had the very long-delayed conversation with Dev about what happened when I got pregnant."

"WHAT? You talked with him? When was that?"

"Like, no more than twenty minutes after I told Eric he was a racist and walked away from him. With him bruising my arm – look at this!"

"Oh honey, what an emotional night. I can't imagine. How did it go with Devin?"

"Heavy. Okay in a way. I think he was hoping to hear that I wished I hadn't had Shakti and that we would be together now."

"Really?"

"It's a hunch. But I let him know I had no regrets. There was no missed opportunity for us to have gone on forever." Liv closed her eyes and put her hands on her face. "But how bizarre is that really, the Eric Devin collision."

"I get it. A short bizarre time in which strands from your life all came together."

"Exactly. So maybe that's me, Mom. I just can't pull off a viable relationship, at least not at this point in my life."

"Liv, don't get overly dramatic. I still think you'll meet someone when Shakti starts first grade at a new school."

"Right, the divorced father looking for a mother for his kid." Liv stood up. "Just forget it for now, I don't want to hear about it. I don't want to be fitting into someone's job description. I just want to get on with my own life and soon enough that will mean grad school." She took another visible breath and focused on Katherine. "For now, it's Grandma, you, and Shakti."

"Speaking of your grandmother, the visit to the church really exhausted her. Then, while she and Grandpa waited at Ryan's with little Jeff and the sitter, she kept saying she wanted to go home. I was so glad Mimi had gotten a sitter, so she could take care of the kids and your grandparents could rest and I could wait on them for a while. They're both pretty tired today." Katherine began to pull down chips for a snack. "It made me aware how much she's gone downhill even since they moved over here. Sad. It's hard to see."

Liv, relieved that the focus had shifted, moved toward the hallway to her old bedroom where Grandma was staying. Turning, "How long, do you think?"

"Maybe a couple of months? I seriously doubt she'll make it to Christmas."

On the drive home, Shakti brought up Colleen. "Nanny's really sick, Mom. She's not the way she used to be. She told me that she might die."

"She did?"

"We had a talk about it while you were in the kitchen with Grandma. I don't understand why Nanny's going to die. Or what happens when she dies."

Liv was reminded that before her summer fling with Eric came to dominate her thoughts, she'd started this conversation with Shakti. She'd been going to research Buddhism but gotten side-tracked. Now the need was there to get this Eric thing out of her system, maybe journal about it, and make Grandma her focus. And Shakti, and what lie ahead for them as a family. This whole preoccupation with finding a husband and father had been a colossal waste of time. And she reminded herself, if I'm delaying school, I should use this time well for our family.

The soundtrack for her return drive home could have been a symphony's change in movements from allegro, a spirited clashing with herself for getting involved with Eric, into a slow adagio of death knocking at their family door. *I need to be present for my family, to be there for Mom, to know how to guide Shakti through this. Grow up. Elyse has moved on. Others are launching their work like David. Stop wasting time on men.*

Friday, September 21

Elyse and Liv opted for a pizza night out. They had yet to fully debrief since the newlyweds returned from Hawaii and their week-long honeymoon. "Cory's already swamped with work. I'm so glad you could come out tonight."

"Did you bring pictures?"

"Just some on my camera from Hawaii. But nothing from the photographer yet. I'll show you mine on the computer monitor later."

"I'm dying to hear...how was it? The honeymoon?"

Elyse slouched down against the red leather cushion of the booth. "Honestly?"

"Of course."

"It was a mixed bag."

"Tell me the good parts."

"The good parts were that we both slept a lot, relaxed on the beach with Pina Coladas, and ate great food. And we talked about everything. About the future, house, kids, things we'd like to make happen in our lives. How we'd support each other."

"That all sounds wonderful."

"Yes, it was all good," said with a soft smile but absent a lilt in her voice.

"So, what's the mixed part?"

"It was a little rough, hard at first because he felt the wedding had gone, well, first he said 'south' but when I reminded him that was politically incorrect, we agreed that it had gone sideways. And, I just still felt mad, actually still feel that way, about his mom's and his reactions to me having a good time. I kept saying, 'lighten up.' He kept fretting that his mom wouldn't have anything more to do with me."

"That's not all bad, is it? I mean they're east coast anyway."

"Oh, the stuff in the future, trips one way or another at the holidays, visits with kids. He feels like the relationship, which hadn't really existed at all before the wedding, well, it's not ever going to happen."

"You wouldn't be the first person to have in-law issues. She was probably looking for reasons to dislike you."

"True. Anyway, so the beginning of the trip was less than festive shall we say?" Elyse refrained from revealing that they didn't make love their wedding night. "But he picked up after a while. And I was super good about accommodating his reduced mobility. Very wifely. You would have been proud of me."

"So, now it's on to real married life."

"Exactly. And he's stayed at work late every night. I've been busy too. We have budgeting to work on this time of year for next year." Elyse's lackluster eyes bespoke low energy. The last two weeks of intentional actions to be a good wife, menu planning, incorporating washing his clothes into her free nights while he worked, and doing more errands because of his foot, left her feeling drained. Weighed down. Liv was quiet too. "What about you and Eric? What happened at the end? I was drunk as you know only too well, but I don't recall seeing him at the end."

"That's because he left. In a heat."

"Why, what happened?"

"I called him a racist."

Elyse visibly perked up. "You what? Why?"

Liv's account of not only the encounter with Eric, but also with Devin, brought Elyse alive. "Ryan's on my case, a little standoffish. He doesn't want my break-up with Eric to affect their business relations. Although, really in my opinion, it should. Anyway, Eric apparently said at some point to Ryan that I owe him an apology. I told Ryan, no way, but I didn't go into details. It's not my place to say something that might cause Ryan over time to decide to let Eric go. For now, Ryan thinks I must be in the wrong."

"Did you tell Mimi?"

"No. I've been sort of aloof about the whole thing."

It began to feel like old times between the two of them. "I'm encouraged now that I can count on you to keep life interesting for me."

Interesting? While you've settled into an enviable marriage and family life to come, I'm the 'interesting' single mom side show? She wasn't in the mood to go there tonight though. Liv wanted to share with Elyse how hard it had been to see her get married. How her marriage left Liv feeling lonelier; and that it helped to hear Elyse was not getting as much time from Cory as she wanted. They could still go out like this, just the two of them. *Am I being narrow hearted? Not sympathizing, but taking comfort in her complaints?* No doubt, the whining comforted Liv that marriage would never be the panacea.

Elyse meanwhile was discomfited by a small wave of envy. Liv was still free, free of having to make nice to in-laws, free of having to manage expectations about a husband. And still free to fashion her life. In the moment, Shakti seemed inconsequential to Elyse. Liv had her options open when it came to men. Thinking these thoughts embarrassed Elyse: how shallow I am, how ungrateful for Cory, for all our plans to create a life. There was her control drama again, to be in charge of her own life and even better, have a big say in his.

"It's odd of us to be so quiet." Liv wanted to ditch her negativity. "Let's go see those Hawaii shots."

Friday, September 28

"Hey, the official photographer's proofs are here now. Can you come over and see them? They're not bad and there's a couple of us I love."

When Liv saw them that night while Cory worked late at the office, she loved them too, especially the one of her and Elyse and Shakti, taken right before they left the little room. They had opened the door and the photographer pleaded for just a few shots. They all looked so relaxed and happy, but more than that: looking one at the other, Elyse at Shakti, Shakti at Liv, Liv at Elyse, there was a palpable circle of love. "That's the one I want! Eight by ten for sure." Liv flipped through the others again, taken after the wedding. She thought she looked like a ghost haunting the scene. There were some sweet head shots of Elyse and Cory alone. "One of those too."

Elyse was enthused for the most part, while pointing out the fake looking smile on Cory's mom. "That woman didn't like me then, even before the party."

"Oh Elyse, get over it."

As they worked through their thrown together pasta dish, Elyse, irritated at her lack of skill in the kitchen, served penne that hadn't cooked enough: "I'm trying to get better at this dinner-for-the-man-every-night thing." Elyse brought up David. "By the way we took him out yesterday for dinner. Have you two gotten together yet?"

"No, I haven't heard from him. He said he'd call before he left."

"It was hard. I felt like we'd never see him again."

"Oh, come on. The world is way too global these days. Of course, we'll see him."

"You think he'll come back and live here?"

Liv had been asking herself the same question. "Honestly, no. I think he's headed for big things someplace, but not here."

"Yeah, so pretty uncertain if we'll ever see him again."

"That bums me out. Ever since that dinner we all had together, I've been wondering if anything could happen between us."

"I was afraid of that. I never should have said anything to

you in the car, about his having a crush on you."

"Can we change the subject?" Liv finished eating, leaving Elyse's very dead, overcooked green beans on the plate.

As Elyse rose to take the plates away, she asked, "So changing the subject, what about Eric?" It came out in a slightly unnatural voice as though what was intended to be a low-key inquiry was something she was extremely interested in.

Liv was only too aware Elyse was trying to reopen a closed case. "Nothing."

No point trying to cozy up to this. "I mean, I've been thinking about what happened and that we all had too much to drink, and also...well, maybe what he said did not have to be construed as racism."

"Excuse me! How so?"

"Well, if you dated only brown-eyed guys, a girlfriend might say to you, "You're really into dark-eyed men. Or, she likes them tall, dark, and handsome. Or he's attracted to blondes. I mean what Eric said about your liking them dark doesn't have to be taken as a racist remark – if you get what I'm saying?"

"Sure, I understand what you're saying. But there was this snide tone of voice, and sort of a sneer on his face. It just came off as clearly racist."

"Well, I'm just saying, it doesn't mean he meant it that way."

"What is this? Why are you trying to absolve Eric?" Liv got up and went to the other side of the room. "Is it because of what I just said about David? Are you thinking I like dark-skinned men too?"

"Liv, CALM DOWN. My only point is that Eric was or is available. He lives here. He's not going anywhere. He's very attractive, I mean if you like that Nordic look, which by the way I don't, so does that make me racist?"

Liv sat down. "So, what are you saying – that I blew it?"

"No, no, no. It's that maybe Ryan's right. Maybe you should contact Eric and see if you might want to back down, if you took it the wrong way? Maybe?"

"Shit. I have no interest in talking to that asshole."

"Liv, this is me, remember the one who was there when you walked away from Devin and didn't talk to him again all that time. Is this what you do? Is this your MO? To walk away and never have the full conversation?"

Liv was listening harder now, her mind on pause while she took in what Elyse said. "And I walked away from Rama too. But at least I let him know about Shakti."

"Right, him too, so yeah, is walking away and never getting closure your specialty?"

"You don't have to get nasty."

"I'm not being nasty, I'm being your best friend. And I'm telling you Eric was a reasonable option and you shouldn't just cut him off without really knowing for sure."

Liv didn't want to think about it. "I'll think about it."

"Give it some thought. One more phone conversation wouldn't be that hard. And it would help with Ryan, that you smoothed it over a bit."

"Maybe."

Monday, October 1

Do I call? Stop by – no there might be another girl there. Write? not how one communicates with Eric. Okay, I have to call. She assumed he'd be busy Saturday, maybe have a girl still over Sunday morning. Was the afternoon or evening better? Well, Monday night it was. She practiced what she wanted to say, and not say, before she dialed.

He picked up right away. She'd really been hoping for his voicemail, so she could leave the ball in his court. "Hi, this is Liv."

"Oh." Silence while she waited for it to sink in. "What's up?"

"Look, we all had a lot to drink at Elyse's wedding."

"Speak for yourself."

So he wasn't going to make this easy. Honestly, she had zero interest in him at this point, but made herself do it because Ryan asked. And to avoid awkward scenes in the future. And to prove she was a more mature person. And a little bit because Elyse's line of thinking made Liv slightly curious – less about him and more about her own ability to read people correctly.

"Okay. I had a lot to drink. And I was feeling emotional to begin with. And you said something that made me think...in the moment...that you were racist."

"Yep, that's what you called me." No way was he going to make this easy for the bitch, now that he figured she was missing him.

She really didn't want to apologize because she still thought she'd been right. "Well, I've thought about it and I may have misinterpreted what you said."

"What did you think I said?"

Shit. "I thought you were putting my dancing with David together with Shakti having an Indian father and...and putting me and them down, as though they were lesser human beings based on their skin color. And that you thought I was like perverse or something for not noticing and discriminating against them. Like I had some abnormal fixation on 'dark men' as you said, rather than the truth of it, which is that I accept each person for who they are regardless of their skin color."

"Really," said not as a question but a statement that connoted the idiocy of the person who had just said something.

Eric was caught between wanting to lash out and confirm that he had been saying she was a nigger-lover or stringing this out to give her a hard time. But he also needed to factor his boss into the equation. All in all, better to let her think she was mistaken and blew the relationship – or whatever it was they had going. "And so..."

Liv was irritated now. *Bastard.* What did he really believe? "I guess it was also because Shakti thinks you didn't like her."

He decided he didn't want to be having this conversation. He could care less about her or the damn kid. But...the boss issue. "Look, if you're trying to apologize, then just say you're sorry. If you're just bored on a Monday night after a lonely weekend, then all I can say is too bad." At last, the adrenalin was flowing, and his fight instinct propelled him. Time to talk tough. "And if you just want me to screw you, I'll call you when I'm in the mood."

"Fuck you!"

"No, fuck you, and fuck you to any white woman who hits on me just because they aren't getting what they want from the colored guy in their life." He was thinking of Linda on the yacht now which really made him mad. If Liv had been there in front of him, he would have slapped her. And fucked her from behind. And then thrown her out.

Liv held her cell phone away from her body and stared at it. *I was right. He is a racist.* She ended the call.

After dinner the next evening upstairs, she pulled Ryan aside. "I just want you to know I did speak to Eric."

Ryan looked interested. "So, things are cool between you two?"

Liv still didn't lean toward getting Eric in trouble at work, not only for his racism which his Hispanic boss would not appreciate, but for his lack of anger management skills. "No. I doubt, actually I really hope I never see him again. If you ever invite him over, please count us out."

"Sis..." Ryan put his hands on her shoulders and changed his tone to a consoling one, "...I never thought you two would really work out. I don't judge either one of you."

"Good. That's cool."

"The fact is Eric's showing a lot of initiative about our developing a specialty in boat electronics and telecommunication. Said he might even take a few classes to up his game. This could turn out to be important to the business. I don't know if you've noticed, but there's a lot of bad economic news – we could be headed for some kind of melt-down that could put everything from home ownership to small businesses in jeopardy. "

"Really? You're right, I haven't been focused on that at all."

"Yeah, it might make it harder for Mimi and me to afford this house, so I'm watching it pretty carefully. Anyway, the techie millionaires around here probably won't feel it much, the rich guys always do fine. Having a business with more high-end services might help us weather some bad times."

Liv was quiet.

"What is it? Are you sure there isn't something I need to know?"

Liv met his eyes. "You know what Mom says about how you can just move to the side in a controversy and let people do themselves in, the Aikido thing?"

"You mean that stuff she learned in some corporate training session?"

"Yeah. My point about Eric is that I don't know if my issues with him will show up on the job. If and when they do, then you can decide what to do about it."

"Fair enough. Thanks for letting me know, and for making the effort."

"I needed to do it."

"Hey, as long as we're talking, down the road…when Grandma has passed on… I'd like to find ways to have Grandpa over more. I want to take him down to Fisherman's Terminal now and then, let him hang out at the shop, go out for an evening sail with me."

Once again, Liv was struck by the bond Ryan had forged with the grandfather he hadn't known for so long. "Nice. Where would he sleep?"

"That's the thing. There's these blow-up airbeds and we might put one in the third bedroom…until a new baby comes along. Or maybe…"

"Or maybe he could sleep in my room sometimes? Or in the living room?"

"Yeah, I mean we just need to be flexible and welcoming so that he likes being here."

Liv smiled. "Well, it's not like I have any hot prospects

right now. Sure, I'm open to helping. It's going to be a rough time for him."

"That's what I'm afraid of. Not that your dad isn't around the house during the week sometimes, but he's mostly staring at a computer screen or on the phone."

"Right." Liv had a flash of Grandpa living with them, eventually having his own room. Maybe the kids would need to share a room. "We'll make it work somehow. Who knows, if I'm at school or the library at nights, maybe he and Shakti could do some reading together."

"There you go." Ryan pulled her into a bear hug. "I love my family."

Liv hugged back hard, which felt like tofu against a slab of red meat. Her heart was healing as the gratitude for her brother pumped in and pushed out the toxin of Eric.

Sunday, October 14

David called after eight that night. "Liv, hi. Can you talk?"

"David! I'm so happy to hear your voice. Does this mean you've taken a job somewhere?"

"Yes, yes I have. I'm headed back to Africa finally."

"To Sudan?"

"No, it will be to the refugee camps in Kenya. It's all quite amazing. The International Rescue Committee and the UN refugee agency have several research projects that they've wanted to do for some time and the New York office of the Rescue Committee got a one-year grant from the UNHCR funding the studies. I leave in two or three weeks. First for New York to be briefed on my projects, and then to Nairobi."

"God, that's so great for you. Will they let you travel so you can be looking for your family?"

"No, not really. The research is at the big camps in Kenya, Dadaab, which is the world's largest refugee camp, and Kakuma, where I was. But I can do my search on my own time."

"Honestly, I've got mixed feelings, but I am happy for you. Really."

"I know. I'm still not believing it."

"I want to see you before you go."

"Of course."

Liv was about to suggest including others or arranging a party. What came out was, "Why don't you come here for dinner? Do you have a car?"

"No. Are you on a bus line?"

"Oh yes. Not far. And I can drive you home. What is your time like between now and when you leave?"

"Incredibly busy. I need to empty out my apartment, give away or get rid of what's there, see friends one more time."

"Sounds as though you're never coming back."

"That may be true. Once I start doing work there who knows what it might lead to."

Liv's chest felt pain like heartburn. "Hmm. I suppose that's likely." They were quiet. Liv was reaching to say more. All she could muster was, "What about a Friday or Saturday night for dinner? Saturday would be the best for me."

"Sure. Next Saturday I'm going to a party Jonathan is

throwing with our neighborhood crowd. You could come to that if you want instead of all the trouble of dinner?"

Party. It reminded her of a wedding debacle. Plus, she wanted a little quality time with David. "What about in two weeks then?"

"Yes, that would work."

"Come at six then. I'll email you the bus lines and directions. In the meantime, say hello to Jonathan for me."

"I will. I think it won't be long before you get an invitation to his wedding."

"Agh. Weddings. I've had enough."

David had helped close out Elyse's wedding scene with Selena and Liv, and knew something was awry with Liv, that her date had disappeared, and that she'd been drained at the end. All that Selena said was that Liv had been upset with her date. "I guess Elyse's wedding ended badly for you. I'm sorry."

"Don't be sorry. It was for the best. Just upsetting at the time." Liv considered stopping there. But didn't. "So back to square one."

"What does that mean?"

"It means that I'm supposed to be finding a father for Shakti and I'm not getting anywhere." There was silence at the other end. *Now I did it.* "I mean, you know, ever since I became a single mom, my parents have been on my case to get married and create a traditional family life for Shakti."

"Is that what she wants?"

"Yes, I think so. She's old enough to notice that the other kids in first grade, they mostly have fathers. And of course, she sees Ryan all the time. Why do you ask?"

"Just that I guess in my case, ONE parent would have been heaven. She's lucky to have you. I know the model is mother AND father, but honestly so many children in the world today have to do with none, or one. Or lucky to be raised by grandmas. Look at what AIDS has done, is doing in Africa."

"I know. I've read about it."

"And in many African countries, it's not unusual for women to not be married and have children. I see it more here too."

"But do you think that's right?"

"It depends on the woman I guess. But for the child, what I missed for so long is having anyone to care about me. Except you know what's saved us all who have made it, is our brothers and sisters in the camps. Shakti, she has many people who care about her. She'll be fine."

Liv wanted to say, what about me? But David wouldn't understand. "Good to hear a different point of view than what I usually get."

"Americans reach for the moon, and some get it. But most of us, if we can survive, and have something, even one thing that's positive in our lives, then we live on hope. And look at you, you have many positive things in your life. There is always hope for you." They were quiet. "Sorry for the lecture."

"No, no need for sorry. I know you're right." Liv looked down at the coffee table. The books she'd bought a while ago at the East/West Bookstore on spirituality were there. In the last few weeks, she'd begun talking to Shakti about the different stories people tell about what's behind the door, the door Liv compared to death. "Oh, David, when you come, I want you to tell Shakti what you believe about death, about life and death. My grandma is dying, and we visit with her almost every weekend. So Shakti is really curious about the whole subject."

"Interesting. Good, I think. The time is appropriate for her. But why do you want her to hear what an African thinks. Aren't you Christian or Catholic?"

"I was raised that way. And Grandma is a strong Catholic. But Shakti's father, I think he was Hindu although honestly, I don't know. I've talked to her about the belief of reincarnation. And I'm reading more about Buddhism. I think it's good for her to hear other people talk about their beliefs."

He laughed. "Honestly, I haven't given it a lot of thought. I grew up in a more animist culture, but then there were Christian missionaries and rituals of different kinds in the refugee camp, so I did some of that. I'll think about it."

"Plus after she goes to sleep, I do want to learn more about your upcoming work and thoughts about finding your mom and sister."

"There's not too much to say for now. But sure, we'll talk."

"Look for my email then."

"Okay. Thanks. My angel."

Saturday, October 27

The evening of her dinner for David, Liv was nervous; she wasn't used to having people over. Now that Shakti's tastes were evolving and mac and cheese, hot dogs, and sloppy Joe's no longer had to dominate the menu, she was only beginning to focus on cooking. What would he like? She decided on her mom's broiled salmon with butter, lemon juice, and brown sugar, corn, and mashed potatoes. The fish would require her attention up to the last, but David and Shakti could be playing.

When they finally settled down at the table, Liv raised her glass of beer to his. "Here's to great good luck every single step of the way!"

Shakti raised her glass of milk, adding, "No lions or crocodiles." She knew his story and its fearsome details were embedded in her young mind.

"Right! If I go my whole time with no lions or crocodiles, I will be so, so happy."

"What will you do in Africa, Uncle David? Why are you going away from us?"

"For a couple of reasons, Miss Shakti." He didn't really want to talk to her about going back to help desperate people in camps, to find an old friend or two who hadn't made it out, to learn if there was any way he could help. He recalled what Liv had asked about his beliefs. "I need to go to know with more certainty what happened years ago to my mother and sister."

"Are they lost?"

"No, most likely they died when the...when the bad men came. My father died then in the attack. But I'm not sure what became of my mom and my sister, Amer. I need to know for sure to live my life."

"My Grandma is dying."

"Has your mom told you about the rituals that will happen when she dies?" From her quizzical face, he saw that his choice of words did not connect. "Rituals are things people do to help people get to the next life or world. So, if my family is for sure..." here he looked to Liv and saw her encouraging look to keep going, "...for sure dead, then I want to do my part to help them get to the world of our ancestors."

"What's that? Is it the same as heaven?"

"Help me, Liv, I'm not sure how to talk about this."

Liv thought the conversation was going well. Shakti knew the word ancestors, sort of, but ancestor world was a new concept. "Shakti, you know how we've been talking about what will happen to Grandma when she dies?"

"Oh yes. She says she's going to heaven. And she'll see all her old friends. And she won't be sick anymore."

"Right. And that's what Grandma, what many, many people think is on the other side of that door we talked about. Do you remember that?"

Shakti looked unsure, twisting her nose and mouth a bit. "Sort of. You said that when we die it's like opening a door. But no one really knows what's on the other side. And people say different things about it. But no one really knows."

David looked approvingly at Liv. "Shakti, your mom is a very smart person to tell you about this."

"Oh, she tells me about a lot of things. I want to know about my father too. And Mommy is teaching me about India and…what are those other words you used that I don't understand yet?"

"You mean the farming talk? 'Agriculture' and 'sustainability'?"

"I know farming, Mom. That's like what Old McDonald does."

"Yes, and do you remember we talked about 'ecology' and the 'environment'?"

"A little."

David looked befuddled. "What's that got to do with the door?"

Liv laughed. "Absolutely nothing. It's a separate set of nighttime talks we're having about Shakti's father, and how he was involved in sustainable agriculture in India. We take little bites at a time to understand why I was in India, what I was like in college, what my internship there was about. Sort of a thousand and one nights of tales." All to avoid me having to talk about her father until I figure out what to say, was what Liv would have added, her hope being that Shakti would get bored and her curiosity about India and her father would diminish for a while. Liv focused more intently on David's eyes. "I'll tell you more later. Where were we? The door conversation. So, David, what do you think happens when someone dies and steps through the doorway?"

He laughed. "I have given this some thought since our call – which was good as I don't think about this too much, except when I think of my family. For us, in our Dinka tribe in Sudan, I'm finding it strange to think of the passage from life to death as going through a door."

"Do you believe there's another place or space dead people go to?" Liv was genuinely curious.

"In some way, it's the same space that we're in. There's a change in what you might call a person's life force. As someone becomes sick, they're losing life force."

Liv shifted her gaze to Shakti. "We can see that honey, right, with Grandma. She's not the person she used to be."

David considered his words. "When a person dies, it's like she is still with us. She is our 'ancestor' now, like my mother, if she is dead. And our ancestors still live on and can talk to us. We just can't see them or talk to them in the same way. It's a good thing to be an ancestor. But you must be given...do you know what a funeral is?"

Shakti shook her head no.

"Okay, to become an ancestor your family has to do certain things to honor your passing, so that you can enjoy the ancestor world, and not just be a lost ghost wandering around."

Shakti was staring hard at David now.

Liv was confused too. "Is the ancestor world like Grandma's heaven?"

"No, not really. It's being in this world. Just in a different way."

Liv continued, "Like being invisible. But I can talk to you?"

"Yes."

"And what did you mean about the funeral, David?" Switching her attention to Shakti, Liv said, "Grandma will have a funeral after she dies. It will be in her church, you know the church there near our house? You've been there...."

Shakti interrupted, "Like the church where Auntie Elyse got married?"

"Yes. But instead of it being happy..." Liv cringed inside thinking how not happy the wedding day had been, "...it will feel sad because we're saying goodbye to someone we love." Shakti started to tear up. "To her body, sweetie, not to her spirit. Remember, the spirit goes through the door."

David wondered if this was too heavy for a little girl. But he could see on the other hand that Liv was trying hard to prepare her. "Shakti, the funeral can feel sad, but we do it so the spirit can become an ancestor and stay with us, but only invisible."

Liv sent him a look of gratitude and took a deep breath. "What's the difference between an ancestor and a ghost? If you don't do funeral rites for your mom, does she become 'a wandering ghost?'" David was pained to have this spotlight shining on him now, to have a piece of his psyche exposed. As he took a sip of beer, Liv saw his affect change. "I'm sorry David. I get interested in these things, and I'm asking you to talk about something you may not want to."

He smiled. "I'll answer part of it. Shakti, from my people's viewpoint, a funeral is very important. Like I said, the rites, the rituals...." He still wasn't sure about the word.

Liv jumped in. "You know how you spread the rose petals to make the way for the bride? And how Elyse and Cory said vows, spoke their promises to each other?" Shakti nodded. "Those are rites or rituals when someone gets married. And when we die, the priest, if you're Catholic like Grandma, he does the rites that go with dying."

"So there's no rose petals and no bride or groom."

"Right. There's the person's body in a ..." God, how should she explain a coffin? "...in a very beautiful long box called a coffin with flowers on top." Liv watched her daughter's eyes grow large. "I'll show you a picture, sweetie. Anyway, the priest will say special prayers for your grandmother. And people will say nice things about her. Those are funeral rites." Liv could see Shakti's mind at work by slight facial twitches and movement of her eyes.

"Will Gramps be there? What will he do?""

"He'll be sad. You should stay close to him and hold his hand." Shakti lowered her head. "David, so without a funeral, you were saying that the person becomes a wandering ghost? Honey, you know about ghosts."

With that her mood altered. "Ghosts! They're scary! They come out on Halloween."

David's own emotions had been stirred by all this and he was looking to end the conversation. He didn't like to think of his family members as ghosts, that had haunted him long enough. He just wanted to find out if anyone was alive and if not, to create his own funeral ritual for them. Many of them in the camps had done a ritual for the people they knew were dead. He felt certain that it was his dad's ancestral power that had seen him to safety, to this country, and through law school. His dad wanted him to go back. "In my tribe, if a person becomes a ghost, it is a scary place to be too, cut off from your family, your clan, your community. But with the proper funeral, as your mother said, then you are with your family and not out there alone."

On balance, Liv was satisfied that she had encouraged this conversation. She knew she could build on it with Shakti in the coming weeks. Truth be told, she resonated with David's ideas herself. "Thank you for talking about this. I feel like it helped me and Shakti to hear what you said. What do you think, sweetie?"

"I don't want Grandma to be lonely and without us. So even though the funeral..." she stumbled a bit with this new word "...funeral sounds sad, we need to do it."

"Exactly, Shakti. You're a very good learner." David looked at Liv admiringly, impressed by her mothering. Of course, he'd always been impressed by Liv in so many ways: the kindness in her eyes when she helped them in Tukwila getting resettled, her lithe gazelle-like figure, her voice as soft and warming as a desert breeze at times, punctuated with laughs and smiles that soothed him. She'd been such an encouraging voice through his college years, sometimes harping on the need to study more and do really well. Overall, she'd been a beneficial influence on him: at first an angel guiding him in this strange and difficult country, then a friend he could always count on. Suddenly, he felt sad to be leaving her.

He'd been emotional too at the party last week with Jonathan and their friends, even crying. Jonathan had laughingly said, "Oh, so you're not a man of steel, you actually have a heart." Maybe it was for the best, to feel again. David had endured so much, devastating loss in the attack, fearsome dangers on the walk, desperation in the camps, acculturation challenges here in this country. Only by not feeling, by compartmentalizing his thinking, had he made it, made himself ready to go home to open doors to his past. The feelings were being set free now, his stiff fiber breaking down. There'd even been nightmares. Everything that had shriveled and died within him as he survived was being brought back to see the light of day. A liberation and expansion of emotions that were strange. For all his accomplishments, he had little practice managing them beyond deep suppression. The time here with Liv was stirring his insides.

Liv was clearing the table and noticing how quiet David had become. "Shakti, time for bed. Please go wash your hands and face. No bath tonight. I'll come read you a story." David began pushing back from the table. "Do you mind waiting? It will only take fifteen or twenty minutes for me to get Shakti to bed. Why don't you sit outside – it's not so cold tonight and the stars are out. You've got a parka? Enjoy the air. Do you want some hot tea?"

"I'm fine. I'll just stay here on your sofa if that's okay. There's plenty of books for me to look at."

As it turned out, instead of Liv reading a story, she wound up answering more questions that Shakti's mind was already puzzling out. "Mommy, when Grandma's an ancestor like David said, will she come visit me?"

"In a way. Not so you can see her. But you may feel her."

"What will it feel like?"

Oh dear, was Liv's first reaction as she took Shakti's hand. "Well, it won't feel like this."

"Mommy, remember when Auntie Elyse got married, but before, and the three of us were in a little room. And we held hands and breathed?"

"Yes, I remember. Why?"

"I wasn't feeling your hands after a while. It was just like we were one person. And it made me so happy! Did you feel that, Mommy?"

Liv thought back, recalling that it calmed them all. "In a way."

"Maybe it will be like that when Grandma comes to visit me? Maybe if I think about her and take a deep breath like this..." Shakti did her best deep breath, "...we'll be together then."

How wise she's becoming already. "That's beautiful. It will be like that, just like that." Liv touched under her eyes to dab the moisture away. "Maybe you can tell your grandma that sometime."

Shakti smiled. "We can make a plan."

Liv peeled away from the bed and reached the door before the voice came again. "Mommy, I'm glad Uncle David came to see us. I really like him."

"I do too. Now sleep tight."

When Liv returned to the living room, David was looking relaxed on the sofa with a book open. He looked up. "Is she asleep?"

"Most likely. Sometimes she cheats a bit and gets her toy flashlight and reads, but my hunch is she's got other things on her mind tonight if she's still awake."

"That was a heavy conversation."

"You think so? I suppose. Every weekend, we're with her Grandma in Redmond and those two get talking, meanwhile Shakti seeing her get sicker and sicker. Within weeks, at the most a month, Grandma will pass, and Shakti will be experiencing it all." Liv sat on the sofa too turning her body toward him. "What book is that?"

He held it up and looked at the cover again: *"The Four-Fold Way."*

"Oh, let's look at what it says about the fall. I love the way it brings together a lot of cultural traditions and comes up with a theme for the season."

David flipped some pages. "Ah, fall is the way of the teacher."

"What's the mantra or saying?"

"Be open to outcome, not attached to outcome." David read a little, then paused. "This really speaks to me. Funny that I picked this up. Like this first part, it's talking about trust and being comfortable with uncertainty, and then it gets into detachment. See, here it says most people think of detachment as 'not caring,' but that it really is 'the capacity to care deeply from an objective place.' That resonates with me. Then look here, it gets into 'ancestor spirits!' How strange is that!"

"Let me see." Liv pulled the book closer to her and started reading an excerpt. "This is so beautiful David. I think it's about you: *'Oh, may this be the one who will bring forward the good, true and beautiful in our family lineage; Oh, may this be the one who will break the harmful family patterns or harmful nation patterns.'"* She turned her eyes to his, enjoying the intimacy of being shoulder to shoulder as they sat and read. "Maybe what you said is true, your ancestors want you to make this journey, they're counting on you."

He read over her shoulder, "'*All my ancestors live undiminished in me and will continue so to live, united with me, in my descendants.*' "She heard a choke in his voice. "That's empowering to me. It's synchronicity that I picked up this book."

"I know, that happens to me a lot with that book. So back to the mantra, let's ask ourselves, where do I need to be open to outcome?"

David didn't have to think about that. "It's obvious for me, isn't it, that I don't know what I'll find out, if anything, about my family. I think I'm open to their being dead, but harder for me is to not be attached to finding out one way or the other. I really want to know."

"And if you don't find out after trying, then what? Have you thought about doing some rituals based on assuming they're dead?"

"I would need someone to assure me that it's okay to do that. Otherwise I think I would be doing something that hurts them, sending them to the ancestral world before they're ready to go."

"But maybe it's a ritual for you? To bring closure."

He didn't look convinced. "Maybe." David looked at her and then as though a veil lifted looked more deeply. "And what about you Liv, where do you need to be open to outcome?"

Liv was seeing him too with a more assessing eye: how incredibly dark his skin was, the sheen of it, the starkness of the contrasts of his teeth and the whites of his eyes. How very different he was from her. So elegant in a way, compared to her fluffiness as though she were a tabby cat sitting next to a sleek panther. "For me, right now, I'd say I need to be open to looking afresh at my life, to not being attached to notions of getting married, of giving Shakti a father, settling down the way say Mimi and Ryan are. Maybe I need to be open to a different lifestyle as a woman. It's looking like I'll be back in school at UW in January. Maybe that will be a part of a new beginning for me."

"What will you study? You're going for a master's?"

"Yeah. I'm thinking - although mind you, I'm not really attached to this as an outcome..." Liv laughed touching his arm, "...I'm thinking I want to be a storyteller. To tell the stories of people whose voices aren't being heard. Poor people, vulnerable people. Like some I see at work. In the nonprofit world, it's critical to share people's stories in public relations and grant applications. Just the other day, I learned from Selena that more nonprofits are looking at lobbying, at talking to elected officials about what needs to change. So, I'm pretty set to start a marketing and communications master's at UW."

"It's interesting what you said about 'giving up' on getting married. If that's what you really want, you shouldn't give up."

"I'm not sure what I do want anymore. It just seems like I've been holding on too much to some socially pre-determined intention about what to do with my life. I should be more open." Her heart beats increased. She wanted to touch him but was afraid of embarrassing herself and him. "Let's go sit outside with some hot tea and take in the cool night air." They went out to the plastic armchairs facing west, to a view dotted with lights on Queen Anne and downhill out to the bay. Then total darkness where the water and mountains were. They pulled their chairs close and leaned back to see the sky, neither feeling any need to talk. Liv was wondering: if he was available, would I try?

David was reflecting on how unsettled he was inside, a newfound awareness of emotions that intrigued him but slightly repelled him: *I don't want to go there, to that space of feeling.* Yet Liv did seem so open to him. Just talking with her, with his friends the past weeks about going home to find out what happened to his family, he sensed their thoughts more – and their feelings that he was on a fool's mission. He'd made a success of himself here, had community here, and now perhaps, perhaps there was even an opening to be with Liv? *Why am I leaving now? What is the likelihood I'll find out anything?* The trail, whatever footsteps in the sand they made twenty years ago, there was no way he'd find out anything about his family. They were simple women of a clan. Who would know anything of them? He looked at Liv's profile made only slightly visible by the backlighting from her apartment. *This woman is real. She's been a mother to me, a sister, and a friend over so many years. Why am I attached, yes, actually holding on to the notion that nothing more can exist between us? Maybe I should be more open to outcome?* He moved his arm from the chair and took her hand in his.

Liv was in a semi-meditative state where she was inviting him to touch her. When she felt his hand take hers, she wasn't sure what world she was in. *So, this is what he feels like, his long, slender hand surrounding mine.* She opened her eyes and looked down to see that yes, her fair hand was now covered in dark. Indeed, he had taken her hand. She turned her head slightly and smiled.

Neither wanted to break the coupling. They kept their eyes closed and let their skins melt away. Pulses communing, seeking sympathetic rhythms. As Liv's thoughts slipped away, the last was of the union she and Shakti and Elyse felt before the wedding, breathing together. There was only the up and down, the back and forth of blood circulating between them. She felt his pulse throughout her body, receiving his life force into hers.

David experienced a release, as though he'd stepped out of a heavy skin. He envisioned a lion shedding its coat, its scowling face, and its lumbering moves, to reveal a cub, playful, ready to frolic, happy, yes happy, to be alive. He felt tears, a witness on his cheeks to an incredible tenderness in the evening air. He could finally, really breathe. Breathe without fear. Breathe for the enjoyment of it. Breathing that expanded beyond his body into Liv, into the space around them. There was so much joy.

They sat for a long while. Liv came back first. *What was that?* A journey to another world of being? Words were inadequate. There was nothing to be said or done. Except she squeezed his hand.

With the slight pressure of her fingers, he called himself back. Slowly. He didn't want to leave. Shrinking back to his body was discomforting, being summoned to such a tiny, confined space of being. He finally opened his eyes. Then he squeezed back and released her hand to stand up. Stretching his arms high and his torso tall, he stamped his feet, then turned and offered his hand to Liv inviting her to rise. Their bodies flowed into a deep embrace.

Liv knew how this must end. They could go no further. She gently pulled back and looked up. "I need to get you home."

David looked into her eyes with contentment. "I have never felt so home."

Her face lit up in the dark. "Never forget then. This is home."

She pulled him back into her flat shielding her eyes and laughing, "Too bright!" Liv went for her handbag and car keys, and they walked out to the car.

"Liv, I need to walk."

"But it's so far down to Rainier Beach."

"That's not far at all. I need to walk like I used to walk. With the uncertainty and yet the hope that my walking will bring me where I should be." He looked around, up at the sky. "There is joy in the night air that I couldn't accept when I walked before."

"Are you sure?"

"I cannot be contained in a car right now. I need the night sky. I need the effort. I need to walk into my future, as I did once before. To become the one I need to be, the one my ancestors want me to be."

She searched her heart for the right words. "My love goes with you. Forever."

They embraced again. He lifted her chin. "I will walk with you in my heart." And with that, he turned and started off.

Liv watched him until he turned a corner, wondering when she would see him next and what might unfold. Her mind was still, her spirit confident, accepting that she could wait. Even wait a very long time.

That night lying in bed, she relived the experience of spiritual love under the stars, recalling every detail of their being together, burning it into her memory. Her sleep was fitful. A dream took her back to India and her only other experience of love that existed in a space/time warp, her times with Rama. But in her dream state, it was David who came to her in a royal purple robe, her long gossamer gown opened in the front. They let their garments slip down to be naked before each other, moving gently together into a simple bed veiled in white. He lifted her to bring her closer to his body. As they were losing themselves in their coupling, she heard Shakti's voice, 'Mommy, who's that? What are you doing? Mommy, I need you!' Liv woke abruptly, thinking Shakti had cried out in the next room. Rising and finding her daughter sound asleep, Liv realized that Shakti's voice was in her fantasy. *Is there no fulfillment, even in my dreams?*

She stopped at Elyse's Sunday evening on her way back from Redmond, ostensibly to pick up the photos she'd ordered. Mimi, who'd also stopped by for a visit with Grandma, agreed to take

Shakti home with her.

Liv and Elyse had already debriefed the call with Eric weeks ago. Now Liv was feeling the need to talk about what happened with David, although wary that discussing it with her friend would somehow be sacrilegious. Yet, Liv knew that by virtue of what had passed between her and David last night, she'd entered a holding zone where sexual frolics and detours would be suspended, pending developments. And she wanted to let Elyse know.

Elyse had known that David was coming to dinner. "How was it? Tell me how things went. Have you by any far flung chance caused him to rethink going?"

"You know that's impossible, not even right. Of course, he's going. It's what he needs to do. For his ancestors." Liv went on to share with her the highlights of their dinner conversation on ancestor spirits, and how the sayings in the book fit with that.

While Elyse found some of this in Liv's woo-woo vein, she indulged it without rolling her eyes or making faces. She knew David's truth warranted respect. "So back to square one. No Eric, no David. Are you depressed about it all?"

Liv calculated how to lay out the relationship she believed existed now with David. "No, I'm not depressed. I think there is something with David going forward."

"Did he promise to come back? Is the final job offer good for only a year or something?"

"No, I don't know how long he'll be gone and I'll be surprised if he ever comes back."

"Well, you're not going anywhere, are you? I mean, not to be overly-negative, but that does seem impossible, that you and Shakti would go off to live in Africa?"

"Yes, I agree. But I might very well go to visit him. Not that we talked about it like that. But why not? I could take a trip to Africa and see him there."

"What shifted? What makes you feel like you're going to have a long-distance relationship with him?"

Liv didn't want to tarnish the experience with David by talking about it. "Let's just say, we broke through a barrier of only being friends, that we both acknowledge the potential for something more."

"No juicy details?"

"I don't want to go into it."

"But you do want to talk about it around the edges?"

"Well, I'm claiming a connection with him. He's the man in my life for now. We're together in our hearts. He has old family wrongs to attend to, but that's not such a strange affair, is it?"

"Not in years gone by, I suppose. That does simplify life in a way. You've found your love, but the relationship only takes up psychic space, and comes with no demands on your time. I guess there's something to be said for that."

"I'm just saying, that's the way it is for now. Not that I wouldn't want to be around him every day. But for now, it's just not what's possible." *Love requires patience. I didn't know that.*

"So, no set-ups in the foreseeable future?"

"Right. I'm changing my focus to the tasks in front of me. Grandma. School. And how I can take a trip to Africa next year."

Thanksgiving

By Thanksgiving, they all knew the end was near. At first, it was unpleasant at times as Katherine, and especially her sister El, challenged the approach of the hospice workers who started to visit, refusing to accept that the concept of palliative care meant more morphine over time and less consciousness, letting go sooner rather than later.

Liv stayed as open as she could to everything going on, learning about how different people dealt with dying in such diverse ways. She saw the futility in her aunt's approach. El was insistent on trying to keep feeding Colleen, while Liv's mom and dad talked about how animals just went off to die and refused food and water. Liv saw a role for herself in trying to reduce friction in the household between them all. She listened in on all the sidebar conversations, and began to identify which conversations focused on the technical work of the dying process and which were the tough challenges. Her mom discussed with Aunt El at length which church they would use, given that the majority of Grandma's friends were based in their old neighborhood in Seattle on Beacon Hill. The few from their retirement condo on Bainbridge who would want to come, why make them drive all the way to the church in Redmond? More heart-rending were the dialogues moving into the adaptive work of coping with Grandma's absence, like Ryan consistently doing emotional check-ins with Grandpa. Liv fit in as the support person around the edges, ensuring the care-givers were getting relief, doing her own share of basic care for Grandma, and encouraging Shakti in small ways to keep the others' spirits up.

The Friday after Thanksgiving Liv found herself alone with Grandma while others were out shopping or running errands. As Liv sat by the bed, letting her thoughts drift to David and his latest brief email, her grandmother awoke with a burst of energy. The coughing bout was severe but then she was fully present as the morphine dose wore off. Liv inquired as to pain, but Grandma replied, "I hate being so doped up. I want to see if I can do a better job of handling this pain." Liv helped prop up her head and adjust the pillows to make her more comfortable. She applied cream around Colleen's nostrils where they were chaffed from the oxygen tube. Suddenly, Colleen caught hold of Liv's wrist and stared at her. "I want to ask you something."

Liv was taken aback, but murmured, "What is it?"

With clarity that was refreshing, Colleen, in brief bursts of speaking, began her probe. "I think you know, Liv...when your mother as a teen had Ryan...I didn't place him through an agency...my friend Helen and I arranged for her son Carl and his wife...they couldn't have children...to take him... I never told your mother...but I think she knows...do you know if she knows?"

"I don't. But if I guessed, she probably has figured it out too."

"Do you think she holds it against me...should I ask her to forgive me...It was all done with the best intentions...I was always there as a bridge for them to meet...but your mother wanted him to decide what was right for him...and then it took him so long to decide to meet her."

"I suspect she's forgiven you a long time ago, Grandma. You shouldn't be worried about that." Liv lent over and laid her head on Colleen's chest. "We're all together now, and that's what matters."

Colleen sighed. She was feeling more pain, but still was determined to maintain clarity of mind. When Liv pulled back, she was surprised that her grandma stared at her again. "What about you, Liv, and Shakti...will she be able to find her father if she wants to...are you keeping a bridge open?"

"Yes, there is a go-between, a friend I have in India. Shakti's father could contact her. And I have a journal for Shakti and a letter from him for when she's older."

"So, you may do as I did...keep to the side and wait... leaving it to them to say when it's time to meet?"

"For now, yes. When she's older, maybe eighteen, I might decide to give her a nudge."

"Maybe I should have nudged more... But waiting for Ryan to make a move seemed best." Her tentative eyes sought Liv's.

"Yes, Grandma. That's what I'll do too, wait for a grown-up Shakti to want to meet her father."

Colleen grimaced at Liv. "I'll take that pain pill now."

As the weekend passed, little did Liv know about the conversations Shakti was having with her grandparents. Grandpa looked at Liv as they sat to watch the History Channel: "What in the world are you teaching that girl about? She asked me about coffins today. She asked if they were a bed for the dead that you could move around." And in one of Grandma's last spells of lucidity with Liv: "Do you know I'm headed for the ancestral world?"

"Oh Grandma, is that what Shakti talked to you about?"

Between racking coughs, Grandma managed a feeble hint of a smile. "We've made our appointments to talk. I'm to visit her in the evenings in bed... and ask about her day... and give her a good night kiss."

"Maybe I'll join you!"

With the hint of a sparkle in her eyes, Grandma gave a long, appreciative look at Liv. "I'd like that." A pain came then. When it passed, she pressed Liv's hand. "You made the right choice sweetheart about Shakti. You really did. I'm so proud of you."

Liv would recall those words as the last she had with her grandma.

Wednesday, December 5

Grandma Colleen passed midweek. Grandpa had been sleeping next to her the last few nights. He felt she was already gone to him, and cried each night by her side, speaking to her of times they'd shared: when they first met at the big naval reserve building on south Lake Union, his return from the war to find she had baby Eleanor, the hard times when both their girls got pregnant during the same year, El aborting and Katherine giving up Ryan. He liked talking about how they all hung together and how Ryan was back in their lives, how Liv had done what Colleen had with El, and kept the baby. "What a pistol she is – you never know what's going to come out of Shakti's mouth." And then, he awoke that Wednesday, looked at her, and knew she'd left. For all the collective suffering of the preceding months of care, the pain he felt was nonetheless huge and encompassing, at the same time sharp and pointed. A wail came out that shocked him. He sobbed as he held her closer.

So it was with Katherine and El, they knew it was coming, they'd been having crying spells for months. And yet when she passed, the sorrow was fresh and strong knocking them over like a gale wind. There is nothing like the loss of a mother. The one who created you, brought you into life, and held you and loved you through every bump and scrape, every hurtful remark of childhood, every disappointment of adolescence, and every shared decision of womanhood.

While Liv had braced herself to be there for them, she too was not ready for how deeply she felt the loss. She sensed that the wound to her heart was of a mythic nature: the passage of time and lives, the legacies, the generational turn over, her aunt and mom now being on the front lines to go next, indeed that someday she would have to watch her own mother pass. But her grief was less visceral than her mother's and she focused on soothing her and El as much as she could.

The wake was traditional. Liv abhorred the ritual of the open-faced casket and had to suppress her own opinion about cremation being far preferable. Elyse came to the wake, so at last Liv could speak her mind. "I hate this casket thing. There's only one thing that gets said: people go up and say…"

"I know, 'it doesn't look like her.' I know Liv, it happens in my family too. What do they expect? It's crazy. What did Shakti do?"

"I talked to her about rites, rituals, and explained that for some people, it helps them, because they see with their own eyes that the person is really dead."

"Was she afraid?"

"Not really. I held her up to see, and she leaned over to look. She said, 'That's not Grandma.'" She also said, but Liv didn't share this part with Elyse, that "Grandma is already going through the door, Mommy. She's moving into the ancestral world. I don't think she's here right now though. I don't feel her."

The day of the service however, in St. Edward's Catholic Church, Shakti leaned into Liv and whispered, "I feel Grandma here. She gave me a little kiss."

As the mass wore on, Liv realized her lack of connection to it. Years had passed since she'd stopped going to church. Now this year, good God, she'd been in church for a wedding and a funeral. And needed to bring Shakti into the world of religion, spirituality, and beliefs about life and death. *She's growing up.* Liv reflected on how she was shaping her daughter's mind with all her bedtime talks and fly-bys of world religions. *And then, whoosh, she'll be grown, and her mind will be shaped by so many others. And I'll eventually die, and then she'll die. Really, what is the point of us all carrying on over births, and weddings, and deaths? It all passes. We could be in an accident, something bad could happen to Shakti. And the people who love us bear the loss, and the world just moves on.*

These morose sentiments accompanied the parade of believers walking past to take Holy Communion. Liv, unsure of her beliefs, chose to sit; and feeling the cold, burrow deeper into her parka. Which returned her thoughts to *The Four-Fold Way*, her bedside companion last night. A more austere time and space than summer had arrived, a time called 'the way of the warrior,' a time when one must 'show up and be present.' This wintery mantra brought forth an image of a grove of tall trees, barren of leaves, but defiant. *I'm one of those trees. I need to stand on my own despite the heavy winds. Just as I am.* Time to let go of trying to lock a man into her life and create a controlled outcome. Ludicrous in hindsight. Her life didn't need to follow some pre-determined script which others had written.

Which made her think of David. *How can I show up and be present in a relationship when he's so far?* Liv held a thread of email contact with him, he sharing vignettes as he could of his work in and around the refugee camps, but not having consistent access to email. All she knew is that in a few weeks, he was taking time off to travel towards southern Sudan and try and learn what happened to his family. He'd made some contacts with refugee agencies and was going to talk to long-time camp workers. It seemed more than hopeless, but he was being methodical in exploring every angle. What if they had gone west to Chad? What if they simply had folded into another clan? Often Liv feared terrible trouble would cross his path. The simplest thing in Sudan could turn into a nightmare: a breakdown of his rented vehicle in an inauspicious location, a robbery, some wild guy with an AK-47 shooting him.

To distract her worries, she brought her attention to the altar. The crucifix hung cold and cruel. Her gaze traveled to the side altar where Mary, mother of God, was enshrined. *Mary, you know about mothering. About loss, about mothers and sons, about suffering, about having your child die before your eyes.* Liv squeezed Shakti's hand and whispered to her. "That's Jesus' mother, Mary. Remind me to tell you about her." The statue was a traditional version, painted to endow Mary with eyes as blue as the cloak over her draping white tunic. Liv silently critiqued the lack of verisimilitude to a Palestinian woman, then was moved by comforting thoughts of children crowning the Blessed Virgin, recollections that dated to her early years of church-going. Shakti looked at the stone figure and tugged at Liv's sleeve. "It's just a statue, Mommy."

"Later." Liv overrode Shakti's discordant observation and offered a prayer to Mary that David would find his mother and sister. Mothering. In this moment, it was enough to be a mother. Liv had a place to stand, a role to play. *Maybe my life isn't about me, maybe it's my role in relation to Shakti's life. Maybe she's going to be the person I've wished I could be, taking on the world, and making it better.*

Holding her eyes softly shut, her internal space expanded with deep inhalations and exhalations. *I am one with all of this, only a tiny drop of water in a great wave of life.* As if standing in the path of a tsunami, Liv experienced the futility and arrogance of struggling to make the wave go some other direction. *I just need to go with the flow. Let it carry me.*

The mass was concluding with the jingly sounds of the priest swinging the chains of the golden censer of incense over the casket. A fragrance of frankincense wafted in the air, a smell today of Grandma's passing, of a lifeless body beginning its return passage, of a metamorphosis into nothing. The experience of impermanence moved through Liv as sonorous music might, conveying meaning beyond words: a sense of acceptance of the way life is, of change and passing, of surrender. She was at peace.

Continue to follow Liv's coming of age
(check *NonprofitGirlTrilogy.com* for publication dates)

Nonprofit Girl Trilogy, book three
Shakti Rising

**When the universe speaks,
are you listening?**

A mature woman, Liv is successful in her career, and content in her relationships. But at 15, her daughter Shakti has begun a demanding coming-of-age that challenges her mother's comfort zone. Throw in a job villain, transitions of aging parents, and her eco-manfriend's priorities, and the world conspires to flood her out of her backwater existence into an emotionally strenuous, psychologically complex, and spiritually transforming river of events. A distant grandmother in India emerges to shift the trajectory of Liv and Shakti into a whole system change of life, ripe with new possibilities – and an abiding love.

In this, the final novel of the *Nonprofit Girl Trilogy*, Shakti's life begins to unfold, and Liv owns her accomplishments as a nonprofit woman.

Did you miss the beginning of Liv's story?

Nonprofit Girl Trilogy, book one
Nonprofit Girl

If you had an unwanted pregnancy, what would you decide?

When Liv, 21 and about to graduate into a career of nonprofit work, returns from India and discovers she's pregnant, she needs to make choices that will define her life. What should she tell her live-in boyfriend Devin who is not the father? Does she want to have an abortion as her best friend Elyse urges? If not, will she give up the baby as her mother Katherine did?

Set in Seattle, with flashbacks to her time in Mumbai and affair with Rama, watch Liv's new-found feminism shape her decisions. And hear a legacy from the women in her family that gives her the courage to stand for her own values.

This coming-of-age story begins the *Nonprofit Girl Trilogy* that evolves into a family saga spanning 15 years and populated by strong women of all ages.

About the author:

Ann uses her own nonprofit career experiences, volunteer work with the International Rescue Committee in Seattle, her home of thirty years, and romantic experiences to create Liv's story.

Currently residing in the Washington, D.C. area, she's taught business courses at George Washington University and uses her J.D. to be a citizen advocate with RESULTS to help alleviate the worst aspects of domestic and global poverty.

You can learn more at www.nonprofitgirltrilogy.com

If you would like to blog about your personal motivation or inspiration for being a nonprofit girl or woman, please contact Ann at annstil@aol.com

Visit me on social media

Made in the USA
Lexington, KY
17 February 2018